WHAT LIES IN THE DARKNESS

(SHADOW COVE MYSTERIES, #1)

JESSICA SORENSEN

What Lies in the Darkness
Jessica Sorensen
All rights reserved.
Copyright © 2016 by Jessica Sorensen

ISBN: ISBN: 9781939045867

For information: jessicasorensen.com
Cover design by MaeIDesign

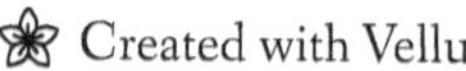 Created with Vellum

ONE

"Hi, my name is Makayla Evingston, or Mak as my friends like to call me. And I'm here to tell you about a little project I'm working on, a project I fully intend to prove is true." I comb my fingers through my long, brown hair, sweeping tangled strands out of my eyes. "Now, not a lot of people know this, but Shadow Cove has the highest rate of kidnap-ping and murder crimes in all of America." I angle the web camera downward to get the glare off my face. "But that info isn't going to show up in any records. In fact, most of the records I've obtained for this project show an extremely low number of kidnappings and murders. But I've recently come across some top secret documents that show a startling amount of mysterious disappearances and deaths that have happened here. Yet most of them were never released to the citizens of Shadow Cove. In truth, the kidnappings were always put down as runaways, and almost all of the deaths had a very brief investigation, despite the mysterious activity surrounding each one."

"Mak, please tell me this isn't for your history project." Everleigh's heart-shaped face pops up on the screen like a springing Jack-in-the-Box. Her blue eyes are filled with worry behind her square-framed glasses, and her mouth is curved into a disappointed frown. "Please tell me you're just messing around."

"What?" I swivel around in my chair. "I think it has a good angle for the assignment—murder as part of the town history. You've gotta admit, it's pretty catchy."

"I know you like to play the journalist angle with every-thing, but unless you have facts about this theory, it won't get you an A in history. In fact, Mrs. Maralline will probably fail you." She repeatedly combs her fingers through her curly, brown hair, a nervous habit. "And, as your best friend, it's my duty to make sure you don't turn that video in."

It's so like Everleigh to be all dutiful. She doesn't just do this with me, but with all of her friends and sometimes even teachers. While most people find it annoying, I've known Everleigh long enough that I'm used to it. It's actually kind of nice to have a friend always looking out for me.

"Hey, maybe I do have proof," I argue. "Maybe I've been collecting information, and all the evidence points to one thing: there's a conspiracy in Shadow Cove. The kidnappings and murders *are* being covered up."

I'm being over the top, but I have to think outside the box in order to win an argument with Everleigh. And by outside the box, I mean, way, way outside, all the way past the moon and the stars to where aliens live. Why? Because Everleigh is super smart, although her genius stops at questionable subjects that might not be provable by reading a book, questionable subjects like aliens and conspiracy theories. I guess everybody has their way of understanding. Mine are the mental notes I file away in my brain.

Here are some of the basic mental notes I have on Everleigh:

Full Name: Everleigh Rosenbloom.

Age: Seventeen.

School Status: Senior at Shadow Cove High.

Known For: The genius in our group of friends and pretty much all of Shadow Cove High.

Hobbies: Homework, science, computers, and basically anything with electronics.

Parents: Dad teaches PE at our high school and coaches the football and soccer team. Her mom died in a car accident when she was ten, right before her family moved to Shadow Cove. Because of this, Everleigh has taken on the mom role and spends a lot of time cooking, cleaning, and worrying about stuff normal seventeen-year-olds don't have to.

Siblings: Finn, her younger brother who is the opposite of Everleigh and focuses mostly on sports achievements instead of grades. He's his dad's pride, adored by most of the town, and has dated at least half of the cheerleading squad this year alone.

"Do you have facts about your murder theory?" Everleigh asks, looking genuinely interested.

God, I wish I did. Then maybe I could prove my dad isn't a complete nut job.

I sigh. "No, but one of these days, I'm going to find proof that a cover-up is going on in our town." I rotate the chair around, thrumming my fingers against each other, and use my best evil villain tone. "And when I do, I'm going to take down everyone involved."

"You sound just like your dad ..." She presses her lips together at the mention of my father. "I'm so sorry, Mak. I didn't mean to bring him up."

Despite the ill knots winding in my stomach, I wave her off. "It's cool." I turn back around in the chair to power down the computer and hide my sullen expression. "I don't mind talking about him."

Which is true. I don't mind chatting about my dad as long as he isn't being ridiculed, something Everleigh would never do. As for the rest of Shadow Cove ... Well, let's just say a lot of people around here weren't very fond of my dad before he disappeared.

"Have you ...?" Tentativeness fills her tone. "Have you heard from him?"

I shake my head. "No, nothing's changed."

Okay, that's not entirely true. A lot has changed—at least in my life—since the once loving, doting, awesome father I knew just up and vanished into thin air. Up until then, he was a great father, husband, and spent most of his time working as a reporter for the *Shadow Cove Daily News*. The position made him extremely unpopular amongst the town residents.

Honestly, I kind of don't blame some people for disliking him. My dad did have a habit of making other people's dirty laundry the main focus of his articles. Like the time he reported on Mr. Wellford getting busted for hiring a prostitute, which led to his wife divorcing him and taking over half of his ten point five million dollars, which led to the bankruptcy of his company and the unemployment of about fifty members of our town. Yeah, total domino effect. So, when my dad disappeared a little over six months ago, not too many people were upset. Me, I almost fell apart.

My dad and I were always close and shared a love for journalism. Sometimes, during the summers, he'd let me go dig up facts with him and do interviews. Those are some of my best memories and the ones I try to hold on to.

The last time I saw him haunts my mind every single day. He looked so worried and upset, frantically sifting through some of his old files and notes. I wasn't sure what he was looking for as he rambled about some sort of conspiracy theory, too frazzled for me to dare ask.

I should've. I really wish I had said something. Instead, I made a mental note to ask him later, after he calmed down. But, by the time I came home, the house was empty, and it stayed that way until my mom returned from working the night shift at the hospital.

She didn't seem too concerned that he was gone—he'd done that a lot over the last year, ever since my brother died. After a few days of still being MIA, though, my worry grew, and I drove down to the police station to report him missing. No one seemed too eager to find him, and after doing a brief search, the sheriff declared my dad left of his own free will, that he abandoned his family.

Everyone, including my mom, accepted the answer. Not me. I know my dad. While he believes in some crazy ideas and pissed off a lot of people, I know he loves me and would never have just left without at least calling and checking in. I can't accept anything else, not without hard evidence.

Tears fill my eyes as I think about the last six months without him. Not wanting to turn into a big, old cry baby, though, at least not in front of Ev, I suck back the water-works and change the subject.

"I think I need to take a break from this project and regroup my thoughts, maybe come up with another angle."

"Do you want my help?" She reaches for a worn spiral notebook on her computer desk, practically bursting with excitement. "I came up with a list of topics for the project.

I'm only going to use the two I underlined." She flips open the notebook then hands it to me. "You're welcome to use any of the rest. The broadest topics are highlighted in pink. Any of those will more than likely guarantee you an A as long as you do the work properly and thoroughly."

I crinkle my nose at the sight of the fifty-plus topic ideas, each as boring as the next. "Thanks, but your ideas might be a little too smart for me." I shut the notebook and toss it aside on the desk. "Wanna hit up the skate park with me for a little while? It'll probably help me figure out an idea for the project."

Her excitement goes *poof*. "Mak, you always do this."

"Do what?" I feign dumb as I slip on my sneakers.

"Avoid doing big projects until the last second."

"Well, at least I'm consistent," I joke.

"You can't flunk history. If you do, then you won't be able to graduate." Her frustration gradually shifts to deviousness. "And then you'll have to spend the summer retaking the class and listening to Mrs. Maralline's monotonous tone. Is that how you want to spend your last summer?"

"I don't know ... Hey, did I tell you what Finn did in Biology yesterday?" I ask, pushing to my feet.

She waves a finger at me. "Don't change the subject. You always do that, too."

"I know." I tug my knitted maroon beanie on my head then slip my studded backpack over my shoulders. "It's a great distraction when you don't necessarily want to talk about something. Some of the people my dad used to interview would do that to avoid answering questions that were making them uncomfortable. My dad referred to it as a guilty tick, and when he spotted it, he'd dig his claws in."

She narrows her eyes at me. "You just did it again."

Dammit! She's too smart for her own good.

"Fine." I raise my hands in surrender. "Give me today to de-stress and kick some ass on the half-pipes. Tomorrow, I'll re-stress by draining my soul and working on the project."

"*Draining your soul?* Isn't that a little bit overdramatic?" Shaking her head, she sighs in defeat. "Fine, I'll give you today to have some fun. But tomorrow, you're going to finish that project. I'll stay with you all day and night if I have to in order to make sure you do it."

I salute her. "Yes, boss, sir. But only if you try to have some fun today, too."

She nods, and I grab her hand.

"We can pick up Embry and Kennedy on the way," I say, yanking her out the door with me.

Embry and Kennedy are our two other best friends. We've been friends since elementary school, and together, we are a very different, very awesome group. Although, the people we go to school with haven't realized how truly awesome we are. Then again, it's not their fault they aren't awesome enough to realize this for themselves.

"Hold on." She wiggles her arm from my grip and snatches up her laptop. "I think I'll work on my English midterm while we're there."

"That's what you consider fun?" I question then shake my head. "You know what? Never mind. Silly question."

"No question is a silly question," she states seriously as we step out of her bedroom.

"My dad used to say that, too." I almost smile at the reminder of my dad. Then I remember all the questions he was asking the police right before he vanished. Questions about my brother's death, about a conspiracy, secret societies, sacrificing rituals, strange, otherworld things going on. Questions that seemed to make people uneasy. He swore half the town was in on it: rich, poor, business owners, homemakers, even some of the police.

Sometimes, I wonder if asking those questions led to his disappearance.

TWO

After Ev and I hop into my car, I steer toward Embry's house because it's closer, unlike Kennedy's, which is located on the posh side of town. Out of our four friends, Kennedy's family is the only one who's wealthy. The rest of us are lower-class.

Shadow Cove does have a middle-class, but it's the smallest of the classes. Most people either own businesses in the community, or work for one. And the workers make Jack shit, while the owners roll in their pools filled with hundred dollar bills. Don't believe me? Just drive across town. One-half of the land is dotted with lavish two- and three-story homes and in the center of town is small section of quint subdivisions of cookie cutter homes where all the middle class live. Then when you cross Main Street, the subdivisions shift into single-story, run down, in desperate need of some maintenance homes, and the families who live in them struggle daily to make ends meet.

"Do you ever think they'll fix the sign?" Everleigh asks as I roll through a four-way stop. I'd come to a full stop, but for the last year, one of the stop signs has been lying broken on the ground, so I don't know if it really counts anymore.

"What? The stop sign?" I ask, and she nods. "I don't know. It took them, like, three years to fix the yield sign down on Fifth Street."

Ev frowns. "Why don't they take care of this town better?"

"Oh, they do," I say, sarcasm dripping into my tone. "You just have to go to the other side of town where all the stop signs are shiny and new. I even heard they have traffic lights and everything."

She chuckles, setting her computer on the floorboard. "Traffic lights, huh? Wow, that's super fancy."

"Oh, yeah, totally fancy." I flip on my blinker. "Way too fancy for us common folks. We probably couldn't even figure out how to use them ..." The humor dies from my tone as we pass the old wooden sign that points to the dirt road leading to Shadow Cove Lake. The lake where my brother's body was found.

I almost forget how to breathe as I recollect the days leading up to his death and those afterward.

Some people consider my brother's death a great tragedy. The few people who showed up to his funeral spoke of how he was too young to die and how heartbreaking it was that he was in such a dark place the few months leading up to his death. And they were right. My brother was in a dark place right before he died. The colorful, joking, loving, goofy brother I grew up with had withered into a sullen, depressed, moody guy I barely recognized. He lost enough weight that his ribs were protruding and his face was sunken in. His once 4.0 GPA slipped dramatically. He was quiet and withdrawn, spending hours locked in his room. When he would come out, he was snappy and irritable.

My mom and the school's guidance counselor thought he was depressed. My dad had another theory: that my brother got into trouble with some secret society in Shadow Cove. A lot of people in the town gossiped about him selling drugs. Me, I didn't know what to think. Still don't.

Whatever was going on with him, he ultimately took his own life. At least, according to the final police report, he did. I was there when the officer told my parents and rambled on and on about my brother until there wasn't anything left to say. The conclusion was pretty simple, though.

Full Name: Sawyer Evingston.

Age: Eighteen.

Time of Death: 12:38 p.m.

Date of Death: January 17, 2014.

Cause of Death: Overdose of morphine.

My mom easily accepted this conclusion. My dad, not so much.

"That doesn't explain why he was found in the lake," Dad argued after the detective finished his speech.

"More than likely, he injected the drugs near the lake—either on the shore or up above on the cliffs—and either fell into the water or the waves pulled his body in," the detective answered in a tolerant tone.

My dad loosened his tie, his face turning bright red. "This is such bullshit! He's only been dead for a week. A week isn't long enough to investigate a murder case."

My mom glared at my dad. "James, do not bring that stuff up right now."

My dad gaped at her. "Are you being serious? Our son is dead and these"—he waved his hand at the detective sitting on the other side of the desk—"yahoos are saying he killed himself without looking into all the facts. How would his body fall into the lake? Better yet, why would he choose to overdose near a lake when he hated water? And where did he even get the morphine? Plus, he had those scratches on his arms." He shot the detective a look. "Was that even looked into?"

I wasn't too surprised by my dad's questions. He always had a knack for questioning everything. It's what made him great at his job, but kind of ruined his people skills.

"I can assure you, Mr. Evingston, that the case was

looked into thoroughly, and there is no evidence of foul play," the detective said. "This isn't one of your stories. We don't stretch the truth here in order to please people. We stick to the facts, and we're very good at what we do."

"Good at what you do, huh?" My dad leaned forward in the chair. "Tell me this, then. If you guys are so great at what you do, why does half the damn town practically get away with murder?"

"That's enough!" My mom's outburst startled everyone. She slung her purse over her shoulder, rose to her feet, and stuck her hand out to the detective. "We appreciate every-thing you and everyone else has done. Now, if you'll excuse me, I need to get home and finalize the funeral arrangements."

My dad looked like a kicked puppy as she stormed out of the room without so much as a backward glance.

He cleared his throat several times before turning back to the detective. "Close the case if you want. I'll just start my own investigation"—he pushed to his feet and headed for the door—"because I know there's more to this, whether you know it or not." He signaled for me to follow him. "Come on, Mak; let's get out of here."

I wiped a few tears from my eyes and followed him out, his words and threats echoing in my mind. Was there really more to my brother's death? Did he really not commit suicide like the police said?

Later, my mom took me aside and explained my dad's irrational behavior was due to stress from my brother's death. Maybe she was right, but that didn't stop my dad from going into full-on detective mode for the next six months, trying to solve the mystery around my brother's death all the way up until he vanished off the face of the earth. And now my brother's death remains a mystery, along with my dad's disappearance.

That's all my life is anymore: unanswered questions, confusion, and a desperation to find out what happened.

"Mak, did you hear me?" Ev asks, yanking me out of my thoughts.

I blink dazedly at her. "What?"

"I said I just texted Embry, and she's at Kennedy's, so we don't have to go this way." Concern masks her expression. "Are you okay? It felt like you just spaced out for, like, five minutes straight."

I probably did space out for five minutes, but I'm not about to tell her that. Ev is already afraid enough of my driving.

"I'm cool," I lie breezily as I pull the car to the side of the road to flip a bitch. "I'm just tired. I've been sleeping super shitty lately."

"You're not having nightmares again, are you?" Her attention drifts to the screen of her phone as it buzzes.

"No. I just have a lot on my mind with midterms and this skating competition coming up," I lie for the tenth time today.

Sure, the skating competition hangs over my head like a dark, grey, "ha, ha, you're never going to come up with the money" cloud, but that's not what's been hindering my Zs. Ever since my brother passed away, a very vivid reoccurring nightmare of him drowning in the lake haunts me. Instead of jumping into the water and helping him, I just stand on the shore and watch him die. The odd part of the dream is when Sawyer's ghost appears beside me. Sometimes, he asks me why I didn't help him, to which I never know how to reply. Sometimes, we talk about nothing important, like the weather or how things are going with my skateboarding. Sometimes, we don't talk at all, which is worse because it reminds me of our relationship during the last few months he was alive.

I told Kennedy, who's really into dream interpretations, about it once, and she suggested that my dreams might represent guilt. Guilt over what, she wasn't sure, but I have a hunch it might have to do with what happened the last time I saw Sawyer.

"I need your help, Mak," he said, barging into my bedroom.

I was lying on my bed, working on math homework, and had barely glanced up. "What's up?"

He shut off the music playing from my stereo and shouted, "Will you look up at me when I talk to you!" His anger startled and pissed me off.

"If you want something, you can just ask," I snapped, irritated he was yelling at me for no good reason. He had been doing that so much lately, and his bad attitude was starting to wear on my nerves, and everyone else's for that matter. "You don't need to yell at me. If you want something, just ask."

"I just ..." He massaged the back of his neck tensely. "Never mind." Then he hurried out of my room.

I moved to chase him down to apologize but froze. For the last few months, all I'd been doing was apologizing to him, so I let him go, figuring I'd give him time to cool off before trying to talk to him.

I never got the chance. That was the last time I ever saw him. To this day, I don't know what he needed help with or what he wanted to talk to me about. And the guilt gnaws away at me every single day.

"Mak, stop!" Everleigh shrieks, her voice laced with pure terror.

I jerk back to reality and realize I'm about to fly through the fancy, schmancy stoplight. I pound my foot on the brake, and the tires skid as my car grinds to a halt.

"Holy shit," Ev breathes, her eyes wide as she stares at the red light across from us. Taking a few measured breaths, she releases her death grip on the seat. "What the heck just happened?"

"Whoopsie." I shrug. "Sorry. I wasn't paying attention."

She works to compose her erratic breathing. "Maybe I should drive."

"Nah. I can handle this." I tap the side of my temple. "My head's back in the game."

"It scares me to think of how long your head's been out of the game."

"For, like, thirty seconds, tops."

"Liar."

"Okay, maybe a little longer." I drive forward as the light turns green. "But I promise I won't do it again."

I make good on my promise, keeping my focus on the road as we weave around the jagged hillsides that curve around the coastline and make a right turn into Kennedy's driveway. I ease the car up to the towering iron gate and honk my horn while Ev sends them a text to get their butts out here.

I could press the buzzer to get in then drive up to the front door, but Kennedy's stepmom isn't a huge fan of me, something she proves when she wanders outside to collect the mail.

She's dressed in a white jumpsuit, her blonde hair pulled into a tight ponytail, and she's cradling a yappy, little dog like it's her baby. When she spots my car at the gate, she shoots me a nasty look. Whether it's at my piece of shit car or me, I'm unsure. Probably both.

"She's such a weirdo," Ev remarks, her face twisting in disgust as Mrs. Wellingford lets the dog lick her lips.

"Ew, I think they just touched tongues." I gag. "I'm so glad she's only Kennedy's stepmom. Could you imagine if that were her real mom, and that's what Kennedy would turn into?"

"No way," Ev disagrees. "Kennedy would never turn into that. She's too much of a good person."

"True," I agree, sliding my square-framed shades over my eyes. "Kennedy is the best."

We sit at the gate for another couple of minutes, getting the stink eye from Mrs. Wellingford when my car backfires.

I smile at her and secretly flip her the bird, but the movement offers zilch gratification since she can't see it. If I did actually grow a pair of lady balls and flip her off for real, she'd probably call the cops on me. That might sound absurd, but she's already done shit like that a handful of times. Like when we were being too loud out back, and she claimed she thought we were intruders to the police. She knew it was us, though. She freakin' saw us go back there!

By the time Kennedy and Embry come wandering out, the wicked witch of a stepmom has glared at me half a dozen times. The second she spots Kennedy, though, she focuses her evilness on her, pulling her aside to say God knows what. When Kennedy walks away, she looks fuming mad.

Watching Kennedy and Embry hike down the paved driveway is an odd sight. The two of them are completely opposite: Kennedy with her long, blonde hair; white miniskirt; and pink tank top, and Embry with her newly dyed, blazing red hair; heavy eyeliner; black shorts; black T-shirt; and black clunky boots.

"God, she's such a bitch," Kennedy says as she slides into the backseat, glaring at her stepmom through the windshield.

"What'd she do now?" I ask as Embry gets in.

"Oh, you know, the usual." Kennedy fastens her seatbelt. "Told me I look like shit, that I need to lose weight, that I need to stop spending money, that I'm too spoiled." She rolls her eyes. "Like she has room to talk."

"She told you to lose weight?" I ask. "*You?* Jesus, you're, like, a size two."

Kennedy dismisses me with a flick of her wrist. "It's not that big a deal. I know she's just jealous because she can't eat whatever she wants and stay skinny. I heard her bitching about it to my dad the other night. You should've heard them. Apparently, he didn't say the right thing, and she flipped out and started screaming at him. He called his lawyer the other day." She raises her crossed fingers. "Fingers crossed it was about a divorce. They're hitting the two-year marker, so I bet it is."

"Your dad's so predictable." Embry cracks the window, letting the warm, salt-kissed air blow into the cab. "Has he ever stayed married for more than two years?"

Kennedy nods, staring out the window. "My mom and he were married for almost nine years."

The cab grows quiet at the mention of Kennedy's mom. The woman ditched her and her dad for the pool boy. Kennedy was eight at the time, and we'd been friends for about a year. That day, she broke down on the playground and started crying.

"My mom ran away," she sobbed through the tears.

I was so confused. Parents weren't supposed to run away, were they?

"I'm sure she'll come back," I told her. "Parents don't just leave."

She dragged her hand across her face to wipe away the tears. "My dad said she's not coming back. He said she traded us in for a hot, younger piece of ass, took half of our money, ran away to Italy, and is never coming back." Her hands shook on her lap as she stared at the dirt beneath us. "What if she never comes back, Mak? What if I'm stuck in the big house with my dad, listening to him yell all the time?"

"He doesn't yell all the time," I lied. "Just most of the time."

She gave me a *really* look. "He yells *all the time* ... at me, the maids, the cook. I even heard him yell at the mailman once for leaving a package too close to the door." Tears bubbled in her eyes. "I'm so scared. I don't want to live alone with him."

I wanted to comfort her, but I wasn't sure how. My parents rarely yelled at me, and my mom and dad had been happily married for as long as I could remember, so I couldn't relate to her situation. Still, I knew I needed to comfort her.

I reached over and took her hand. "I know it's scary, but everything's going to be okay. I won't let your dad yell at you, and I won't let you be alone in that house too much. If you have to, you can come stay with me. I'm sure my mom and dad won't care."

She gripped my hand tightly. "Thanks, Mak."

I held up my end of the promise, too. Whenever Kennedy's dad got too cranky, she would come spend the night. He never seemed to mind when she took off, and to this day, Kennedy has more freedom than most kids our age. She's never said it aloud, but his neglectful attitude wears on her, and sometimes, she purposefully gets into trouble to get his attention.

"Hopefully, he'll wait a few months before getting remarried this time," Kennedy says, rolling down her window. "And find someone who's at least ten years older than me."

Embry slips an arm around her shoulder and gives her a side hug. "Remember what we talked about? Don't let the man get you down. Or the bitch. Things will get better." A Cheshire cat smile spreads across her dark red lips. "But, if they don't, I'll just have to make someone pay."

Kennedy chuckles. "Thanks, Em. That really means a lot, especially coming from you."

I know what she means. Embry is the badass of our group. And by badass, I mean, she's skilled in all sorts of martial arts and has made people pee their pants with her death glare. Literally. Don't believe me? Ask Sophie Burdely, the captain of the cheerleading squad. She also loves pissing her parents off, mostly because they love to ignore her unless she's done something wrong.

Grinning, Embry opens her mouth to say something, but the words never leave her lips. Her attention darts to the left side of the street as four cop cars whiz by us. When they reach the end of the road, they veer west down a narrow dirt road, heading in the direction of the lake. For a heart faltering moment, I swear to God I see Sawyer standing at the end of the road, simply staring at me. As quickly as he appeared, he vanishes into thin air.

I swallow hard, reminding myself that Sawyer is dead. I didn't really see him, just an old memory of him that stems from seeing the police cars.

"I wonder where they're going," Kennedy mutters, twisting around in her seat to gawk out the rear window.

Embry frowns, her worried gaze flicking in my direction. "It looked like they were going up to the lake."

I swallow hard. "Yeah, it did."

Kennedy twists around in her seat, fixing her concerned eyes on me. "They were driving so fast. It has to be bad, right? Like, an accident or something?"

I shrug, clutching the steering wheel. "Maybe."

"It could be a routine drill," Ev suggests, setting her phone on my console.

"They don't usually turn on the sirens for that, do they?" Kennedy asks, tucking a strand of hair behind her ear.

Ev gives me an edgy, sidelong glance. "I don't know."

The cab grows quiet as the three of them throw anxious glances in my direction, as if they're afraid I'm going to break. I want to tell them I'm fine, that it was just a couple of police cars, for crying out loud, but the words get lodged in my throat as the memory of my brother's death resurfaces.

We were driving around that day, too, and saw the

police cars zooming in that direction. I made a joke about how they must have been racing and the winner won all the donuts. Kennedy laughed her ass off, and Ev corrected me that the donut/cop thing wasn't true. When I got home an hour later, I found out the real reason the police had been in such a hurry. An anonymous caller had phoned in that there was a body near the shore.

"Wait. I thought you knew everything, Ev," Kennedy jokes through the pitying silence, throwing a smirk at Ev.

"Not everything," Ev quips with a grin. "Just almost everything."

Kennedy laughs, and Ev smiles.

The two of them banter back and forth, trying to solve the mystery of whether the cops are reacting to an actual emergency. I know the answer, though.

They only turn on their sirens for an actual emergency, something I learned the day my brother died.

THREE

"Mak, I love you so, so much, and I love that you love skating, but I really dislike hanging out here." Ev frowns at the ramps, grind rails, and half-pipes.

"That's because there are guys around," Kennedy says, opening the door to get out of the car.

"That's not why." Ev chews on her thumbnail as she eyes the groups of guys skating and loitering.

"That's totally why." Kennedy grins at Ev. "You've been afraid of boys for forever."

"So what if she has?" Embry chimes in. "If you ask me, guys aren't that fantastic."

"Oh, they are for certain things." Kennedy flashes the two of them a mischievous grin. "Trust me."

Embry rolls her eyes. "You're so all talk."

Kennedy laughs. "Maybe. But maybe not."

"I'm not afraid of guys," Ev gripes, her gaze drifting to the skate park. "But would it hurt for more girls to hang around here?"

"Sometimes, they do." I silence the engine and stuff the keys into my shorts pocket. "I wish more would. Maybe one day they'll all realize how awesome this place is."

"I wouldn't go with awesome," Kennedy says, stretching her arms above her head. "No offense, Mak, but I think this place is pretty lame."

I climb outside underneath the greying sky and bump the door shut with my hip. "Then why do you come here?"

"To support my awesome, best-skater-girl-in-the-world best friend." She winks.

I can't help smiling, my worries of cop cars and lakes dwindling more with every one of her jokes. That's one of the things I love most about Kennedy. She has a way of making you forget all the bad stuff going on in your life.

"She is pretty badass, isn't she?" I say with a teasing grin.

"She really is." Smiling, Kennedy skips off and meets Ev and Embry at the front of the car while I head to the trunk to collect my skateboard and iPod.

By the time I have all of my stuff, they've made plans to get some snow cones from across the street.

"If you're lucky, maybe we'll bring you back one," Kennedy teases before the three of them take off toward the main road lined with stores that sell overly priced goods.

"You better! Or I'll steal yours!" I shout back then turn around and hike toward the closest half-pipe, walking near the powerline posts on my way to scope out the new missing persons' flyers that have been put up. There are always new ones, yet no one ever gets found. Either they stay missing and everyone assumes they ran away, or they wind up dead somewhere. The usual cause of death? A drug overdose.

Today, three new flyers have been stapled to the posts. Three new girls missing, all just a year or two older than me, and two I knew when they still went to school.

"What's happening to you?" I mutter. "Are you really just disappearing to escape Shadow Cove, or is there more to it?"

I wonder the same thing about my dad all the time.

Sighing, I tear my attention off the flyers and continue my walk across the parking lot to the skate park.

It's sort of intimidating to approach an area where twenty or so guys and zero girls are hanging out, but I'm used to it. I've been coming to this place since I was about seven years old when Sawyer first taught me how to skateboard. I caught on quickly and was soon doing more tricks than he could. He was so proud of me and always supported me by coming to every one of my skate competitions. At least, until the few months leading up to his death.

I smash my lips together, recalling the police cars I saw earlier. What if someone else drowned in the lake? Will it be one of those girls on the flyers? Will the truth actually make it to the public this time? The only reason my brother's death did was because my dad reported on it. There have been many other cases of people drowning in the lake that hardly anyone knows about, according to the few research notes my dad left behind. I know he had a lot more notes about the lake and the deaths that happened there—files of them, actually—but either he took those with him, or they were destroyed. Either way, I was never able to find all of them.

"Well, well, well, look what we have here."

My lip twitches at the sound of Dixon's voice—aka, my number one nemesis in the world. Not just because he's constantly tormented me ever since middle school, but because he picks on anyone he deems unworthy. I've seen him lock people in lockers, dump food trays on people's heads, and once, in middle school, he tripped a girl in the cafeteria, which wouldn't have been so horrible; except, she was wearing a skirt and ended up flashing everyone. Oh, and did I mention that girl was wearing an oversized pair of underwear with kittens on them? How do I know this? Because I was the girl!

My lip curls in annoyance as Dixon skates toward me. He's wearing designer jeans, a T-shirt, and shoes that probably cost more than my car, and on his face is a my-shit-don't-stink smirk.

He grinds to a stop, kick-flipping his board into his hand. "Haven't seen you around here lately," he says with a conniving grin. "Thought maybe you finally figured out you're a girl."

I grind my teeth. The only reason I haven't been at the park much is because I've been busy taking on odd jobs, like mowing lawns, handing out flyers, waving a sign around in front of the café—anything to bring in extra money to help pay the bills. I've tried to find a permanent part-time job, but most store owners seem skittish to hire me because of a rumor going around that I like to shoplift. A rumor I'm pretty sure Dixon started, but I have no proof.

I open my mouth to insult Dixon's technique and take his ego down a notch, but a voice rises over mine.

"Dixon, leave her alone," Rylen—Dixon's kind of, sort of friend and my kind of, sort of other nemesis—intervenes.

He walks up to us with his board tucked under his arm. He's rocking a grey knitted cap over his chin-length black hair, his jeans have a tiny hole in the knee, and dirt smudges dot his sneakers. He's not poor by any means. He's just not as flashy about his wealth as Dixon.

Rylen offers me a sympathetic smile. "Just ignore him. He's in a bad mood because a girl handed him his ass during last week's competition."

Dixon shoots him a nasty look, probably because the girl Rylen is talking about is me.

Okay, so maybe Rylen isn't really my archenemy. The guy is actually really nice, but he's also my main competition. He's so good Shadow Cove's local skate shop sponsors him, which means he gets free clothes to endorse, and they pay his skate fees.

I've tried so hard to get a sponsor, but to no avail. The owner of the local skate shop—a twenty-something-year-old ex-skater, pot lover, hippie dude—did tell me once that, if I ever beat Rylen at one of our local competitions, he'd straight up offer me a sponsorship. The problem is that Rylen has some killer moves, and I always come in second place. If I ever want to beat him, I'm going to need to up my game. I just haven't figured out a way to do that yet.

I hold up a hand in Rylen's direction. "It's cool. I've got this." I give Dixon a sugary sweet smile. "So, are you pissed off at me because I kicked your ass at the last competition and every other competition, for that matter? Or are you just pissed because Kennedy shot your sorry ass down at the party last weekend?"

Anger flashes in Dixon's eyes before a malicious smile curls at his lips. "Hey, does your dad still come watch you skate? I know mine does. I'm thinking yours is too busy bailing on your family. What's left of it, anyway."

Usually, I'm not much for violence, but I just about throw down right there.

"Don't you ever talk about my father," I growl, lunging forward to either hit him or shove him. Rylen jumps between us, though, and snakes an arm around my waist, guiding me backward.

"Just calm down," he says. "It's not worth it."

I glare at Dixon from over Rylen's shoulder, my chest heaving with every angry breath I take. "No, I definitely think it is."

"Mak, think of the rules. If you get into a fight here, you'll get banned." His lips quirk into a smile. "And I can't lose my best competition. It takes all the fun out of winning."

I wrestle back a smile. "Fine, whatever. I won't kick his ass *today*, only so I can kick your ass at next month's competition."

"Good." He removes his arm from around my waist and steps back, a pucker forming at his brow. "Wait, what about the competition in two weeks? Aren't you entering?"

I shake my head, trying not to sulk. "Nah, I don't have the thousand bucks to enter."

Normally, competitions don't cost so much, but this one is the yearly Shadow Cove's Skate Charity Event, one of the biggest competitions of the year. The main market is the upper-class community who can afford the thousand bucks entry fee, which is cool and everything—charity rocks. The problem is it gives people like Dixon another reason to rub his wealth in my face and every other poor kid who dreams of competing. What I wouldn't give to just once have the thousand dollars so I could enter and kick his spoiled brat ass in front of all his family and most of Shadow Cove.

For a few days, I actually thought I might be able to after Kennedy offered to fork out the dough. Then her stepmom convinced her stepdad to cut off her cash flow for a while so she can, as her stepmom puts it, "learn how to take care of herself." This coming from a woman who married for money, something she admitted once when she had a few too many glasses of wine. Fortunately for her, Mr. Wellingford doesn't give a shit and is only looking for a trophy wife.

"Are you sure it costs that much to enter? I thought it was less," Rylen says. "I mean, my mom paid my entry fee, so I'm not positive, but I can double-check."

"I'm sure it costs that much." I sidestep around him and head for the half-pipe. "Thanks for stopping me from getting myself banned."

"Anytime," he calls after me.

Dixon shoots Rylen a nasty look before sidestepping and blocking my way. "So, you're not making it to the charity competition. That's too bad. I'd say maybe you could ask your dad to lend you the thousand bucks, but you'd actually have to be able to talk to him to do that."

I count underneath my breath, doing my best to ignore his jabs, and brush by him with my chin held high.

"Or maybe I could ask my dad to hire your mom," he hollers after me. "From what I hear, she's been selling herself on the corner to make some extra cash."

That isn't true at all. My mom works double shifts at the hospital and doesn't have a single hour to spare. Plus, we're pretty much as broke as we've always been.

I spin around, walking backward to smile haughtily at Dixon. "You don't have to ask him to do that. He already hired her last week. And from what I hear, the dude's got a serious case of erectile dysfunction. I hope that's not hereditary. From the rumors I hear in the locker room, I think it might be."

He glares at me, his hands curling into fists. "Lia needs to shut her stupid mouth and stop telling fucking lies."

I tap my finger against my lips. "Who said it was Lia?"

He looks like he wants to throttle me as he opens his mouth to say who knows what. I don't stick around to listen. I spin on my heels, drop the skateboard, and skate off toward the closest ramp.

I spend the next hour hitting the half-pipes and grinding the rails with my earbuds in and some music cranked up. The longer I skate, the deeper I get in the zone and the more the outside world fades away. I feel like the only person in the world, even with at least twenty other people around. That's what skating does for me. It gives me a break from the crazy reality that is my life.

Eventually, I start to slow things down and focus on practicing my 540 McTwist, my favorite trick to do in competitions. By the time I'm finished, I'm exhausted, thirsty, sweaty, and completely content.

The second the wheels stop spinning, reality catches up with me as Dixon strides up, looking way too happy. And a happy Dixon is never a good thing.

"Looking good out there, Mak." He stops in front of me,

practically bouncing with happiness. "Too bad your mom doesn't seem to think so."

My comeback dies on my tongue. "What?"

His grin broadens as he gives a chin nod in the direction of the picnic tables where my mom is standing with her hands on her hips and her lips pursed. She has her scrubs on, her brown hair is pulled into a messy bun, and she looks super irritated.

Dixon laughs at the sight of my scared expression. "Maybe I should go ask her what she charges an hour. I mean, she's a little on the old side, but she does have that whole naughty nurse thing going on."

Gritting my teeth, I skate by him, purposefully slamming my shoulder into his. When he trips sideways from the impact, I get a morbidly sick sense of gratification. But the feeling dissipates the closer I get to my mom and her death glare.

I rewind through everything I've done today, trying to figure out what has her looking like her panties are all wadded in a bunch. The only reason I can come up with is because I'm here, skating. She's never been a fan but didn't verbalize her dislike very much until after my dad disappeared. It was like she was holding back for his sake then decided, since he is gone, she doesn't give a shit anymore.

"Hey, what're you doing here?" I ask, grinding to a stop. "I thought you were working until midnight."

"I got off early." Her gaze skims the ramps behind me, and then her eyes land on me. Up close, I can see the red rimming her eyes, evidence that she's been crying. "I don't know how you can stand this place. It's so noisy and rowdy."

"It's not that bad." I pop the skateboard up, tuck it under my arm, and offer her a joking smile, trying to lighten her mood. "It doesn't feel as rowdy when you're part of the rowdiness."

She rolls her eyes. "There's so much better stuff to do with your time. You're a smart girl; why can't you start focusing on school more?"

"I'm not that smart." I glance around for my friends and spot them lounging on the hood of my car, slurping on sodas and laughing about something. "Ev's the smart one."

"You could be as smart as Ev if you tried harder, but you don't try at all. That's your problem."

Over the last year or so, my mom has gotten more and more testy toward me. Sometimes, she gets angry for no evident reason. I have a feeling it has to do with losing her husband and son over the course of a year. Whatever the reason, I've learned that remaining silent is always the best choice whenever she gets like this.

"Whatever. Just stand there and don't say anything like you always do," she snaps. "It doesn't really matter. I didn't come here to argue with you about your B average."

"Then why did you come here?" I ask cautiously.

She scowls at me. "Because you need to come home right now. I've been trying to call you for the last hour, but your phone keeps sending me to voicemail."

"I think the battery's dead," I tell her calmly. Inside,

though, my thoughts soar. She seems so upset, more than usual. Did she find something out about my dad? "Is something wrong?"

"Is *something* wrong?" She gapes at me with her arms folded. "No, Mak. *Something* isn't wrong. *Everything* is."

Her loud voice is starting to draw attention, and Dixon is laughing his ass off. Great. Now he's got all the ammunition he needs to make my life a living hell.

"Do you have any idea how worried I've been for the last couple of hours?" she yells. "And all that worry could've been cleared up if you'd just answered your damn phone."

"I-I'm sorry," I stammer. "I didn't mean to let the battery go dead. I just forget to charge it sometimes."

"Well, maybe if you weren't so distracted with this shit" —she flings her arm in the direction of the skate park—"then you'd remember to do half the stuff you forget about."

"I'm sorry," I repeat. I don't know what else to say since I really don't think this is about my phone battery dying. "I'll make sure it stays charged from now on."

"You better." She points at her old, beat-up truck in the parking lot. "Now get in the car. You're coming home with me, and then you and I are going to have a nice, long talk about something."

I point over at my car. "But I drove my friends here."

She scowls at my friends. "Fine. Take them home then drive your ass straight to the house. Do not make any extra stops."

Nodding, I hurry toward my car. With each step, worry

laces my thoughts. After all, the last time my mom told me we had to talk about something was the day she told me my father left us. And I can't help wondering if maybe my dad is the reason the police were hauling ass up to the lake this afternoon.

FOUR

Right before my dad vanished, he spent a lot of time up near Shadow Cove Lake, looking for clues about my brother's death. When I reported my dad missing, I suggested to the police that they look for him there. I'm not sure if they ever did. I thought about going up and looking around myself, but I never got the guts to do it, fearing what I'd find. Or what I wouldn't.

My stomach kinks in knots as images of my dad's body floating in the lake flood my mind. What if he's been dead up there this entire time?

Then Dixon takes it upon himself to shout at the top of his lungs, "Hey, Mak! Last night was really fun! You're damn good in bed, girl!" and the images go *poof*.

I would be grateful that he momentarily got rid of the morbid images in my head, but my mom isn't in her car yet. The look of horror and disgust on her face lets me know I just went from being in deep shit to being buried alive in it.

"Well, at least he said you were good," Kennedy offers as she hops off the hood of my car. She hands me a melted snow cone, and I down it like a soda.

"I don't care about that. But now everyone at school's probably going to think I slept with him." I yank open the driver side door, slide into the seat, and my friends follow, climbing in.

"Maybe not very many people heard him," Ev suggests, drawing her seatbelt over her shoulder.

"Yeah, right. I think the whole town heard him." I flip on the headlights. "Man, this night went from okay to sucky in about two minutes flat."

"Cheer up, buttercup." Kennedy reaches over my seat and pats my shoulder. "We'll get him back. Don't you worry."

That gets me to smile.

"And how do we do that?" I ask.

Embry pops her knuckles. "I could kick his ass. Getting his ass handed to him by a girl would be the ultimate punishment for his stupid, sexist ass."

I consider the thought, but not for very long. "No way. He'd probably end up suing you and pressing charges."

She slumps back in the seat. "Yeah, you're probably right, but dammit, it might be worth it."

Kennedy shakes her head. "Beating his ass isn't enough. We need to kick him where it really counts."

"And how do we do that when his dad always bails him out of trouble?" I ask, steering out of the parking lot.

She half-shrugs. "Give me a few days. I'll think of something sinister."

"Please don't think of something that's going to get us into too much trouble," Ev pleads with her hands clasped. "The last time you came up with a revenge plan, I ended up grounded for three weeks."

"All the best revenge plans require getting into trouble." Kennedy sips her soda with her thinking face on. "I need to dig up some dirt on him. Maybe take a look at his school records, see what he's got going on ... Oh!" Excitement bursts through her. "We could run a background check on him, his dad, his mom—anyone he knows—and see if the Jennings are hiding anything. Then we could plaster the evidence all over the town. Can you imagine a family like the Jennings having to endure the shit you have, Mak?"

A small smile tugs at my lips. "I think I might like the sound of that."

Ev apprehensively shakes her head. "I'm not doing anything illegal this time."

Kennedy juts out her lip. "Come on, Ev. What's the

point of being a computer genius if you don't use your power for the greater good?"

"Hacking into people's personal records isn't for the greater good," she protests. "And do you know how much trouble I'd get in if I got caught?"

"Oh, fine." Kennedy's pout deepens. "I guess I'll have to think of something else equally as awesome."

For the next twenty minutes, Kennedy throws out her ideas, ranging from getting dirt on Dixon from his ex-girl-friends to changing his grades from As to Fs, all of which Ev says nope to. By the time I park my car in front of her house, she hasn't come up with a solid plan, but pinkie promises she'll think of something before skipping up to her front door.

"I think she enjoys this revenge stuff a little too much," Ev says as I back out of the driveway and onto the main road.

"Perhaps." I steer the car back toward the main section of town to drop off Embry next. "But I kind of love her for it."

"Me, too," Embry agrees, propping her knees against the seat back. "You can always count on her to have your back. You don't find that very often, you know. A lot of people will bail out on you when things get ugly."

I offer Embry a sympathetic smile, knowing where her thoughts are heading. Back before the three of us became friends, Embry was picked on a lot for the old, outdated clothes she wore. One day on the playground, Kennedy screamed at all the other kids for being assholes—she had a very colorful vocabulary in grade school. That was enough to scare the shit out of most of the people, and for a while, everyone backed off.

Then, when Embry went Goth in middle school, the ridicule started up again. By then, though, Embry had gotten into martial arts, and after getting into a fight with one of the popular girls, the entire school was scared shitless once again and backed the fuck off. Of course, the popular girl went home and lied to her dad about who started the fight, and Embry ended up getting suspended from school because of it. She's been more careful since then about throwing her fists around. Still, it's always nice to know that, if a fight ever broke out, she could kick some serious ass.

Fifteen minutes later, I've dropped off Embry and am pulling up to Ev's house. She gives me a look of sympathy and a pity hug, as if this is the last time she'll ever see me. It might be, depending on how angry my mom is when I get home.

"Facetime me tonight if you can," Ev says as we idle in front of her house. "And let me know what's going on. I've never seen your mom so upset."

"I have. Twice." I grip the living daylights out of the steering wheel. "And those were some really, really bad times."

"I'm sure she was just worried when you didn't answer your phone," Ev insists, although she looks pretty worried, too. She collects her laptop from the floorboard then opens the door to get out. "My dad sometimes gets weird about stuff like that, too."

I force a smile, and she frowns.

"No fake smiles," she says. "We talked about this, and you promised me you were going to stop."

My plastic smile turns into a bummer frown. "Yeah, I know. I'm sorry. I just ... I don't know. I'm really worried. I mean, she's upset a lot and everything, but she hasn't acted this irrationally since my dad took off."

She hugs the computer to her chest as she lowers her head into the car and offers me a hopeful smile. "Maybe she's upset because she heard from him."

"Maybe," I say, not really believing my words.

The truth is, I often wonder if the next time I see or hear about my dad will be when his body shows up somewhere. It's a morbid thought, but for all I know, my dad's body could be stuck at the bottom of the lake, secured down by chains and bricks.

Sighing, I wave good-bye to Ev then back onto the road. I spend most of the drive lost in my thoughts, only snapping out of my daze when I pull up to my house and spot a shadowy figure standing on the front porch that's smothered by darkness. I instinctively tap the brake as a drop of fear laces through me.

As the car slams to a sudden stop, I nearly bash my head on the steering wheel. Thankfully, I manage not to crack my head open and hastily blink at the house. Just like when I thought I saw Sawyer, the shadowy figure has vanished, leaving me wondering if I really saw anything to begin with. Maybe I'm just hallucinating from the stress, something that happened both after Sawyer died and my father disappeared. I had to go on meds for a while, but the side effects made me tired all the time, so I stopped taking them despite the doctor's orders.

"God, I hated taking those pills," I mutter to myself.

After I calm down, I park the car in the driveway, deciding to keep the hallucinations a secret for now. I don't want to spend my days doped up again. Besides, I'm sure seeing the police cars is probably what triggered it. Hopefully, I'll feel better by tomorrow. I just hope things don't get out of hand like the last time when I had trouble distinguishing between what's real and what's not.

FIVE

I take several breaths to prepare myself before opening the door to my house, feeling super nervous about talking to my mom. Most of the lights are off, and the soundlessness makes me question—okay, makes me naively hope—that perhaps my mom had to return to work.

"In the kitchen!" she shouts, crushing my hope into smithereens.

I set down my skateboard and bag then enter the kitchen where my mom is sitting at the corner table with her reading glasses on and bills scattered out in front of her.

"So, would you like to explain to me why you think you're old enough to have sex?" she asks without looking up.

Dammit, I was hoping she'd skip over that and talk about why she was so upset at the skate park.

I slump down in the chair across from her. "I didn't sleep with Dixon, Mom."

She sifts through a thin stack of papers. "Then why does he seem to think you did?"

"He doesn't." I blow out a frustrated exhale. "Dixon Jennings is just an asshole who gets his kicks and giggles from making my life a living hell."

She peers up at me. "Dixon *Jennings?* As in, the Jennings who own every dealership in Shadow Cove?"

"Yeah, that would be the one," I say with as much disdain as possible. "Why?"

"Oh, it's nothing." She sets the bills aside and gives me her undivided attention. "It's just that, if you were dating a guy like him, I'd be okay with it."

"By 'guy like him,' do you mean a sexist, rich, spoiled brat? Because that's what he is."

"I'm sure he's not that bad. And he seems to like you."

I eye her over suspiciously. "Are you drunk?"

"No." She tosses a stack of envelopes down onto the table and removes her glasses. "I just know that sometimes, when a guy likes a girl, he teases. Just like Dixon did to you."

"You mean, when he practically told everyone I was sleeping with him when I'm not? Or when he insulted dad and Sawyer?" I resist an eye roll. "Yeah, sounds like he likes me a whole freakin' bunch."

A frown forms on her lips. "He insulted Sawyer?"

I do my best to ignore her lack of interest in my dad, reminding myself that to her, he abandoned us. "He always does. And he insults you, too."

Her face scrunches as if she just swallowed something sour. "What exactly did he say?"

"I'd rather not tell you."

"Mak, just tell me. I'm a grown woman. I can handle it."

Reluctantly, I give her a recap of what Dixon said. I expect her to get angry, but when I'm finished telling the story, she simply thrums her fingers against the table, seeming lost in thought.

"Well, I'm sure he didn't mean it," she finally says. "And I'm sure his father never told him that. Don is a wonderful man. I'm sure he wouldn't spread rumors about me."

Yeah, right. Dixon's dad is more of a sexist douche than his son, something he proved when he ran for mayor and declared that women belonged at home and should spend their time supporting their husbands. Needless to say, he didn't win, but people still buy cars from his dealerships.

I shake my head. "Dixon's dad is a jerk, and you know it. Remember when he ran for mayor?"

She stacks the bills evenly and sets them aside. "Don is the only reason we still have a roof over our heads."

I blink at her. "What are you talking about?"

She rises to her feet. "Nothing. Never mind. Forget I said anything."

I swiftly scoot the chair back from the table, causing the legs to grind noisily against the chipped linoleum floor. "No way. You can't just drop something like that on me and then walk away."

"I can do whatever I want, Makayla." She uses my full name as a warning that I'm about to push one too many of her buttons. "Now, if you'll excuse me, I need to take a shower and get to bed. I'm working the morning shift and part of the evening shift tomorrow." She sighs. "It's going to be a long day."

A thousand questions burn at the tip of my tongue, but pushing my mom for information will only cause her to shut down more. So, I keep my trap shut, but that doesn't mean I'm dropping the subject. I'll just wait until she gets into the shower before snooping around.

She pauses in the doorway and turns back around. "Oh, about what happened earlier at the skate park." Her tone softens slightly. "I didn't mean to yell at you. It's just that a girl was brought in who was pronounced dead on arrival. I heard the call come in over the radio, and they didn't have her name yet, but her description fit you, so I sort of panicked. When I tried to call you, and your phone went to voicemail, I nearly lost it."

All of my irritation toward her melts in an instant. If I were in the same position, I probably would've lost it, too.

Hell, I barely kept it together when I saw police vehicles driving toward the lake.

"I'm so sorry." I cross the room toward her. "I didn't mean to let the battery go dead. Ev and I were working on a project for most of the day, and charging it kind of slipped my mind."

She wraps her arms around me, pulling me in for a hug. "Just try to keep it charged from now on. I worry about you."

I bob my head up and down, hugging her back. "I know you do, and I promise, from now on, I'll try my hardest to keep my phone charged at all times."

She steps back, her eyes a bit misty. "I don't know what I'd do if I lost you, too."

A small smile touches my lips. "Well, I don't plan on going anywhere anytime soon."

"Good." She smooths my hair out of my eyes like she did when I was a little kid then gives me a strange look. "You've been feeling okay, though, right? I know it's been a while since you stopped taking your medication. I just want to make sure you're doing okay without it."

Crap, it's like she knows what happened today.

I nod, trying to remain calm. "I'm feeling really great, actually."

"Good." A hint of wariness floods her eyes before she turns to leave the room.

"Wait, Mom," I say, and she pauses. "What happened to the girl? I mean, how did she die?"

She doesn't turn around, but her back stiffens. "I'm not sure … Her body … was found in the lake."

"The lake?" I whisper. "Shadow Cove Lake?"

"I'm sure it was just an accident. Nothing we need to worry about. Nothing *you* need to worry about," she adds. "Now, I'm going to go take a shower. Don't stay up too late, okay? I want you to get a full night's rest." She doesn't wait for me to answer before hurrying into her room and shutting the door.

It's a suspicious move that leaves me wondering if she's lying.

SIX

LOCATION: THE SECRET SPOT IN MAK'S DAD'S
OFFICE
TIME: 11:54 PM
DATE: SATURDAY, MARCH 20TH

Before I leave the kitchen, I raid the fridge for some food. Unfortunately, no one has been shopping recently, so it's basically empty except for some bottles of juice, eggs, and a few cupcakes my mom brought home from a work party.

Not wanting to cooke, I grab a cupcake and a bottle of juice, then head to my dad's office.

There's a small nook hidden behind a bookcase in there that no one knows exists except for me and my dad. This makes for the perfect spot to do some snooping around in my mom's computer files and emails to find out why the hell she thinks Don Jennings is the reason we're not homeless.

The problem is, she recently changed her password. Usually, hers are ridiculously easy to crack. She's super fond of birthdays, last names, anniversaries, etc. But apparently, she's upped her A-game. After an hour of punching in every important number and name I can think of, I'm still locked out.

"All right, Mom, what are you hiding?" I prop my feet up against the wall in front of me and stuff my face with sugary frosting goodness while racking my brain for another route, another important date I may have missed, or the name of someone important to her.

I don't know why I do it, what the heck comes over me, other than I can't stop thinking about my mom's odd behavior earlier, but I end up typing "Don Jennings" into the password box. When the password is accepted, allowing me onto the home screen, my stomach goes *kerplunk*, and a little bit of puke burns in my throat.

"Oh, my God, is my mom having an affair with ...?" I nearly gag on a bite of cupcake and I start coughing, sprinkles flying everywhere.

No! There's no way she'd ever do that. Not when my dad has only been gone for six months. Not with the biggest douchebag in town. There has to be another reason his name is the password. Could it be because he saved us from being homeless? How did he do that, exactly? And why? What would be his ulterior motive? A guy like Don

Jennings wouldn't do something out of the kindness of his heart.

Clearing my throat several times, I compose myself and get to work. I start by raiding her bill files first and checking our monthly estimated bills Excel reports. Nothing seems different there, so I move on to her monthly bank statement. The last four months look kind of normal, except that her paychecks from the hospital seem a little bit low. Maybe she got a pay cut, or started working less hour. That doesn't explain why she's been gone the same amount of time as she always does. And besides, we haven't been making less money. My confusion only deepens when I get to a deposit made five months ago.

"Holy jackpot." I squint at the hefty cash deposit made back in November, about a month after my dad took off. "Ten thousand dollars! What the fuck!" The words leave my mouth way too loudly, and I quickly slap my hand over my mouth. I listen for signs that I've alerted my mom, but the house remains quiet.

Lowering my hand, I scroll through the transactions, wondering where the money went. Half of it went toward the next few months of rent, and then I get a bad taste in my mouth when I see a high amount was spent at Mayfield Luxury Hotel and Spa. I don't remember her taking off to Mayfield on that weekend. In fact, she supposedly works back-to-back shifts and is usually gone so much I don't see her for days on end. Apparently, she snuck off on a vacation, though, which I'd be completely fine with—she works her butt off and deserves a vacation—but why do I get the feeling she took the vacation with the person who gave her the money?

No! Stop thinking that, Mak! Your mom isn't shacking up with Don Jennings!

Still, I can't help thinking about it. A lot. And a thought crosses my mind, not about Don, but about Dixon. He's always disliked me, but lately, he's acted extra douchey. What if it's because he knows about the affair?

"Ugh." I grimace, feeling disgusted and beaten down.

After searching through the rest of the files and finding nothing else that seems suspicious, I move on to her emails, finding she's currently deleted most of the messages in her inbox and sent files. Does she know I snoop around? She has busted me a time or two before.

Giving up for the night, I set the computer aside and turn toward the far back wall to a few newspaper clippings tacked up, along with a handful of Post-it Notes covered in my dad's messy handwriting. The notes are random dates and times, and the newspaper clippings are help wanted ads for a gardener, a dog walker, and a housekeeper. If my dad didn't love his job, I'd think he was job searching. But he loved being a reporter as much as I love skateboarding. And besides, I saw the wall before he disappeared. There were so many sticky notes and torn sections of newspapers that the tan paint wasn't even visible. What compelled him to take some down and leave some up is beyond me. I have a hunch they carry some sort of importance because of something my dad said to me right before he flew off the radar.

"Mak, if something ever happens to me, just follow the trail, okay?" he said to me in a panic. "Just be careful. Don't let them find out you're on to them. I think that's what happened to your brother."

By that point, my mom had started calling him crazy, and I overheard her talking to one of her friends on the phone about sending him to the Shadow Cove's Treatment Facility. I worried that she might be right, but I didn't have the heart to say anything to my dad. I just nodded and agreed to follow this alleged trail.

About a month after he disappeared, I wandered into the hidden nook and spent hours staring at the notes and clippings, attempting to make sense of them. Then, one day, it dawned on me. My dad used to refer to his research as a trail to his article. He'd put most of the research on this wall. So, what if the leftover research on this wall is the trail?

The problem is, I've been staring at the wall for months now, and I can't even find a starting point. I'm afraid of where the trail will lead me when I do figure it all out, and I don't know if I'll be brave enough to follow it.

SEVEN

LOCATION: SHADOW COVE HIGH
TIME: 7:54 AM
DATE: MONDAY, MARCH 22TH

I spent most of the rest of the weekend cleaning the house as an apology to my mom for not answering my phone and for going through her computer files. Sure, she may never know about the last part, but that doesn't mean I don't feel a little bit guilty for doing it. I also tried to bring up Don Jennings a couple of times to get to the bottom of what's going on, but every time I so much as mentioned his name, she shut down the conversation.

Her odd behavior raises the suspicion factor immensely. I don't want to believe she's having an affair with him, but what if she is? Not only is that gross, but it makes both of them cheaters.

After looking through her emails on Saturday, I did a search online for a report on the girl who drowned. Nothing came up, and my frustration bubbled.

Back when my dad reported for the newspaper, he had to fight to get certain stories printed. A lot of the "more complicated and unsettling stories," as his boss and the mayor put it, weren't allowed in print. Topics like deaths, robberies, and other illegal activities were often swept under the rug. Most of the time, my father had a pain in the ass time interviewing people because hardly anyone wanted to discuss a story that didn't show the pleasant side of Shadow Cove.

On Sunday, I work on my project with Ev for a little bit, and then checked online again to see if the story popped up, but nope, nothing. I ended up asking my mom again about the incident, but she insisted on knowing nothing, not even the girl's name. I think she might be lying since she refused to make eye contact.

On a more positive note, I haven't hallucinated again. Thank God. Plus, as a double bonus, I managed to chill on Facetime with my friends, during which Kennedy informed me she's come up with a few fabulous ideas to get Dixon back. When I asked her what the plans entailed, she told me —and very evilly, I might add—that I'll have to wait until Monday morning to find out because she had to check on a few things first.

Needless to say, by the time Monday morning rolls around, I'm more than bursting with eagerness.

"Why isn't Kennedy in her car?" Ev asks as I park my beat-up 1989 Camaro next to her nearly brand new Mercedes.

I shrug, just as perplexed as her.

Since Kennedy lives so far away from Ev, Embry, and me, she normally drives to school by herself. But since she loathes almost everyone we go to school with, she typically hangs out in her car until the three of us arrive. Why she'd wander in by herself today is a mystery. I have a feeling one of her revenge plots might have something to do with it.

"Do you think I should dye my hair purple?" Embry asks randomly from the backseat. She has a compact mirror out and is frowning at her reflection. "I think I'm sick of the red."

"You just dyed it last week." Ev slips her seatbelt off and rotates around to face her. "How can you be sick of it already?"

Embry snaps the compact mirror closed then tosses it into her worn messenger bag. "I get bored easily. Besides, Emilia Greyferson was talking about dyeing her hair the same color." She grimaces. "I mean, seriously, where's her originality?"

I smile to myself. Embry is all about originality. Just look at her outfit: red, clunky boots decorated with skulls and buckles; fishnet stockings; a pleated grey skirt; and a torn black T-shirt. The girl loves being the unicorn of our school.

"Even if Emilia dyes her hair red, I think you'll still be a unicorn," I tease Embry as I dig my buzzing phone out of the pocket of my torn black skinny jeans.

Kennedy: Meet me by the Rewards Board ASAP. I have an official Take Dixon Down Revenge Plan.

The Rewards Board is a place where students can post ads for lost items, tutors wanted, tutors for hire—things like that. Teachers and the administration often post announcements there, as well. The digitalized board is flashy and showy, stretching across half the wall near the main office. Why Kennedy would want us to meet her there is beyond me. I put my phone away and collect my car keys and bag, ready to find out.

"Kennedy wants us to meet her by the Rewards Board," I announce, reaching for the door handle.

Ev and Embry trade a perplexed look before collecting their bags and books.

Embry slings her messenger bag over her shoulder and scoots toward the door, asking, "Why? Did she lose something?"

I push the door open to get out. "She said she has an official plan to pay back Dixon."

"Maybe her revenge plot is up on that board," Embry suggests with a wicked grin.

"God, I hope she didn't post something on the board about Dixon," Ev gripes. "If he finds out Kennedy did it, he'll go after her."

"And we'll be there to have her back." Embry grins, hops out of the car, and starts across the busy parking lot toward the school.

Ev and I follow suit, jogging after her. When we reach her side, we slow down and match her pace as we make our way up the sidewalk and to the double entrance door, doing our best to ignore the nasty looks and whispering gossip being thrown in our direction. I can't hear everything being said, but I've dealt with the town's mockery long enough that I have a pretty good guess: 1). They're making fun of Embry's outfit, calling her a devil worshipping freak or some shit like that. 2). They're making fun of me, the girl whose dad abandoned her. The girl whose brother committed suicide. The girl no one wants to be around. None of this is new; I've heard it all before. 3). Kennedy has done something to Dixon, and word has already spread around the school. Or 4). Word has gotten around about Dixon shouting that we slept together.

"You know, after years of this shit, you'd think they'd get tired of it," Embry mutters as we ascend the wide stairway that leads to the entrance doors.

People file around us, moving as far away as possible, like we're carriers of a viral plague. Even some of the people who used to be my kind of, sort of friends—before my family became the town gossip—join in the gawk fest. That, I find a bit irking. I mean, we're not friends with them or anything, but we have a mutual understanding to never, ever gang up on each other.

"Is it me, or does everyone seem really grossed out by us today?" I ask Ev and Embry as I open the heavy door and step inside the school.

Ev and Embry join my side, and we start up the hallway toward the Rewards Board. Eyes flick in our direction as we pass the rows of lockers and people surrounding them.

"It's definitely not you," Embry mumbles, her clunky boots squeaking against the black and white checkered floor.

Ev chews on her thumbnail, keeping her head tucked down, her brown hair a veil around her face. "I hate it when they stare like this. It gives me anxiety."

I loop arms with her and tug her close to my side. "Chin up, Ev. Don't let them know they're affecting you."

She lifts her chin but remains tense as we walk down the hallway side by side.

"*Attention students,*" the secretary's voice flows through the intercom. "*Due to an increase in locker theft, we would like to advise students to make sure they're lockers are shut and locked securely during class hours. Thank you.*"

"Well, that's new," I say, trying to ignore the continuous gawking in our direction. "Thievery at Shadow Cove High?" My voice drips with mockery. "Are the rich kids getting bored or something?"

"It could be some of the poor kids," Ev says. "I know you don't like to think that, Mak, but maybe they're doing it because they need money. And we can't exclude the middle class either. Anyone could be a suspect"

I sigh. "I know."

By the time we get to the Rewards Board, Kennedy is waiting for us with an impatient look on her face, casting glances at her diamond encrusted watch. Above her, the infamous massive marquee sparkles with digital numbers and letters—a request for a tutor, followed by a phone number to call.

I've never used the Rewards Board before, but I do know that, in order to get an ad up there, a student has to go into the main office and put in a request with the secretary. However, a few times, students have hacked into the system and rigged the marquee to show an ad about the local gossip around the school.

Before my brother died, he was the subject of a false ad. *"Sawyer Evingston has drugs in his locker and was selling crack down at the corner this morning."* This was before Sawyer started getting really depressed, back when he was a happy, joking brother who in no way came off as a drug dealer. Still, the cops were called in, and Sawyer was searched and questioned. Nothing was found, but the incident gave the school even more of a reason to torment my too-nice-for-his-own-good brother. Now, whenever I see the Rewards Board, a little bit of hatred for this school burns inside my chest.

"Oh, my God, you guys took forever." Kennedy's designer heels click against the floor as she shoves her way through the mob. "What's with everyone today?" She stops in front of us and raises her tone. "Didn't anyone ever learn that staring's rude?"

"Didn't you learn no one gives a shit about anything that comes out of your mouth?" Hunter, a senior who plays lacrosse, shouts at Kennedy from across the hall.

Kennedy rolls her eyes, sliding her leather purse higher onto her shoulder. "Shut up, Hunter, or I'll tell everyone what you did last summer at Tia's birthday bash!"

Hunter's eyes pop wide, and then he hurries down the hallway in the opposite direction.

"Okay, what did he do at the birthday bash?" Embry wonders with delight in her eyes.

Kennedy waves her off. "That's another story for another day. Right now, we have bigger problems to worry about."

"You mean, why everyone's staring at us like we forgot to wear pants or something?" I ask, doing a double-check that I fully have my outfit on. Sneakers: check. Torn skinny jeans: check. Plaid shirt with all the buttons done up: check.

"Exactly." Kennedy taps her polished pale pink fingernail against her glossy lips. "Did anyone do anything interesting this weekend?" She glances accusingly at Embry. "Did you kick anyone's ass?"

Embry mulls the question over for slightly too long. "Not that I can remember."

"I know I didn't do anything to piss anyone off—well, besides my stepmom. So that has to mean ..." Kennedy turns toward me with an exaggerated smile on her face. "Mak ...?"

I mimic her smile and tone. "Kennedy ...?"

She laughs, shaking her head. "What did you do, and who did you do it to?"

"I didn't do anything." I draw an X over my heart. "I promise."

Her meticulous brow arches. "Are you sure you didn't piss anyone off? Like, say ... by snooping around in someone's bedroom or hacking into someone's emails?"

I press my hand to my chest, mocking offense. "Now, why would I ever do something so horrible?"

"Um, because you love snooping around and finding out people's dirty secrets," she says. "You've been doing it since we were eight and your dad showed you how to crack passcodes."

Man, she knows me too well.

"Okay, maybe I do snoop a lot." I swipe a strand of hair out of my face and sigh. "But I promise I didn't do anything this weekend." Except for with my mom's computer, but I'm not ready to tell them that my mom accepted money from Don Jennings and that she might be having an affair with him.

"Hmmm ..." Kennedy contemplates this. "So, if none of us did anything wicked this weekend, then maybe this is about Dixon yelling that you're great in bed."

I pull a face. "God, I hope not. The last thing I want is for anyone to think I'm sleeping with Dixon Jennings."

"Hey, why didn't anyone ask me if I did anything bad?" Ev asks with a hurt look on her face.

Kennedy threads her arm through Ev's. "Aw, my dear,

sweet Ev, we don't ask you those things because you're the sweetest person in the entire school, and you never do anything bad, so no one ever gets upset with you."

"That's not true," Ev starts to argue then sighs in defeat. "All right, maybe I do follow the rules all the time and try to be nice, but that doesn't mean people don't get upset with me. Just look around. Everyone in this school seems upset with us right now."

I peer around, measuring people's expressions. "No, they're not upset. They're pissed off."

"There's a difference?" Embry asks, fiddling around with a clasp on one of her leather wristbands.

"Upset means we probably hurt their feelings," I explain. "Angry means we did something they think is godawful to them."

Embry considers this then shrugs. "Well, I say fuck them. If they want to be pissed, then let them be pissed. We don't need to stand around and give them the benefit of witnessing us squirm." She spins toward Kennedy, her red hair whipping behind her like a cape. "So, what's your big plan?"

Kennedy's eyes light up with glee as she claps her hands together. "Oh, my God, it's so brilliant." Her gaze skims the main entrance, and then she leans in and lowers her voice. "We have about twenty minutes until the first bell rings. Let's talk in the secret spot. Too many people are paying attention to us right now."

We nod, and then the four of us make our way outside,

past the outdoor building where detention takes place, and to the back section of the school beside the dumpsters.

"I still can't believe no one's found this place," Ev remarks as Embry and I inch the smaller dumpster away from the side of the school, uncovering a door to a stairwell that leads to a basement.

Embry was the one who found the spot at the beginning of our freshman year after someone threw her art project away. She went out to the dumpster to search for it and stumbled upon the hidden door. Curious, she asked me to pick the lock. When we discovered the door led to a stairwell that hadn't been touched in years, we declared the area our secret spot, a place we go when we need to have private conversations or just need a break from mornings like this one.

"Even if someone did find it, they wouldn't have a clue how to get in." Kennedy unzips her purse, digs out a hairpin, and hands it to me. "Because they don't have Mak's awesome lock-picking skills."

"Nope, they sure don't." I grab the hairpin from her, crouch down in front of the rusty metal lock, and work my awesome lock-picking magic.

Once the lock unclicks, I return the hairpin to Kennedy, pry open the door, and usher everyone into the darkness.

"*Be careful Mak,*" a deep voice whispers in my ear. A voice that sounds an awful lot like Sawyer's. "*Once you start, you can't go back.*"

EIGHT

LOCATION: THE SECRET SPOT
TIME: 8:17 AM
DATE: MONDAY, MARCH 22ND

My heart is pounding in my chest as I fumble to get the door locked, and then I tug on the cord above our heads. Soft light filters around the flat section of space above a flight of stairs that winds down to a very cobweb-covered basement. I quickly glance around, looking for a sign of where the voice came from. My lack of surprise when I only see my friends is unsettling.

It's starting again. Shit.

I only panic on the inside. On the outside, I'm the epitome of calm.

Embry fans her hand in front of her face, gagging. "Man, it always reeks in here like fish and rotten eggs."

"You should be used to it by now." Kennedy leans to the side and checks down the stairway before unzipping her purse and retrieving a crumpled receipt. "So, here's how we're going to get back at Dixon." She hands me the crumpled receipt with a proud smile on her face.

I force a smile and skim the purchase on the receipt. "Um, thanks, but how is a pair of five hundred dollar shoes going to help us get back at Dixon?"

"*Five hundred dollars,*" Ev mouths with wide eyes.

"Hey, I got a twenty percent discount." Kennedy taps the total amount for the purchase. "And the shoes aren't my plan. This is." She flips the receipt over and hands it back to me.

A phone number is written across the back in glittery pink ink.

"Some dude gave you his phone number," I say with amusement, "on the back of a receipt. How very old-school of him."

Kennedy stares at me, unimpressed. "It's not a guy's phone number. It's a phone number off the marquee for a lost laptop ad. And for your information, Miss Smartass, I had to write it down because my phone battery died while I was typing it." She points a finger at me with a sassy smirk. "And you should be grateful that I know how to do old-school, or else we wouldn't have this awesome plan right in front of us."

"But what is the plan, exactly?" I smooth the creases out of the receipt. "This phone number doesn't explain much."

A sinister grin spreads across her face. "You need a thousand bucks to enter the skate competition, and the reward for this lost laptop just happens to be a thousand dollars. So, I figure we call the dude up, ask a few questions, and then go looking for the laptop ourselves. You're good at this detective stuff, Mak." She bows to me, and I laugh. "Something like this should be a cakewalk for you, oh great one."

She's right. I do kick butt at detective stuff, but I still have reservations about this.

"I'm just finding it a little weird that there's a thousand-dollar reward." I assess the phone number on the receipt. "That's more than my laptop costs brand new."

"High-tech ones can cost up to, like, five to six thousand dollars, Mak." Ev slides her glasses up the brim of her nose. "I'm sure a lot of the people who go to Shadow Cove High have high-tech ones. Even the computers in the library probably cost a couple thousand."

"Okay ... Still ..." I chew on my bottom lip, mulling it over. I don't know why I keep thinking of the voice I heard when I first stepped into the secret spot. While I know it wasn't real, the warning it whispered haunts my thoughts. "I know I'm probably sounding super overanalyzing right now, but I can't help it. I'm worried there might be more to this than a lost computer. I mean, if someone can afford a five-thousand-dollar computer, they should be able to replace one, right? Why offer such a big reward to get an old one back unless there's something really important on it?"

"The files on the computer are probably irreplaceable," Ev tells me. "Photos, school assignments—things like that."

"Sex videos," Kennedy adds with a giggle. When I roll my eyes at her, she shrugs. "What? You know that's Dixon's phone number, right?" She grins. "And he's such a dirty man-whore. I bet he has a ton of sex videos stored in his computer."

My jaw nearly smacks the concrete. "What the hell? How did you ...? What did you ...? Huh?"

"Don't worry; you don't have to say it." Kennedy beams proudly. "I know I'm awesome."

"Awesome, yes. But this ..." I glance down at the receipt. "It's like the stars aligned perfectly. I need a thousand dollars to enter the skate competition so I can kick Dixon's ass in front of his whole family, and he's the one who's going to give me the entry fee. Plus, I can snoop around on his computer before we give it back and see if I can get some dirt on him. It's so perfect." I suddenly frown. "You don't think he's setting us up, do you?"

"I seriously doubt Dixon put up the ad, hoping we'd see it and call his number so he could set us up," Kennedy says. "I love you, babe, but sometimes, you overthink things too much."

"Hey, the trait can be annoying sometimes, but it's useful sometimes, too," I point out. Of course, deep down, I know she's right. I am overthinking this, all because some creepy-ass voice that isn't real whispered a warning to me. "I'll try to tone it down a little."

"Good." Kennedy rubs her hands together. "Okay, who gets the honor of making the call and convincing Dixon to give us enough info for us to start the search?"

The four of us exchange a wary look as the light above us flickers on and off.

"Fine, I'll do it. This is my thing, anyway." I reach for my phone in my pocket, but Embry smacks my hand away.

"He'll probably recognize your voice." She blasts me with a pressing look. "You two talk a lot."

"More like argue," I clarify. "But, yeah, you're probably right."

"I'd offer to do it," Embry says, scraping some black fingernail polish off her thumbnail, "but I have sucky people skills."

"True dat." Kennedy laughs, and Embry playfully shoves her, causing her to stumble. Once she regains her balance, she sticks her hand out to Embry. "Let me borrow your phone. I'll do it." Once Embry hands over her phone, Kennedy looks down at the receipt in my hand and punches the digits into her phone. Then she flashes a smirk at Embry as she puts the phone to her ear. "Good thing I have excellent people skills."

Embry sticks her tongue out at Kennedy while I rush to dig a pen out of my backpack. Biting off the cap, I quickly jot down some important questions Kennedy needs to ask.

1). Where was the laptop last seen?

2). *What was the date and time the laptop was last seen?*

3). *What kind of laptop is it? What does it look like? Is there anything on it, like a decal or something that will make it stand out?*

4). *Would anyone want to steal it for some odd reason, or does he think he just misplaced it?*

5). *Is there any other helpful information he can give us?*

By the time I finish scribbling down the last question, Kennedy has Dixon on the line.

"Hi, I was calling about the lost laptop ad you posted," she says in a fake, flawless southern accent. She pauses as Dixon says something to her. "No, it's not that. I was actually calling because the school has a team of specialists coming in to do an investigation about the increasing number of pricey lost items. There's a bit of concern from the faculty that these items are being taken intentionally." She bobs her head up and down as Dixon yammers her ear off about something. "Yes, I see. Well, that's terrible, but it's not uncommon. There've been a lot of complaints about the security cameras around the school premises experiencing power outages, and we're looking into that, too, to make sure they haven't been hacked into." She snaps her fingers at me, signaling for me to hand her my list and a pen. "I would greatly appreciate it if I could ask you a few questions about your missing laptop so I can cross-reference the date and times with the security camera outages."

Everleigh and Embry cover their mouths to conceal a

laugh. Me, I smile like the freakin' Cheshire cat as I hand Kennedy my list and a pen.

Grinning, Kennedy crouches down, sets the receipt on the ground, and begins asking the questions on the list. She jots down a few notes before telling Dixon she'll be in touch. Then she hangs up and bounces up and down.

"God, that was such an adrenaline rush." She hands me the receipt now covered with the notes she took. "I was seriously worried he wouldn't buy the story, but I think I sold it pretty well." She points a finger at me. "I finally found a use for all those boring detective shows you make us watch all the time."

"Told you they'd come in handy one day." I smile, skimming over the notes. "So, according to this, the last time he saw his laptop was Friday morning?"

"Yeah, he said he put it in his locker before second period, and by third period, it was gone." Kennedy flicks the receipt in my hand. "He insists no one knows his locker combo, but that doesn't mean someone couldn't break into it."

I rub my lips together, thinking. "Did he go to the main office and ask them to check the security footage?"

Kennedy nods. "And that's where things get really shady." She leans in as if she's revealing a scandalous secret. "Apparently, the cameras shorted out at the exact time the laptop was stolen."

"That can't be a coincidence." Ev steps up beside me to read the notes on the back of the receipt. "Cameras don't usually short out like that unless there's a power outage. And the school has a high-end system, so it should have a backup recording system."

"Maybe the secretary doesn't know about that," Kennedy suggests. "That's who Dixon said he spoke to."

"That could be a possibility." Ev anxiously thrums her fingers against the sides of her legs, dazing off in deep thought. "Ms. Finkleson isn't the best with electronic devices. One time, she called me into the office to show her how to use the calendar program on the computer, and it took an hour before she figured it out."

"Maybe you could offer to help her find the backup data for the cameras," I propose. "And then, while you're at it, you could sneak a look at the footage of when the computer was stolen."

Ev hastily shakes her head and shuffles back. "No way. Do you know how suspicious it'd look that I even knew the camera system went down? Plus, I don't do well under pressure."

"True." I rub my jawline, the wheels turning in my head. "Hmmm ... What if I went in and reported something stolen around the same time as Dixon? When Ms. Finkleson tells me the cameras went down, I can ask her if she can check the backup system."

"And what will you do when she has no idea how to do that?" Worry creases Ev's brows. "Because she will say that."

I tap my ear. "I'll put an earpiece in, and you can walk me through the process."

Her frown deepens. "And where do you plan on getting this earpiece?"

My lips curl into a grin. "Leave that to me. Just be ready by lunchtime to put this plan into motion. It's the best time to do it, anyway, since Ms. Finkleson usually is the only one in the main office. The fewer people who see us messing around with the security system, the better. In fact, Kennedy and Embry, you two should chill outside and keep an eye out on things. Make sure no one, like Dixon or one of his friends, comes wandering in there. I don't want them putting two and two together and figuring out what we're up to."

Kennedy salutes me, and Embry gives me a fist bump.

"You got it," Kennedy says. "Though, I don't really think any of Dixon's friends are smart enough to put two and two together."

"Better safe than sorry," I say. "We don't want any accidental slipups happening."

"Hey, that's what my mom said to me when we had our first sex talk," Embry remarks, and Kennedy snorts a laugh.

Ev releases an exhausted sigh. "Guys, this seems a little extreme for a revenge plot. Isn't there a better way for Mak to get back at Dixon?"

"Not a way where she can get back at Dixon and have enough money for the skate competition. And getting to compete is half the point of this," Kennedy says. "Look, Ev, this needs to be done, not just for Mak, but for the greater good of our fellow losers. Dixon has spent too many years running his mouth and tormenting the school."

Ev continues to frown. "And what if something happens? Like, what if Ms. Finkleson catches on to what you're doing?" She shakes her head, causing strands of hair to fall into her eyes. "She may be computer illiterate, but she might figure out something's up when you ask her to look at the footage of Dixon's locker."

"Excellent point, Ev. I didn't even think of that." I twist a strand of hair around my finger, mulling over the dilemma. "What we need is a way to get her out of the office so I can peek at the footage once she gets the files open. Like a distraction that makes it so she has to run out of the office for a moment ... like a fight going on or something."

Embry's hand shoots up in the air, her boots thudding against the concrete as she jumps up and down. "Oh, me, me. Please pick me!"

Kennedy swiftly shakes her head and mouths, *"Don't let her do it. She'll end up getting detention again."*

"Not a real fight," I clarify, and Embry's hand falls as she pouts. "Like a fake cat fight between two best friends. Now, all I need are two best friends who are amazing at acting and pretend fighting."

Kennedy and Embry exchange a deliberating look, a shrug, and then a nod of agreement.

"I guess we can do that," Embry says. "Just as long as I win the fight. I do have a reputation to uphold."

"Like you could really kick my ass in a fight," Kennedy says then zips her lips when Embry arches a brow at her.

"So, we're good, then," I tell Ev. "Once she gets into the backup system, I'll sneeze, and then Kennedy and Embry will start fighting just outside the office. Just make sure to scream a little."

"Yeah, so you can both get detention." Ev restlessly taps her foot. "A fight isn't going to work. You need to do something more inconspicuous that won't get Kennedy and Embry detention."

"Good point, Ev." I aim a finger at her. "Way to be an active participant in this devious, delinquent plot."

Ev lifts her glasses up and presses her fingers to the brim of her nose. "I'm just trying to make sure you guys don't get expelled so I don't get stuck going to this hellhole by myself."

"Oh." Kennedy steps back, covering her mouth with her hand, mocking being aghast. "Ev just said hell."

Ev gives her a dirty look, but her lips quirk, and I can tell she's starting to soften.

"I could always just pull the fire alarm," Embry offers. "The one near the back of the school is out of view from the cameras. I should be able to get it done without anyone knowing."

"How do you know that?" I question.

"Remember that time the alarm went off during the Biology final last year?" she asks, and I nod. "Well, I may have forgotten to study, and I may have asked for a bathroom pass so I could pull the alarm and get the final postponed until the next day."

"That was you?" Kennedy smacks her a high-five. "I owe you a huge thanks, Em. That stunt saved my pretty, little behind from flunking Bio."

"You didn't study, either?" Embry asks.

Kennedy rolls her eyes. "Duh, I was with you the night before. Remember? We snuck into that club."

"I can't believe I'm just realizing how much trouble you guys get into," Ev gripes. "And I'm sure this office stunt is going to be another thing to add to your list."

Embry drapes an arm around her shoulders. "Don't worry, Ev; if shit hits the fan, Embry, Mak, and I will take the fall. You won't be anywhere near the office, anyway."

Ev nervously combs her fingers through her hair. "It just seems like you guys are enjoying this a little too much."

Embry, Kennedy, and I trade an amused look.

"Nah, I think we're enjoying this just the right amount," I reply. "Even you can appreciate taking down the school's worst evil villain a teeny, tiny bit. Just think about all the times he's tormented you personally."

She wavers then nods. "All right, I'm in."

I smile and force her to give me a high-five.

Maybe she's right. Maybe I am enjoying this too much. The truth is, our revenge plan kind of reminds me of the days when I helped my dad get a story. Sometimes, we'd have to do stakeouts or make sneaky phone calls like Kennedy just did to Dixon. Some stories were a real pain in the ass. My dad would have to go undercover to get to the bottom of the real truth, and I'd be his eyes and ears. He was always so good at it, and I've often thought it would be great to be like him: chasing stories, getting to the real truth, solving some great mystery.

I just cross my fingers that I can be as good at this undercover thing as he was and that all the trouble will be worth it. And that my sanity has returned to normal.

NINE

So, yeah, our school has its very own super swanky recording room where aspiring artists can create videos, take photos, paint, record music, or whatever else their little artists' hearts desire. The room is also fully stocked with all kinds of gizmos and gadgets that these artists can use. And what I have my sights set on are the walkie-talkies the school's video camera crew uses when televising sporting events.

While I in no way, shape, or form have a good reason to

be in this room, I'm currently pretending I do. With Embry's camera strapped around my neck, I stand outside the shut door, waiting for the red light to click off and for the person occupying the room to clear out. According to the schedule on the door, they have exactly one minute left. Then there'll be a ten-minute break when the room should be empty, giving me just enough time to slip in and steal a couple of walkie-talkies and an earpiece before hightailing it back to class. If anyone stops me in the hallway and asks what I'm doing, I have a freshly signed bathroom pass in my back pocket.

Exactly one minute later, the red light flips off, and the door swings open. I straighten and am preparing to walk in when Rylen strolls out of the room with a guitar slung over his shoulder. When he sees me, his lips pull into a smile.

"Hey, Mak." He tilts his head to the side as he glimpses the camera dangling around my neck. "I didn't know you were into photography."

I decide how to play this. Rylen knows me enough that he might be able to tell if I'm lying.

"It's actually a new hobby," I say. "Embry's really into it, and she's giving me a few pointers." When he peers around the empty hallways, I add, "She's actually waiting for me in the quad. I'm supposed to pick up some equipment for us to use."

He shoves the sleeves of his grey thermal shirt up. "That's cool. I mean, that she's helping you. And photography's pretty fun. I think you'll like it."

"Are you into it?"

"I'm not hardcore into it, but I've taken a few classes." He pats his guitar. "Music's more my thing. And skateboarding."

"Well, aren't you just a man of many talents?" I flash him a teasing grin.

For some reason, he seems embarrassed. Is it because he's talking to me? He's associated with me at school before, though. Perhaps whatever has turned everyone into gawkers has made him second-guess being nice to me.

"But, anyway, I have to get that stuff out to Embry ASAP. Maybe I'll see you at the skate park later."

I'm moving to head inside when he sidesteps, causing me to bump straight into him. I start to trip back, but he curls his arm around my waist and steadies me.

"Sorry," he says quickly. "I didn't mean to run into you. I just wanted to ask ... to make sure you're okay."

"Um, yeah." I'm so confused, not only by his question, but by his invasion of my personal space. "Why wouldn't I be?"

"Because of what happened to that girl." He studies my puzzlement, and then his eyes widen. "Shit, did you not know about that?"

I start to shake my head, but then it clicks. "Wait, are you talking about the girl who drowned in the lake?"

He relaxes, stuffing his hands into the back pockets of his black jeans. "So, you did hear about it, then?"

"Yeah, my mom was working at the hospital when she was brought in."

He turns all squirmy again. "Did you hear who it was?"

I suddenly feel extremely nervous, too. "No. Do you know?"

He massages the back of his neck tensely. "Um, yeah ... it was ... Bria Brookenrose."

"*Bria?* My brother's old girlfriend, Bria?" I say, probably too loudly.

He nods, and while my mind races with questions, only one leaves my lips.

"Do you know how she died?"

"Well, I don't know for sure, because there hasn't been anything in the paper about it, but there's a rumor going around school that ..." He sweeps his dark strands out of his eyes, looking like he wants to be anywhere but here. "That she killed herself because of some pact she made with your brother."

For a moment, the only noise I hear is the hammering of my own heart slamming against my chest. Then thoughts begin to flood my mind.

Bria killed herself? Bria, the girl Sawyer was dating right before he died, took her own life, too? Bria killed herself because of a pact with my brother? Does that mean my brother killed himself because of a pact?

"It might just be a rumor," Rylen breaks the maddening silence. He stares at me as if he fears I'm about to shatter.

"You know how shit is around here. Someone says one tiny remark, and suddenly, the entire school is blowing up with gossip. Don't let it get to you, okay? You're too strong for that."

"Yeah, I know." I distractedly click the camera lens on and off with my brows furrowed.

Even if it is a rumor, there has to be a starting point that sparked it. What got the ball rolling, or rather, who?

I rub my aching chest as reality sinks in. Bria is dead. The girl Sawyer once said he loved is dead. Just like him.

Tears sting my eyes, and I hurriedly wind around Rylen. "I have to go. Embry's waiting for me."

He opens his mouth to say something, but I quickly yank open the door to the recording room, slip inside, and shut myself in.

While Rylen is a nice guy, he does hang out with the same crowd as Dixon, and the last thing I need is to break down in front of him.

Taking a few measured breaths, I collect myself and focus on the task at hand. I cross the room to a locked glass shelf with all sorts of high-tech gadgets. When I spot a pair of walkie-talkies and an earpiece, I dig my student ID card out of my pocket and slip it between the lock and the frame around the case. With a slight wiggle, the lock glides open, and I easily slide open the glass.

I quickly grab what I need, hide them in my bag, and then hightail my behind out of there with time to spare. After I'm finished with the plan, I'll have to sneak in and return the items without being spotted. I'm not a thief, contrary to what this town believes.

The second I step out of the recording room, Dixon and a couple of his friends walk by.

Great. Please don't let them spot me. Please don't let them spot—

"Hey, Mak," he greets me with a chin nod and a sly smile.

Dammit!

"I heard your brother spread his craziness before he offed himself and convinced poor Bria to kill herself, too," Dixon continues. When he passes by me, he spins around and walks backward. "Tell me, was he always such a crazy-ass motherfucker, or did he go off the deep end when everyone at school found out he was selling drugs?" When my fingers fold into fists, his smile broadens. "That Rewards Board can be such a bitch, can't it? Anyone can put what-ever they want up there, even false accusations about some loser selling drugs."

His friends snicker and slap high-fives with each other.

"That was you?" I grit each word out, battling the urge to swing my fist at his face. "You were the one who put that up on the marquee?"

"Now, why would I do something like that? Better yet, why would I be stupid enough to admit I did something like that?" He feigns dumb, but the stupid smirk on his face reveals the truth.

All this time, Dixon was the reason this town thought my brother was a drug dealer.

That asshole is going down!

It takes every ounce of my willpower not to lunge at him and force a smile on my face, instead. "You know what, Dixon? You're right. The Rewards Board can be a real bitch."

Without waiting for him to respond, I stride away. Then, before I walk back into class, I send a text to Embry, Kennedy, and Everleigh.

Step one completed. Step two happens at lunchtime. Meet me at my car promptly at 12:00. We're going to get ahold of that laptop no matter what.

This is no longer just about the money, skating in the competition, or getting back at Dixon for picking on me. This is about getting revenge for my brother. And I'm going to search every single file on Dixon's computer until I figure out the perfect way to do that.

TEN

LOCATION: MAK'S CAR
TIME: 11:58 AM
DATE: MONDAY, MARCH 22ND

"Mak, can you hear me?" Ev's voice fills my ear. "Testing, testing, one, two, three."

I glance over at her sitting in the passenger seat with a walkie-talkie in front of her mouth and a laptop on her lap. "You know, for someone who was so nervous about this plan, you sure enjoy using the equipment."

She clicks the talk button a couple of times. "When I was younger, my mom bought me a set of walkie-talkies for Christmas. It was actually the Christmas right before she died, and we spent the entire day play-spying on my dad and brother." A sad, wistful look crosses her face. "I really miss those days. Everyone was so happy all the time, and we actually did stuff together. These days, we can't even find the time to sit down and eat dinner together."

"I'm sorry, Ev." I lean over the console and give her a hug. "I know what you mean, though. My mom and I barely spend any time together now that my brother and dad are gone." When I sit back in my seat, I notice her expression has tensed. "What's wrong?"

"It's nothing." She runs her fingers through her tangled locks as she stares out at the people roaming around the parking lot.

"Ev ..." I say in a sarcastically stern tone. "Best friends don't keep secrets from each other. We made a pact, remember? Never, ever keep secrets, or else we'll drop dead."

Her shoulders slouch as a sigh eases from her lips. "I'm sure it's nothing, and I know it's not true, but I overheard something during second period ... something about your brother."

I take a deep breath, willing my voice to come out evenly. "I heard about it, too. And I know it's not true." *Don't I?* "And, when we're all done with this Dixon thing, I'm going to find out who started the rumor and track them down."

"I don't think that's such a good idea," Ev says worriedly. "In fact, I think this whole revenge thing might be getting out of hand."

"No way," I disagree, reaching for my bag on the backseat. "I should've done this a long time ago instead of ignoring the shit people said about Sawyer when he died. Maybe if I'd stopped it then, things wouldn't be so bad now."

Pity fills her eyes. "You can't stop every single person in this town from gossiping."

I drop my bag onto my lap. "But I can sure as hell try."

She opens her mouth, but her words are cut off as Embry suddenly hops onto the bumper of my car and begins bouncing up and down.

"Guess what I found out," she singsongs with another bounce. "Kennedy kissed Hunter at the party last weekend, and apparently, he slobbers as much as a dog."

Kennedy strolls up behind her and pokes her in the ribs. "Will you shut up? You're ruining potential blackmailing material."

Embry dismounts from the car and pokes Kennedy back. Kennedy winces then pinches Embry on the arm.

I stick my head out the open window. "Will you two quit acting like two-year-olds? We've got work to do, and the clock's ticking." I make a big show of tapping an invisible watch on my wrist.

Embry dramatically rolls her eyes. "Drama. Queen."

I flip her the bird, and we laugh.

Kennedy skips up to the driver's side and lowers her head to look me in the eye. Doing her best mafia impression, she whispers, "So, this shit is going down now?"

I hand her a walkie-talkie. "This shit is so going down

now. After what happened in the hallway with Dixon, I can't wait to get my hands on his computer."

"What'd the asshat do now?" she asks, handing the walkie-talkie to Embry.

"I'll tell you on our way to the main office." I check the earpiece to make sure it's secure before sweeping my hair over my ear and climbing out of the car. I bump the door shut with my hip then lower my head to look at Ev. "You ready?"

She gives me a thumbs up. "Just please don't get caught."

"Caught? Me? Never." I wink at her then sling my back-pack over my shoulder before walking toward the school with Kennedy and Embry.

As we make the three-minute journey to the main office, I give a brief retelling of what Dixon said to me. By the time I'm finished, Embry looks like she's about to punch someone, and Kennedy is on the verge of tears.

"I really hate this place sometimes," Embry says, opening and flexing her hands. "If it weren't for you guys, I'd probably beg my parents to pack up their shit and get us the hell out of here."

"Mine will never move." Kennedy leans against the wall beside the main office door, eyeing the few people lingering around. "I'll be stuck here until college. But, as soon as I graduate, I'm saying, 'Peace out, bitches,' getting in my car, and never looking back."

"Can you put me in a suitcase and take me with you?" I

joke. "It's probably the only way I'll ever be able to afford to go anywhere."

"Mak, I'd never let you ride in my suitcase." Kennedy's eyes glitter mischievously. "That's where all my clothes and shoes go. But I will cram you in the trunk of my car."

"Aw, gee, how very generous of you. And, as a thank you, I'll return the favor. From now on, you can ride in the trunk of my car everywhere."

"Awesome. I love dark, compact places," Kennedy says. "They're, like, my favorite places ever."

"Says the girl whose bedroom is bigger than my house." Embry peers around the hallway, checks the time on her phone, and then looks at me. "We've only got about twenty more minutes before the bell rings. If you're going to do this, Mak, you better do it now."

"On it. Just remember to listen for the sneeze and then pull the alarm." I test my earpiece one last time to make sure everyone can hear me. Then I breathe out and push open the door to the main office, ready to put step two into motion.

ELEVEN

Like we predicted, Ms. Finkleson is sitting at the front desk with her lunch spread out in front of her. Classic rock floats from the computer speakers as she sings along with the lyrics, tapping a spoon against the desk to the beat.

I shut the door loudly to get her attention, and she startles and nearly drops the spoon she's holding.

"Oh, hey, Makayla." She sets her yogurt down then smooths down her navy blue button-down shirt. "What can I help you with?"

I let my bag fall to the ground and have a seat in the

chair across from her. "I'm pretty sure my phone was stolen from my locker on Friday."

She doesn't seem that surprised. "And why do you think it was stolen? I mean, I know a lot of that's been going on, but sometimes, people think stuff has been stolen when they've really just misplaced the item."

"I know I didn't misplace it. My locker was open when I came out of seventh period on Friday, and my phone wasn't in there anymore," I lie breezily. "I know for sure that I closed my locker before I went to class, and I know my phone was definitely in there because Mr. Brinkling has a shit fit when we bring our phones to class."

"Please watch your language, Makayla," she says, dabbing her lips with a napkin.

"Sorry." I cross my legs and pick at a hole in my jeans. "I'm just so stressed out, you know. I haven't told my mom about my phone yet because I know she'll freak out. But if I don't find it fast, I'm going to have to tell her, and then she's going to stress out about paying for a new one." I glance up at her with a weighted sigh. "Ever since my dad took off, we've been pretty broke, and she's constantly stressing about money." I look down again, letting my hair curtain my face. "So, if there's anything you can do to help me find out who took my phone, I'd really appreciate it."

"Wow, Mak, way to work the sob story," Ev whispers through the earpiece. "That was so good even I believed it."

I want to laugh, but the truth is that my mom would lose it if I lost my phone. That is, unless she has leftover cash from what Don Jennings gave her. But no, the financial records show the money is gone.

I crinkle my nose at the thought then quickly shove the look away. *Now's not the time to be thinking about this.*

"I'm so sorry to hear that, Mak," Ms. Finkleson says. "Your mom is such a sweet person. When my father was hospitalized, it made his day when she was his nurse. She was always so caring and good with him."

"She really loves her job." I tuck a strand of hair behind my ear and look up at her with what I hope is pity-me-please eyes. "She works so hard, too. Too hard, probably. I really hate that this phone thing probably means she's going to have to put in more hours."

"Have you thought about tracking the phone? I know mine has some sort of tracking app on it so I can locate my phone when I lose it."

"Mine's one of those super cheap flip phones, so I doubt it does."

"Oh, I see ... I guess I could pull up the security footage and see if it caught the person who did this. I have to warn you, though, we've been getting a lot of power outages that have ruined a lot of the footage."

My brows pull together. "That's weird. Do you know what's causing them?"

She shakes her head, tapping a few keys on the keyboard, spelling out: *January 15, 1973.* Her birthday, I assume, and probably her password. I make a mental note of that mostly out of habit, but also just in case my plan doesn't go down the way I hope. And hey, you never know when you might need to hack into the school's security system.

"Let's see ..." She glides the mouse around on the mouse pad. "You said it happened this Friday during seventh period?"

"Yes." I inch forward in the chair. "Do you see anything?"

"Hold on." Her lips sink. "Well, shoot. It looks like that happened during one of the outages."

I rest my arms on her desk. "What about the backup data? Can you look at that?"

She glances at me with perplexity etched in her expression. "Backup data?"

"Yeah, a lot of security systems have them."

"Really? Well, that's good to know, but I don't think I know how to access it. Maybe when Principal Mikenely comes back from lunch, I can ask him about it."

"I could do it for you," I offer. "I'm fantastic with computer stuff."

"Not as fantastic as me," Ev whispers in my ear, and I struggle not to smile.

Ms. Finkleson appears torn. "I appreciate the offer, but I don't think I should let you mess around with my computer. It's against school policy."

"That's okay. I can just walk you through the steps," I propose. When she remains undecided, I tack on, "I'd really like to figure out where my phone is before I have to go home today."

She wavers then nods. "All right, tell me what to do."

Right on cue, Ev begins prattling directions off in my ear, which I repeat to Ms. Finkleson. Thankfully, I'm not a complete ditz when it comes to computers and understand most of Ev's directions.

Five minutes later, Ms. Finkleson has the backup footage pulled up and seems greatly appreciative.

"Thank you so much, Makayla." She looks away from the computer screen and smiles gratefully at me. "I wish I knew about this sooner. I have so many students come in here and make reports on stolen items, and about half the time, the security cameras have gone down, so there's nothing I can do to help them."

"That's so weird. I mean, that so much stuff gets stolen around here."

"I used to think so, too, but then I realized that over seventy percent of the kids at this school are in the higher-class income, while the other thirty percent are in borderline poverty level."

"So, you think poor kids are doing all the stealing?" My tone comes out clipped. "And that everyone else are all just victims of our thievery?"

"Oh, no, that's not what I meant. I was just ..." She shifts in her chair uncomfortably. "You know what? Let's pull up the footage of your locker before the lunch bell rings." Looking at the screen, she double-clicks the mouse. "I don't want you being late for class."

"Sounds good to me."

All right, girls, let's get this show on the road.

Sucking in an inhale, I let out a fake sneeze.

"Bless you," Ms. Finkleson says automatically, tapping a few keys on the keyboard.

"Em's on it," Kennedy's cheerful tone echoes out of the earpiece.

I rub my nose and smile at Ms. Finkleson. "Thanks."

She continues to type on the computer until the high-pitched blare of the fire alarm sounds through the school.

Her gaze darts away from the screen to the door. "What on earth? I don't think there was a drill scheduled." She shoves her chair away from the desk, rises to her feet, and pushes the intercom button. "Students and faculty, please evacuate the school using the nearest exit and remain outside until further instructions." She releases the intercom switch and winds around the desk, signaling for me to follow her. "Come on, Makayla; we need to get outside."

I gather my bag and follow her out the door where students are wandering toward the exit doors in a chaotic manner, which makes it easier to get lost in the crowd. Once I'm sure Ms. Finkleson's no longer paying attention to me, I whirl around and slip back into the main office.

"Can someone keep an eye on the door?" I ask loudly over the alarm. "And if she comes back, warn me."

"Already on it," Kennedy replies. "Oh, and FYI, remind me never to believe a damn word you say ever again. Your lying skills are literally terrifying."

I chuckle, swinging around the desk and clicking the

mouse. "Shit. It already went back to the password screen." I crack my knuckles and align my fingers on the keys. "Good thing I totally saw when she typed her password in."

I quickly type in January 15, 1973, gaining access to the home screen. She didn't shut the security program down, so accessing the videos is fairly easy.

I find the video files for Friday and scroll to the footage taken close to noon, around the time Dixon said he believes his computer was jacked. I click through the different areas the cameras are angled at until I find the footage taken close to his locker. Then I push fast-forward and watch for anything suspicious.

About one minute in, the fire alarm silences, and the air grows quiet.

"Shit, I'm running out of time," I mutter, double-clicking the arrow to speed up the fast-forward.

On the black and white video, kids zoom back and forth across the screen, hurrying to classes, lollygagging on the way to their lockers, standing around and wasting time.

"Mak, hurry up," Kennedy warns.

I impatiently drum my fingers against the desk. "Come on, come on, come on."

"Mak, get your ass out of there *now*." Urgency rings in Kennedy's tone. "Ms. Finkleson is heading toward the entrance doors."

"Just a sec." I lean forward, squinting at the screen as something catches my eye. I click the rewind button to backtrack a few seconds then let the video play at normal speed. "What in the world—"

"Mak!" Kennedy screeches in my ear. "She's walking up to the main office door!"

I hurriedly close down the videos, grab my shit, and dash across the office. But right as I move to open the door, it creaks open.

Panic sets in. *I'm so going down!*

I'm starting to back up, scanning the office for a place to hide, when I hear Kennedy's voice on the other side of the door.

"Hey, Ms. Finkleson, can I talk to you for a minute?" Kennedy asks smoothly. "It's really important."

"Is everything okay?" Ms. Finkleson asks in concern.

"Well, you see, there was this thing that happened in the girls' locker room ..." She struggles for words. "A fight broke out."

Tiptoeing over to the door, I peer out of the crack. The two of them are standing about ten feet away with Ms. Finkleson's back toward me.

When Kennedy spies me peeking out, her eyes briefly widen, and Ms. Finkleson starts to turn around.

Kennedy desperately snags her arm and squeaks, "It was such a bad fight, and now I feel really scared about going in there. It's so secluded, you know. No teachers are monitoring the area or anything."

Holding my breath, I open the door wider and inch out into the hallway.

"I'm not really sure what you're asking," Ms. Finkleson says. "Do you want me to see if we can get a monitor in the girls' locker room? Because you'll probably have to discuss the idea with the principal. But if you're worried about the fight you saw, I'd suggest maybe talking to the counselor."

I tiptoe like a madwoman toward the doors that lead outside.

"Thanks, Ms. Finkleson," Kennedy says with relief. "You're the best."

"You're welcome," Ms. Finkleson replies, sounding lost. "Now, if there's nothing else, I really need to ask you to wait outside until I announce that students can come back in."

"Absolutely," Kennedy says. "And thanks again—"

I barrel out the doors and haul ass down toward a cluster of trees where the students have accumulated, crossing my fingers that Ms. Finkleson didn't see me.

TWELVE

LOCATION: MAK'S CAR
TIME: 12:27 PM
DATE: MONDAY, MARCH 22ND

"Oh, my word, what just happened?" Kennedy sputters as I dive into the driver's seat of my car and slam the door.

"I kicked some spy ass; that's what happened." I shuck off my backpack, chuck it into the backseat, and let out a shocked laugh. "I can't believe I just pulled that off. My dad would be so proud."

Ev's expression softens at the mention of my dad. "You found out who took the computer, then?"

I give an exaggerated nod. "Oh, yeah, I definitely found

out who took it. And not just Dixon's computer, but some stuff from other people's lockers, too."

"Really?" She shuts the laptop. "So, who did it?"

I'm opening my mouth to answer her when Kennedy and Embry come jogging across the parking lot, laughing nervously as they say something to each other. When they reach my car, they slam to a stop, and Kennedy yanks open the door to the backseat. She scooches in, and Embry follows, pulling the car door shut.

Kennedy rests her elbows on the console. "That was so close. You're lucky I stepped in."

"I know." I rotate around in the seat to look at her. "I'm kind of proud of you. That was some awesome quick thinking."

"Why, thank you." She beams, but then her smile falters. "Although, I'm kind of worried that we might end up with a monitor in the locker room now."

Ev slants her head to the side. "What?"

Embry scoots forward, tucking a strand of red hair behind her ear. "Yeah, please explain what the fuck just happened and why Kennedy looked like she was about to pee her pants when she ran out of the school."

"I didn't look like I was about to pee my pants," Kennedy protests, swatting Embry's arm. "I was just a little nervous that Ms. Finkleson was going to figure out what we were up to."

"She seemed a little confused with your locker room

story," I say. "But I think she was pretty clueless about what was going on."

"Will someone please tell me what's going on?" Embry begs. "I mean, did it work? Did it not work? Do we know who the thief is?"

"Yep," I say proudly. "When I got to the right spot on the video, I got a clear shot of the thief breaking into Dixon's locker and taking off with the computer and doing the same thing to a couple of other lockers next to his."

"Really?" Kennedy slants forward eagerly. "So, who is it?"

I don't know whether to smile or frown. While I found out who the thief is, I'm baffled over why this person would steal anything, let alone steal from Dixon.

"It was Liam Stallings," I announce through my confusion.

Kennedy's lips part in shock. "Dixon's best friend stole his computer?"

I nod, my confusion deepening. Not only is Liam Dixon's best friend, but he also comes from one of the wealthiest families in Shadow Cove. Why he'd need to jack a bunch of computers is beyond me other than maybe he didn't necessarily want the computers per se, but something on them.

One things for sure, I'm going to do everything I can to find out what's going on.

"Be careful, Mak. You don't know what you're getting

into." I swear I hear Sawyer whisper in my ear, but when I turn around, I see nothing.

But the words ring through my mind, and I question what I'm getting myself into.

THIRTEEN

LOCATION: MAK'S CAR
TIME: 3:14 PM
DATE: MONDAY, MARCH 22ND

After finding out Liam Stallings was the one who stole Dixon's computer, I do everything I can to scrounge up information on him. I spend the entire day searching through files on the computer and asking around about him. I don't hear Sawyer's voice again, but I can shake the words I swear I heard him whisper. I just wish I knew if I really heard him. And if I did, how?

Unable to answer any of those questions, I try to focus on the task in front of me—finding out about Liam Stallings.

Here's what I know so far:

Full Name: Liam Stallings

Age: Seventeen.

School Status: A senior at Shadow Cove.

Current GPA: 4.0.

Extracurricular Activities: Football, lacrosse, newspaper, yearbook staff.

Titles: Homecoming king, voted most likely to succeed.

Means of Transportation: When his driver isn't taxiing him around, he cruises around in a Porsche.

Yeah, the dude's a total overachiever, and almost everyone in Shadow Cove worships the ground he walks on. Not to mention, he's gorgeous if you like the whole blond hair, blue eyes, preppy, collared shirt and slacks look, which I don't. However, a lot of girls do, and Liam spends a lot of time getting his ego stroked by swooning girls.

I try to dig up some dirt up on him during computer class, but his records are perfect, his grades flawless, and he's clean of any probations or arrests, including breaking and entering, and shoplifting. So either the whole stealing computer thing is a new habit, or he's good at covering up his klepto habits.

As soon the final bell rings, Kennedy and I meet at my locker then head out to my car to play stakeout and wait for Liam to exit the school so we can tail him. Embry walks out with us but takes off on foot to her part-time job at the Shadow Cove Cornershop Café, located about a mile away. Ev remains in school to give tutoring lessons, something she does three times a week.

"Are you sure we shouldn't just corner him in the hallway or something?" Kennedy asks with her gaze trained on the shiny silver Porsche parked a few spaces in front of us. "It might be easier."

I collect a bottle of soda from the cup holder and down a swig. "No way. The last thing we need is to try to have this talk while he's surrounded by his friends. And Dixon." I roll down my window as the cab starts to heat up. "He'll never admit anything in front of Dixon, even if we do bring the video up. Our best bet is to follow him around for a bit until we catch him alone. Then we make our move."

"We could always just call him. I have his phone number."

I give her a curious glance. "Why?"

She shrugs. "It's not a big deal. I probably have, like, half the schools' phone numbers programmed into my phone. It's not like I call any of them, though. You, Em, and Ev are probably the only numbers that get used."

I stick out my hand. "Lemme see your phone."

"What for?"

"I wanna see who else's digits you've got. It might come in handy later on."

"Why? You planning on stalking someone else?" She smiles to let me know she's joking. Then she digs her phone out of her bag and punches in her passcode before handing it over. "And while you're at it, just call Liam. This stakeout thingy is getting so boring." She fans her hand in front of her face. "And I'm starting to sweat."

"I can't call him. If I do, then he'll just hang up when I start questioning him. This needs to be done in person." I gradually scroll through her contacts. "And if you're hot, roll the window down."

Sighing, she rolls the window down, letting a warm breeze gust in. "Fine, we'll do this your way, oh wise one who knows everything."

"And don't ever forget it."

I continue scrolling through her seemingly never-ending contact list, making a mental note that, if I ever need to track a phone number down, Kennedy is my go-to person.

She digs a tube of lip gloss out of her purse. "One final question, though, about this little stakeout party we're having … What happens if Liam drives straight home?"

"He won't."

"How do you know that?"

"Because he hates his dad."

Her gaze skates to me, and her lips curve up. "Do I even want to know how you know that?"

I shrug. "Back in, like, ninth grade, we had to do a project together for school. He kept insisting we do all the work at my house, and when I finally asked him why, he told me that he hated being at his house. That his dad is an asshole."

"Liam told *you* all of that?"

"I think he'd been drinking."

"That would make much more sense."

My brow teases up. "What're you saying? That someone wouldn't open up to me unless they were wasted?"

"No." She tosses the lip gloss back into her purse. "I'm saying, Liam Stallings wouldn't open up to anyone unless he was wasted. The guy is seriously as fake as Bridget Stolerfens's tatas."

I gape at her. "Bridget got breast implants? *Really?*"

"Of course she did. She was barely a B cup all through sophomore year. Then, suddenly, she comes back from summer break and her goodies"—she makes a circular motion around her chest—"are bigger than mine. There's no way she grew that much in just three months."

"Huh. The things you learn during a stakeout." I give her back her phone then roll down my window. "So, how long have you had Dixon's number?"

"Since today. I thought I'd save it in my contacts for when we have to call him back and tell him we have his computer." She drops her phone onto her lap and glances out the windshield as Rylen walks by with a couple of his friends.

He waves at us, and I give a small wave back, not wanting to draw attention. But my standoffish move has the opposite effect, and instead of moving on, Rylen says something to his friends then strolls toward my car.

When he reaches my door, he crouches down so we're eye level. "Hey, I'm glad I ran into you." He drags a hand through his hair, making the dark strands stick up in every direction as he blows out a tense breath. "I want to apologize for what happened in the hallway. I never should've brought that shit up. I usually try to avoid talking about the stupid rumors going around school. Anyway, I wanted to make sure you were okay, but then I realized you didn't know and ... I'm just really sorry I upset you."

"You didn't upset me," I promise. "The rumor did. And that wasn't your fault, so you don't need to apologize."

Guilt crosses his face. "Yeah, but I haven't done anything to stop it, either."

"I don't expect you to," I tell him. "Besides, it's not like you could go around and force every single person in this school to stop talking about Bria and my brother. And even if you did, by tomorrow, they'd already be on to the next juicy story."

"Yeah, maybe," he mutters, dazing off with his brows knit.

I cast a mystified glance at Kennedy, who only grins at me like a goofball. "*What?*" I mouth.

Instead of replying, her smile broadens.

Weirdo.

I redirect my focus back to Rylen, who's staring at me with an unresolved look on his face.

"Can I ask you something?" His tone carries caution.

I nod. "Sure. What's up?"

"Well, I ... It's just that ..." He shifts his weight, fidgeting with a studded leather watch on his wrist. "I was kind of thinking that maybe—"

"Yo, Rylen, get your dumbass over here!" Logan, one of

Rylen's friends, hollers across the parking lot. "We need to go before all the good shit's taken!"

Rylen heaves a discouraged sigh. "I guess I should get going. The skate shop just got a new shipment of boards, and Logan's been freaking out all day that all the good stuff's going to get picked over." He starts to stand up then pauses. "You should head down there with us. You could keep me company while Logan looks at every single deck in stock." His lips tilt into a lopsided smile. "He's seriously worse than my sister when it comes to shopping."

"I wish I could go. I could really use some bearings, but I have some other stuff I have to do." Plus, I have a total of eight dollars and seventy cents to my name, which already has to go toward gas. "Sorry."

"No worries." He straightens, stuffing his hands into his pockets. "Maybe some other time?" When Logan shouts at him again, he visibly cringes. "And maybe without Logan."

"Sure," I say, fiddling with the keychain dangling from the ignition. "I'm always down for anything that has to do with skating."

"I know you are." He gives me this weird, indecipherable look before backing away. "See you later, Mak."

The second he's out of earshot, Kennedy erupts in laughter.

"Oh, my God, that was so entertaining to watch," she says through her uncontrollable giggling.

I poke her in the side. "What the hell's so funny?"

"Rylen trying to ask you out." She dabs tears from her

eyes with her fingertips. "And you being completely clueless about it."

"Hey, I know when a guy's trying to ask me out." I pinch her arm, but she only laughs harder. "Oh, will you shut up? You read that totally wrong. Rylen and I are just friends ... No, we're not even that. We're just two people who share a mutual skating obsession and enjoy a little healthy rivalry."

"Oh, my dear, sweet, little, naive Mak. Take it from someone who deals with guys asking them out all the time. Rylen wants you. Badly. He just about asked you out." A giggle slips from her lips as she stares at Rylen's Land Rover backing out of the parking space. "I can't believe you couldn't see it. He looked so nervous I thought he was going to throw up. And then Logan totally ruined it for him."

"Yeah, right. You're so wrong. I mean, can you imagine someone like Rylen liking me? That would be crazy."

"Why? You two have so much in common. He loves skating. You love skating. You're both hot."

I snort a laugh. "I'm so not hot."

"You are, too. You just don't flash it around by wearing slutty clothes." She scrutinizes my plaid shirt, torn jeans, and sneakers. "But you've got killer legs and eyes. Seriously, Rylen couldn't stop staring at your eyes."

"Maybe that's because they're on my face." My tone drips with sarcasm. "And generally, people tend to make eye contact when they talk."

She shakes her head. "Not the way he was. Trust me. And that whole thing about hanging out at the skate shop with him was just a backup plan because he chickened out on asking you out."

I don't know how to process what she's saying, and honestly, I really don't want to. While Rylen is completely gorgeous, nice, and we do have a lot in common, there's no way he could like me in the way Kennedy is implying. Even if he did, it wouldn't matter. We're from two different worlds; his being all shiny, sparkling, and respectable, and mine is all dull, grey, broken, and sometimes borderline crazy. We would never work, and all of his friends—particularly Dixon—would make sure of that.

I straighten in the seat as I spot Liam booking it out of the school. "And there's our man of the hour."

Kennedy tracks my gaze. "Took him long enough. What the hell was he doing in there, playing with himself in the bathroom?"

"You can be so gross sometimes," I tease with my gaze secured on Liam. "Ready to get this show on the road?"

She nods, buckling up. "I just hope he goes some place interesting because, so far, this stakeout has been the most boring twenty minutes of my life."

As Liam nears our car, I snag Kennedy's sleeve and yank her down with me as I duck for cover.

Her eyes pop wide as she moves closer to the console. "Shit. Did he see us?"

"No, but he walked right by the car." I wait about thirty seconds before peering up over the steering wheel, right in time to see Liam hopping into his car.

I sit up in the seat as he pulls out of the parking space and draw my seatbelt over my shoulder.

"Don't follow too closely," Kennedy warns. "Or he might notice your car. And if he does, he'll know it's you."

"Yeah, I know." I shoot her a confident smile. "Don't worry; I've got this."

Liam drives onto the road, and I wait a couple of seconds before following. I maintain a good distance as he drives up the street, heading toward the main section of town where most of the high-end restaurants and stores are located. When he reaches the park, he makes a right-hand turn, veering toward where the fancy shops turn into dilapidated older stores.

"That's weird," I mumble. "Why would Liam head toward the poor side of town?"

"Hey, I come over here all the time," Kennedy protests. "To visit *you*."

"Yeah, I know, but ... Liam doesn't have any friends who live around here."

"Unless maybe he has a secret girlfriend or something."

I throw her a questioning glance. "A *secret* girlfriend?"

"Maybe he's dating a lower-class girl, and he doesn't want people to know about it, or his parents banned him from dating." She slides on her oversized sunglasses. "It probably happens here more than you think."

"Actually, I think about that kind of stuff a lot." I put on my own glasses as the sun shines directly at the front of the car. "I just didn't think Liam would ever be one of those people. I've only ever seen him date cheerleaders and home-coming queens."

The brake lights illuminate on Liam's car as he slows down to park in front of a small, white building on the corner of a back road. Above the entrance door of the building is a wooden, hand-painted sign that reads: Comics, Collectables, Knickknacks, and Everything Shop.

"I wonder if they're speaking literally when they decided to put the word *everything* into the title of their store." I spin the wheel to park my car down near a large oak tree so we're hidden. I push the shifter into park and eyeball the store dubiously. "I've never noticed this place before. Have you? It kind of sounds like a pawn shop."

Maybe that's what Liam is doing here—pawning off the stuff he stole. But why? He can't possibly need the money when he's driving around a car that costs six figures.

Kennedy draws her glasses down the brim of her nose and squints at the store. "I'm sure I've passed it before, but except for the sign, it just looks like an old house, so we probably never noticed it."

"Maybe," I mutter, wariness weighing inside me and only growing as Liam gets out of his car and pops the trunk.

He reaches inside and retrieves a medium-sized cardboard box with an unfamiliar logo on the side. Then, with a frantic glance around the neighborhood, he hauls butt across the yellowing grass and up the stairs of the store. Looking over his shoulder one last time, he raps his knuckles against the door.

"He seems awfully nervous for someone going inside a store," Kennedy notes, slanting forward in her seat.

"Maybe because he's carrying around stolen merchandise and is about to pawn it off."

"You think he's got the computer in that box?"

"There's only one way to find out." I reach for my door handle to get out.

"Wait a second." Her fingers wrap around my elbow. "What're you going to do? Just walk up and accuse him?"

"Yeah, pretty much," I reply, wiggling my arm out of her hold. "But don't worry." I crack my knuckles and grin. "I can be charming when I need to."

"But what about this place?" She scrutinizes the building. "It looks super sketchy."

"I'm sure it's just a store." *At least, I hope so.* "You can stay in the car if you're freaked out."

She rolls her eyes. "Yeah, right. Like I'm gonna let you just wander into some creepy store all by yourself. Just what kind of friend do you think I am?"

I smile. "The best of besties."

She grins, gripping the door handle. "Come on, bestie; let's go get your thousand bucks."

Nodding, I hop out of the car and meet her around front. Then we hike up the sidewalk and cut across the grass to the store, stopping in front of the door.

Kennedy hugs her arms around herself. "Should we knock or just walk in?"

I peer up at the sign and then at the wooden door with

no windows. "I don't know ... Maybe knock." Sucking in a breath, I knock and wait.

We hear a light bang, voices, the rustling of locks being unlatched. Then the door cracks open, and a beady, bloodshot eye peeks out at Kennedy and me.

"Can I help you?" a guy asks, his raspy voice sending a chill down my spine.

I've heard the voice before, but I can't quite place from where.

"Um, yeah, my friend and I would really like to check out your store." I slant to the right, trying to get a better look at him. He inches to the side, shielding his face with the door. "We just weren't sure if this was the entrance."

"Sorry. We're closed," he snaps, moving to shut the door.

I flatten my palm against the door and hold it open. "Look, it's really, really important. My friend's birthday party is in, like, two hours, and we completely let it slip our minds until about an hour ago. We need a present ASAP, but she's really hard to buy for. You know the type—super picky. She's really into comics, and when we spotted your store, it was like a sign from the heavens. So, if you could just let us come in and buy something for her, you'd totally be saving our asses." I give him my best sugary sweet smile, hoping that'll win him over.

He remains silent for a moment, and I start to believe he bought my bullshit. Then he says, "Nice try, Mak, but I know none of your friends are into comics." With that, he slams the door in our faces.

Kennedy gapes at me with bewilderment. "Who the heck was that? And how dare he slam the door in our faces?"

I mentally rewind through what the guy said, trying to match up his voice with someone I know. "His voice was vaguely familiar, but I didn't hear enough to place it to a face."

Tucking a strand of hair behind her ear, Kennedy faces me with her hands on her hips. "What do we do now?"

I check the time on my watch then turn for the car. "We go back to the car and wait for Liam to come out."

Kennedy's head bobbles back as she lets out a groan. "Another stakeout?"

"Yep." A tiny smile touches my lips. While Kennedy may hate stakeouts, and I've never been a huge fan of them, I feel strangely close to my dad at the moment. "And with the way this is going, I'm thinking you better get used to them."

FOURTEEN

LOCATION: MAK'S CAR
TIME: 5:14 PM
DATE: MONDAY, MARCH 22ND

We sit in the car for so long that the sun begins to descend below the hills, and the sky shifts from a vibrant blue to an array of oranges and pale pinks. We ditch the sunglasses and raise the visors, which gives us a better view of the entrance door to the store in question. Nothing happens. At all.

Kennedy yawns, stretching her arms above her head. "Oh, my God, what the hell is he doing in there? Throwing a secret rager or something?" She glances at the time on the clock. "It's been over an hour."

"Thanks for the tenth time update," I joke, scrolling through an article on my phone.

She lowers her hands to her lap and slumps back in the seat. "Sorry. I know I'm being whiny, but I'm not used to sitting still for this long. I like to be in motion." She circles her hands in front of her and sighs. "Maybe we could try knocking on the door again."

"Weren't you trying to talk me out of it the first time I went up there, saying it was too sketchy?"

"Yeah, but that was over an hour ago. *A lot* of time has passed since then. Enough time that I'm starting to rethink my initial hesitance." She ravels a strand of hair around her finger, staring at the building. "You know, we could always just have Embry come over and kick the door down."

I glance at her with my brows elevated. "You know that'd be breaking and entering, right?"

"Yeah. Good point." She unravels her hair and plasters on a bubbly smile. "So, what've you been doing on your phone for the last half-hour? Is it anything I can help with?"

"I'm looking up stuff on this address." I drag my thumb along the screen, skimming through the information I found. "It's weird. There's not a registered owner for this house."

She leans over the console to get a glimpse of my screen. "Maybe the county owns it."

"Nope. I already checked. It's like the place doesn't exist. It doesn't even pull up on any maps."

"That's odd. Could it be because it's old?"

"Maybe ... But it's not that old. Not any older than the

other houses around here, anyway." I thrum my fingers on top of my leg, thinking of what I could be missing.

I wish my dad were here. If he was, he'd know what to do. Hell, he might even have some info on the house.

I scroll through a few more sites, searching for something—anything—about the house. Nothing. That is, until I stumble across a few help wanted ads on the *Shadow Cove Daily News* site. The ghost house is listed on four of the ads with no phone number, just a *please stop by for further inquiries.*

I think about the help wanted ads taped on the wall in the secret spot in dad's office. Is the ghost house listed on those ads, as well? Is all of this connected somehow? Is that where my dad's trail leads? To this house?

One more thing draws my attention. It's an ad some parent put in the paper about their missing daughter. They list the last place she was seen, which just happens to be on this street. I don't know if it means anything, but it's definitely caught my attention.

"What're you thinking, Mak?" Kennedy draws me out of daydream land. "Because you've got you're thinking face on."

"I'm thinking ..." I trail off as the door to the store swings open and a girl steps out.

At least, it looks like a girl. The transparency of her skin makes me question if this girl is from the Land of Reality or Mak's Crazyville. I blink and blink again, and suddenly, I'm no longer staring at a potential ghost, but at Liam. He no longer has a box in his hand, and anxiety is etched into his features as he hurries across the lawn.

I summon a preparing breath before reaching for the door handle. "It's time to figure out what the hell's going on." Then maybe I can hurry and solve this thing, de-stress, and return to Sane Town.

Kennedy tracks my gaze as I shove open the door. Letting out a nervous squeal, she does the same, and we stride across the sidewalk to cut Liam off before he reaches his car.

"Hey, Liam, how's it going?" I say, jumping straight into his path.

He grinds to a startled halt, nearly running me over. "Jesus, Mak. What the hell?" He shakes his head, struggling to catch his breath, and then moves to sidestep around me.

I mimic his move, blocking his way. When he blasts me with a dirty look, I bat my eyelashes innocently. Kennedy inches closer, and together, we corner him against the trunk of his car.

His mouth plummets into a confused frown. "Will you two please quit messing around and move? I need to get to my car."

My smile enlarges as his confusion doubles. "We didn't just come here to mess around, Liam. We need to ask you a few questions."

His Adam's apple bobs up and down as he gulps. "About what?"

I debate the right way to approach this: be blunt or toy around with him until he's so worried he cracks.

What to do? What to do?

I measure Liam up as he tries to charm me over with a half-grin, something I've seen him do to a ton of girls.

Yeah, definitely toy with him.

"Well, for starters, what is this place?" I point at the store.

He quickly shrugs. "I have no idea."

I cluck my tongue. "Liam, Liam, Liam, how are we going to establish any trust if you lie to me on my very first question?"

"Huh?" He scratches his head, blinking at me like a lost baby deer. "Look, I really don't know what you want or why you think we need to establish trust, but I need to go. I'm already late for dinner." He steps toward me, expecting me to move out of his way. When I don't, we bump into each other and bang foreheads.

Okay, that was not my smoothest moment, but whatever.

Time to get to the point.

"Fine, let's do this the easy way, then." I force a dramatic sigh while rubbing the tender spot on my head. "I know you know what's in that store because you went in there about an hour ago with a box full of what I'm guessing is most of the stolen computers at our school."

His face drains of color as he steps away from me. "I don't know what you're talking about. I don't know what this place is. And I don't know about any missing computers. Maybe you guys were seeing things or getting me confused with someone else."

"You know, for someone with a 4.0 GPA, you come up with some dumb lies." Kennedy hops up onto the trunk of his car and crosses her legs. "Come on, Liam; you can do better than that. Tell us you wandered into the wrong place, that you were lost. Hell, tell us you're a doppelganger. That will probably sound more believable at this point."

"What's a doppelganger?" he asks, blinking. "Is that, like, a type of dog or something?"

Kennedy exchanges an *okaaaayy* look with me. "Seriously? This is the guy in line to become valedictorian of our class?"

I refrain from giggling and cross my arms, staring Liam down. "I know you took the computers. I saw video footage of you breaking into the lockers and jacking about five of them, all belonging to your friends, so stop trying to play dumb with me." I smile as he glares at me. "Don't worry; I'm not going to rat you out just yet. I need you to do a couple of things for me."

His gaze skitters from me to the building to his car, like he's going to try to bolt. He probably could, considering Kennedy and I are no match for his height and weight. But then he would be risking the chance of me outing his dirty little sticky finger habit.

"What do you want?" He reaches for the pocket of his slacks, his gaze gliding across my worn sneakers, faded jeans, and plaid shirt that's missing a bottom button. "I'm guessing money."

"Of course you'd guess that, wouldn't you?" I bite back my irritation. "Put your wallet away. You're not getting off that easily."

He shoves his wallet back into his pocket, grinding his teeth, on the verge of throwing a tantrum. "Then what the hell do you want from me?"

"Well, for starters, I want to know why you've been stealing your friends' computers." A cocky smirk rises on my lips as he blinks in shock. "Then, as an added bonus, you can give me Dixon's computer. Then you can tell me what this place is and who owns it."

He studies me suspiciously. "What's it matter to you?"

"Nope." I lift a finger to his lips, shushing him, and Kennedy chokes on a laugh. "I'm the one asking the questions. All you need to do is answer."

The muscle in his jaw ticks. "Fine. But will you please lower your hand? Your fingers smell like cheese."

I remove my hand from his lips and sniff my fingers. Yep. Very cheesy. "Oh, yeah. That's probably from the Doritos I ate in the car while we were staking you out for the last two hours." When he gulps, I dazzle him with a grin. "Yeah, you should be nervous. We've got a lot of dirt on Shadow Cove's golden boy."

He audibly gulps again, wiping his palms along the sides of his legs. "Okay, I'll answer your questions." He throws a hasty glance over his shoulder, and panic floods his eyes as someone draws back the curtain and peers out the window. The lights aren't on inside, so I can't make out a face. However, the person appears tall and has narrow shoulders. "But not here," Liam sputters. Then he leans in and drops his voice to a hushed whisper. "If they know I'm telling you about them, they'll ruin my life."

I want to drill him with questions right now, force him to tell me, but with how jittery he looks, I decide not to for his safety. And honestly, for Kennedy's and mine. While I don't completely understand what's going on, I do know that whoever is in that house has athletic, rich, charming, and seemingly perfect Liam shaking like a cornered cat.

"All right, meet us tonight at the park," I say. "Around eight. And don't be late."

He promptly shakes his head. "I can't tonight. It's family dinner night, and my dad's been seriously monitoring my study hours. I have to put in at least six tonight before I go to bed. And he watches me like a hawk."

"Fine. Then how about tomorrow before school?" God, I'm turning into a softy. My dad would make him divulge the truth before he let him leave "Meet me at my car at exactly eight." I back away from him, and Kennedy follows. "And don't be late, or else the Rewards Board might declare some very dirty secrets of yours."

"Nice touch," Kennedy whispers, gently bumping her shoulder into mine.

"I thought so," I whisper back, restraining a grin.

I waggle my fingers at a trembling Liam before sauntering toward my car.

The second we're back on the road, driving in the direction of the school parking lot where Kennedy's car is parked, I let out a deafening breath.

"He's scared of something," I declare, turning on the headlights.

"Yeah, of you." Kennedy checks her messages on her phone. "I honestly didn't think you had it in you, Mak. I mean, you're not shy or anything, but you're not the kind of girl to boss a guy around and shush him by putting your finger to his lips."

"I was just playing the part. If you want to get to the truth, you have to be pushy, bossy, and persistent." I glance in my rearview mirror, making sure no one is following us. I might be overreacting, but the way someone kept glancing out the window and how Liam looked like he was about to piss his pants has me on edge. "But Liam wasn't just afraid of me ... He was afraid of whoever was in that house."

"Who *was* in that house?" Kennedy asks, tossing her phone into her purse.

"I don't know. I'm really interested in how the hell they know who I am, though."

"Yeah, me, too. Maybe it's someone from our school."

"Maybe." I'm not so sure, though. Something about that voice ... I've heard it before. And not at school.

I replay the voice over and over again as I continue to drive. The raspy tone ... like someone who smokes way too many packs ... And I think there was a tiny bit of a lisp in there ...

Suddenly, it clicks. Lispy Larry. I gave him that nickname when I helped my dad get a story on him. The topic of his article was supposed to be on the increasing drug use in Shadow Cove. My dad had a hunch that Larry, the mayor's son, was in charge of a drug trafficking circle going on. Before my dad made it too far into his research, though, his boss shut the story down. He said it was due to not having enough proof, but my dad overheard the mayor threatening his boss, telling him, if he ran the story, he'd shut the newspaper down permanently.

I never found out if Larry was the head of the drug trafficking or just a little worker bee for someone higher up. But what I'm really interested in finding out is why he's holed up in some ghost house that's connected to a bunch of help wanted ads where a bunch of stolen computers are being stashed. And what does he have on Liam Stallings that made him look like he was about to shit his pants?

FIFTEEN

LOCATION: MAK'S HOUSE
TIME: 8:47 PM
DATE: MONDAY, MARCH 22ND

The second I get home, I sneak into my dad's office while my mom is getting ready for work and check the addresses listed on the help wanted ads.

"Holy mother of jackpots," I whisper as I assess the ad clippings.

Yep, sure enough, the ghost house is listed on all of them. What that means, though, I don't have a damn clue other than my dad's trail on Sawyer's death led him to that house for some reason.

Think, Mak, think. Put the pieces together. What do the

ads, the computers, and Lispy Larry all have in common other than the ghost house?

I don't know that much about Lispy Larry other than what my dad mentioned while we were staking him out. That doesn't mean I can't scrounge through some of his old files and find out more. Plus, a little Internet search can always go a long way.

———

HERE'S ALL the info I can dig up on Lispy Larry.

Age: Twenty-one.

Current Job: Unemployed.

Times in Rehab: Five.

Times Arrested: Zero.

Times He Broke The Law: Eleven.

His criminal activities include theft, fraud, and drug charges. There might be more due to a hunch my dad had that the mayor was buying off the police to keep his son's problems hush-hush.

Most of my information is outdated since I collected it from the info my dad gathered when he was doing the story on Lispy Larry, so I'm not sure what those numbers are now. Then again, I think that might be irrelevant. The fact of the matter is that good old Lispy Larry is not only a troublemaker, but his dad works extremely hard to keep his mistakes out of the public eye. Perhaps that's why the ghost house isn't registered to anyone. Maybe Lispy Larry owns the deed, but with the illegal activity going on, the mayor has erased any record that the house belongs to his son.

I thrum my fingers against the cracked kitchen table, staring at the small stack of papers in front of me—the research I found on Lispy Larry. "So, maybe he's stealing computers and reselling them. It would fit his pattern. But how does Liam play a part in all of this? The two of them aren't friends unless they have a secret friendship affair going on. But if they are friends, then Liam wouldn't be scared out of his damn mind. And why the hell is Lispy Larry placing a shit-ton of help wanted ads in the paper? I doubt he has that many jobs that he needs done ... unless they're really not help wanted ads—"

"Mak, honey, who are you talking to?" My mom wanders into the kitchen, dressed in green scrubs, her hair piled on top of her head in a knotted bun, ready to leave for her night shift. Her gaze drops to the stack of papers, and a disappointed frown forms on her lips. "What're you doing?"

"Just a little research for a school project," I lie, patting the stack of paper.

She stares at the papers with skepticism. "What's the project about?"

"About how drugs affect the human body and mind." I carry her gaze, crossing my fingers she can't see the title on the top paper.

"Oh. Well, that's ... interesting. Let me know if you need any help." She moves toward the fridge to grab her lunch. "I work until ten, so I won't see you before you leave for school." She bumps the fridge shut with her hip then collects her car keys and purse off the countertop. "But maybe we can do dinner tomorrow." Her phone dings, and her brows crease as she fishes it out of her shoulder bag. When she reads the message, worry floods her expression. "I'll make lemon pepper chicken," she says distractedly. "That's still your favorite, right?"

"Sure." I force a smile, wondering why she went from cheery to miserable in the time it takes me to click search. "Sounds good."

"Good." Her eyes remain glued to the screen as she wanders across the kitchen. "Lock up after I leave, okay?"

I nod, but she doesn't even look up to note my answer as she walks out of the house.

Hmmm ... I wonder who texted her.

Probably Don.

Sighing, I drag my butt out of the chair to lock the front door. As I'm sliding the deadbolt, I peer out the window at the top of the door and notice my mom heading for the street instead of the garage.

I press my nose against the glass and squint against the darkness. "Where the hell is she going?"

Glancing left and right, my mom jogs across the street then ducks into the passenger seat of a sleek Mercedes. The headlights flip on, and the car peels away from the curb, speeding down the road and disappearing into the night.

I slump against the door. Who the hell was that? And why isn't she heading to work?

"She could be getting a ride from someone," I try to convince myself. "Not everything is suspicious, so just walk away and go back to your research."

I head for the kitchen, but as I think about how the bank statements showed her paychecks have been less lately, I flip a U-turn and hurry for the front door. Whether it's any of my business or not, I need to know what's going on with my mom, if Don was in that car, and why she looked super worried when she left the house.

Grabbing my bag and car keys from the wall hook, I hightail it to my car. The tires spin as I back down the driveway and onto the road. I cross my fingers that my mom doesn't recognize my car and that she goes straight to work. But I have an unsettling feeling I'm about to discover something about my mom that isn't going to be pretty.

SIXTEEN

LOCATION: MAK'S CAR
TIME: 8:58 PM
DATE: MONDAY, MARCH 22ND

I keep a good distance as I tail the Mercedes through the streets of our neighborhood, over the railroad tracks, and to the center of town. That's a good sign since the hospital is located on the opposite side of town from where we live. My hope rises that she's just bumming a ride off one of her coworkers, like a doctor, which would explain the swanky car. Then my hope fizzles like cheap champagne when the car zooms past the turn-off road to the hospital and heads for the hills, near Kennedy's neighborhood.

I back off a little as the traffic thins, knowing my headlights will be more noticeable now, and continue following the Mercedes as it weaves around corners and past all the neighborhoods, finally coming to a stop at the top of the cliff lookout that stretches above the seaside. While I haven't been to this spot personally, I know kids my age go here to get high, throw parties, and have sex. Since I doubt my mom is throwing a party with the mystery driver, and she gets drug tested at work, I can only assume she's doing the latter.

Yuck. Yuck. Just yuck.

Instead of parking in the same area, I drive further down the road until I reach the next turnoff. Then I climb out of my car and backtrack with my phone in hand. I don't actually want to see what they're doing. I just want to get the plate number so I can run it and find out who owns the car.

Gravel crunches underneath my sneakers as I hike up to the edge of the street, the ocean roaring below and the starry sky twinkling above. The salty air nips at my skin, and every time a car drives by, I cringe, worried the wrong person will spot me. I should probably turn back, but I'm just too close to finding out the truth.

Two minutes later, I reach the entrance to the turnoff and make out the back of the Mercedes. I hunker down, ready to run up to it, snap a photo, and get the hell out of there. As I step forward, though, headlights spotlight against my back. I reel around, shielding my eyes from the light, then inch to the side, figuring someone is just pulling in. When I hear the slamming of a car door, I tense.

"You're in some serious trouble," a deep voice warns. "You need to stop poking your nose into this thing."

For a stupid second, I wonder if I'm hallucinating again, but after blinking at least twenty times, the headlights remain shining across me.

"What thing?" I ask, being honest for once. While I have been poking my nose around in stuff, I don't know which thing he's referring to. My dad's research? My mom's business? My brother's death? Or the computer thefts?

"Don't play dumb with me. Now, you and I are going to have a little talk. Get in the truck." Clunky boots thud against the dirt as the person strides toward me.

The headlights are too bright to make out anything other than his tall silhouette. While I'm dying to find out who this dude is, I don't want to stick around and risk literally dying to obtain the answer.

"How stupid do you think I am?" I ask, backing away from him. "I'm not about to get into a car with a complete stranger who obviously knows more about me than he should."

"Don't you dare run," he barks, jogging toward me.

I spin around and run like a madwoman toward the Mercedes. I don't give a crap if I bust my mom doing the nasty with Don. Right now, getting away from psycho guy is way more important.

"Stop running!" he shouts, chasing after me. "I just want to talk to you."

"I bet you do," I call over my shoulder. "And let me guess, if I get into your truck, you'll give me some candy."

"Goddammit, Mak, will you stop running for two damn seconds!" the guy yells, his boots hammering against the dirt. "I just need to talk to you."

The way he says my name, like he *really* knows me, almost causes me to stop. Yet, considering I'm out in the middle of nowhere at night, I'm not about to risk the chance.

I quicken the pace, rushing for the Mercedes. As I get close, the taillights glow red, and the car backs up.

"No!" I shout, out of breath. "Wait!"

Either they can't hear me, or they thinking I'm about to bust them and are bailing out, because they peel out of there like ... Well, like two people about to get busted for cheating on their spouses.

As the taillights dwindle, I really start to panic. I swipe my finger across the screen of the phone while continuing to run straight for the cliff. No signal. Of course.

Shit! What am I going to do! At this point, it's either jump off the cliff or face the creeper charging me, neither of which sound appealing.

Nearing the edge of the cliff, I slam to a halt and whirl around. "What do you want?" I snap. "If you want to talk to me, we can talk out here."

Pale moonlight trails down on him as he slows to a stop and hunches over, panting for air. "You need to stop poking your nose around in what Liam's doing."

"I don't know what you're talking about," I play dumb

because, hello, I'm out in the middle of nowhere with a big-ass dude threatening me.

"Yes, you do, so back off." He straightens his stance and crosses his arms. "Mind your own business, or you'll end up like your brother."

I stiffen, the pounding beat of my pulse deafening inside my eardrums. "What do you mean, *like my brother*? My brother ... He committed suicide."

"You think so?" He releases a breathy laugh when I gasp. "You have no idea what you're getting yourself into, do you?" He shakes his head, backing away. "Consider this a warning. If you don't stop looking around where you shouldn't, next time, you won't be standing when I walk away from you."

Rage flames through me, potent and violent, a wildfire about to take out a forest. What did he mean by that? That my brother didn't commit suicide? What does he know? Better yet, who the hell is this asshole?

I wait until he gets inside the vehicle and backs out onto the road before I take off, getting my camera ready. When I reach the end of the road, the vehicle is too far away to take a good picture of the plates, but I manage to make out that the vehicle is a grey truck.

I sprint as I fast as I can to my car, rev up the engine, throw on my seatbelt, and slam my foot down on the gas pedal. The tires kick up a cloud of dust as I skid out onto the road. Taking the corners sharp and breaking the speed limit, I manage to catch up to the truck just in time to see it pull into Shady J's Drinkin' and Live Entertainment, a local strip club on the shadier side of town; hence, the name.

I steer my car into the gravelly parking lot of the gas station next door. Flipping off the headlights, I slouch down in my seat, keeping my head low, and watch the driver get out of the grey truck. His back is to me as he strolls across the parking lot for the bar lit up with neon lights and flashy signs of good-time promises.

Once he vanishes into the windowless entrance doors, I slip on my jacket, draw the hood over my head, and get out. Stuffing my hands into my pockets, I dash toward the truck while scanning the area for any bystanders. Thankfully, the thudding music and showy signs have drawn everyone inside.

When I make it to the truck, I check the door handle. Jackpot. Unlocked. Although I do know how to pick a lock if I need to, this way is just simpler.

The inside of the vehicle reeks of cigarette smoke, greasy fries, and body odor. I pull the collar of my jacket over my nose to block out the smell then hoist myself into the driver's seat and close the door. The interior lights click off, but the nearby signs offer me enough light to check the middle console first where I discover a bag of stale fast food rotting away.

"Yuck." I slam the lid closed then lean over to pop open the glove box. Papers spill out onto the floor, and I quickly scoop them up: old receipts, an unpaid parking ticket, and an insurance card. Double jackpot.

According to the car, the truck is registered to Larry Motaling, aka Lispy Larry.

"So, Lispy Larry, you're the one trying to scare me."

Clearly, my being out in front of that store earlier and talking to Liam spooked him. But why? Over stolen computers? Or does this have to do with the drug story my dad was working on? And why bring my brother's death into his threat? Was it just that, a threat? Or does he know something?

I sit in the truck for a moment, listening to the music playing from inside the bar, wondering what to do next. Walk away from this? It seems like the most reasonable thing to do, but at the same time, I really want to know what's going on and if Lispy Larry knows something about my brother's death.

I drum my fingers on top of the steering wheel. "What to do? What to do?"

If my mom were here, she'd tell me to be smart and keep my nose out of places it doesn't belong. My dad, he'd tell me to be safe but get to the truth, because the truth is important.

"Always get to the truth, Mak," he used to say. "Those kinds of stories make the best articles. And you could potentially help a lot of people."

This started out as being about getting back at Dixon, but not anymore. Not after Larry just threw my brother's death in my face. He knows something. I can feel it in my bones.

I mull over what to do for a couple minutes longer

while continuing my search through Lispy Larry's truck. I don't even know what I'm looking for, but when I stumble across a small business card tucked under the seat, I pause.

No name or number is printed on it, just a strange circular symbol traced by a pattern of Greek-like letters. I don't know what the symbols or letters mean, but I know I've seen it before. Somewhere ...

Tucking the card into the back pocket of my shorts, I slip out of the truck and dash back to my car. I'm snapping a photo of the card so I can do an image search when a message pings through my phone.

Kennedy: Hey! I was wondering if I could crash at your place. I really need a break from the craziness for one night.

Me: Of course! I'm actually not at home right now, but I will be in a few minutes, so head on over.

Kennedy: Where the heck are you this late? No, wait, let me guess. You're having a secret lovers' rendezvous at the skate park with Rylen.

Mak: Ha, ha, you're so funny. I already told you nothing is going on with Rylen and me.

Kennedy: Yet.

I start to smile then spot Larry heading for his truck. He walks with a purpose, taking long strides and cradling a duffel bag in his arms like it's the most precious thing in the word. Hmm ... What's in the bag, Larry? Drugs? Money? Computers?

Mak: Whatever. Look, I'll explain where I was tonight when you get to my place. See you in just a few.

I toss my phone onto the console as I slide down in my seat. I stay like that for about five minutes before peeking up over the dashboard. The parking spot is empty, his truck gone, and I'm left stirring in a sea of confusion, determined to swim out of it.

SEVENTEEN

LOCATION: MAK'S HOUSE
TIME: 10:38 PM
DATE: MONDAY, MARCH 22ND

I half-expect my mom to be home when I arrive with some lame ass excuse about being sick and coming home early. Nope. The house is quiet, and her car is still in the garage.

After I change into a pair of plaid pajama bottoms and a clean tank top, I sit down on the sofa with my phone and do an image search on the photo of the card while waiting for Kennedy to show up. The search brings up a ton of results of the same image linked to various different websites, yet, so far, none sparkle any recognition of why the symbol carries familiarity to me.

"Man, this is going to take hours to go through," I mutter as the doorbell rings.

After setting my phone down on the coffee table, I push to my feet and throw open the door with an overzealous smile.

"Welcome to Mak's Bed and Breakfast," I greet Kennedy. "We're the finest bed and breakfast in Shadow Cove."

Kennedy claps her hands. "Oh, goodie. Does that mean you're making me breakfast?"

I nod, motioning her to get her butt inside. "And you're going to love tomorrow's special. Pop-Tarts with a side of Pop-Tarts."

"That's it?" she teases as she walks in and drops her bags on the floor. "It's a good thing I'm not paying you."

I laugh, kick the door shut, and lock the deadbolt. Before I back away, though, I peek out the window to make sure the grey truck isn't lurking in the shadows somewhere. The street is bare except for a few cars parked on the curb, but no trucks.

I turn around, plastering on a grin. "All right, who wants popcorn ...?" I trail off at the sight of Kennedy's face. The porch light was off when she was standing outside, but the bright living room lights give me a clear view of the gnarly welt under her left eye. "What happened to your face?"

"Wow, Mak, you really know how to make a girl feel pretty," Kennedy jokes, shucking off her button-down jacket.

I want to laugh, but the shape of the welt looks an awful lot like a handprint. "Who hit you?"

She lightly places her palm to her face then winces. "No one hit me. I just—"

"Let me guess, fell down," I cut her off with an accusing tone. This isn't the first time I've noticed a suspicious mark or bruise on her.

"I really did, though." She lowers her hand from her face. "Does it look that bad?"

I nod and start drilling her with questions, hoping maybe she'll cave this time and tell me the truth. "How'd you fall this time?"

She chucks her jacket on the armrest of the sofa then smooths out invisible wrinkles in her tank top and yoga pants. "I was walking down the stairs, wearing heels, and you know how that goes."

"I may know how it goes since I suck walking in heels, but not you. You're a pro. Have been ever since sixth grade when you bought those four-inch bright-ass red platforms."

"Oh, yeah, I total forgot about those! I wish those would come back into style. I so rocked the look."

"Don't change the subject." I cross my arms and stare her down. "Tell me the truth, because I know you didn't fall down the stairs."

She sighs, sinks down onto the sofa, and slips her hands underneath her legs.

"I'm pretty sure I know what the answer is, but I'm going to ask it, anyway."

She stares up at me, her eyes pleading. "Can you please just let this go?"

"You know I can't." I sit down beside her. "If I did, I'd be the worst friend ever."

"Yeah, I know." She releases an exhausted sigh. "It was my stepmom."

"*What!*"

"It's not a big deal. We were arguing, things got heated, and well ..." She shrugs. "You know."

"No, I don't know. You want to know why?"

"Not really."

"Well, I'm going to tell you, anyway, because it's important." I twist on the sofa and bring my knee up on the cushion. "It's never okay for a parent or a stepparent to hit their kid, even if you guys were arguing."

"Yeah, I know." She traces her finger back and forth across her lips, staring off into space. "But what's done is done, and now I just want a break from all the drama."

"Was this the first time something like this ever happened?"

"A few times, but like I said, it's not that big a deal."

I stare at her, stunned. This dismissive attitude isn't like Kennedy at all. "Does your dad know about this?"

"Of course he knows." She lowers her tone, mimicking her father. "He knows everything that goes on under his roof." She blows out a breath. "All he cares about is making sure that what goes on inside our house *stays* inside our house."

"Maybe we should report her. Your stepmom, I mean. I could drive you to the police station and help you fill out a report."

"It won't matter. My dad would vouch for my stepmom, and I'd end up looking like a liar. And my dad would get even more pissed off that I aired our dirty laundry." I open my mouth to try to convince her more, but she talks over me. "Look, I just need a few days away from my house until things cool off again."

"Then what happens when they heat up again?" I ask with a stern look.

"I don't want to talk about this anymore." She jumps to her feet. "I'm going to go make us some popcorn. When I get back, I want you to tell me why the hell you were out wandering around town at ten o'clock on a school night. I know this town, and there's nothing to do on weekdays this late except to go to the turnoff and have sex." She points a finger at me, smirking as she backs out of the room. "But the question is, who were you having sex with?"

I roll my eyes at her, and she laughs wickedly before leaving the room. Then I sit back and stare at the dark street outside, questioning what the right thing to do is.

I don't agree with Kennedy at all. Letting this slide—letting her stepmom hit her—is wrong. But I can't go to the police and report the incident without Kennedy being on board. Maybe if I give her the night to sleep on it, she'll change her mind. Or maybe I should talk to my mom about it.

I frown at the thought of my mom. I wonder if she's even at work or if she's spending the night in some sleazy hotel with fancy car man. God, the thought makes me ill.

Deciding I need a distraction, I pick up my phone and return to searching through the sites the images are linked to. "Nope. Nope. Nope." None are even remotely useful, so I mix my method up a bit and type the Greek letters into the engine. Tons of sites pop up, yet one in particular catches my eye. An escort site located in my sweet, innocent little hometown. "What does any of this have to do with computers and Lispy Larry?"

"Who's Lispy Larry?" Kennedy asks, appearing in the doorway with a bowl of freshly popped popcorn.

I tap on the link to the site. "The guy who was in the ghost house."

Her forehead creases. "Wait? How did you find that out?"

I pat the spot on the sofa beside me. When she takes a seat, I steal a handful of popcorn and give her a summary of what happened from the moment I dropped her off. I even tell her about my mom and her secret meet up with the mystery man.

"Wait a second." She holds her hands up in front of her. "You think your mom's sleeping around with some rich guy?"

"Not just any rich guy," I tell her, kicking my feet up on the coffee table. "I think it might be Dixon's dad."

She munches on a mouthful of popcorn. "Hey, she could do worse. Dixon's dad is pretty hot for an old dude."

I shovel up some popcorn in my hand and toss it at her face. "Ew. Never say that again. *Ever*."

She laughs, flicking a piece of popcorn off her shoulder. "Don't pretend you've never thought it."

"Not once." I shake my head a thousand times, trying to clear her comment out of my mind, then finish telling her about the rest of my night.

When I finish, she reclines against the armrest. "That image is in some of the stores around town. The fancier ones, anyway."

"Really?" I ask, and she nods. "Do you know why? And what it means?"

She shakes her head. "I have no damn clue. I just know I've seen it in a few stores here and there." She twists a strand of hair around her finger. "So, when you did a search on the image, it took you to an escort site?"

I nod and show her the open page on my phone. "I don't know what it has to do with any of this stuff with the stolen computers. Maybe Lispy Larry just can't get a date and keeps the card on hand. What I think is really weird is that the card doesn't have a link to the site or anything. I had to type in the Greek letters inside the symbol to get the site to pop up. Seems like a really shitty way to do advertising."

"They're probably running an illegal one and don't want anyone knowing about it."

"What's the difference between an illegal escort service and a legal one?"

"Legal ones offer"—she makes air quotes—" 'dating services.' Illegal ones sell out women for sex."

I want to ask her how she knows this, but I'm kind of afraid of the answer.

She must read my mind, though, because she says, "Back when my dad was a freelance lawyer, he worked a case for an escorting business."

"Was it a legal one?"

"He proved it was, but that doesn't mean it was true. I could ask him, but I doubt that'd go over very well."

I thrum my fingers on top of my knee, looking at the site. The only way to get on it is with an account login and password, yet there's no place to sign up, so my bet is that, in order to get an account, you'd have to speak to the owner directly, which makes the site very hush-hush-like and super sketchy.

"I don't know why this is bugging me," I say. "I should probably let it go ... I just can't shake the feeling that I've seen this symbol before."

She sets the popcorn bowl down on the coffee table and sticks out her hand. "Can I see the photo of it?"

"Sure." I switch to the photo and hand her my phone. Then I scoop up the last of the popcorn.

"I know where else we've seen this," she announces, sitting up straight.

I drop the handful of popcorn back into the bowl. "Where?"

"At that creepy store today." She taps the screen. "It was on the side of the box Liam was carrying."

"That's why it looks familiar to me." I have an ah-ha moment. "Although, I swear I've seen it somewhere else, too."

"Maybe at one of the stores?"

I give her a *really* look. "You know I'm not cool enough to go in fancy stores."

"No way. You're *too* cool to go into those stores." She smiles but the move looks forced. Then she gives me my phone back. "What I want to know is why did Liam have a box with the logo of an escorting business ...a box full of stolen computers."

"I'm not sure." I study the photo, trying to make the connection. "But tomorrow, I'm going to find out."

And I mean that with all my heart. Whether this is right or wrong, I can't let it go, not after Lispy Larry implied he knew something about my brother's death.

"MAK? MAK, CAN YOU HEAR ME?"

I blink my eyelids open and sit up in bed, squinting through the darkness. "Sawyer?"

He materializes in the doorway of my bedroom, the moonlight from outside casting across his face. For a faltering instant, hope leaps inside my chest. Sawyer is here. He's alive. He never died. But he did die, and this is a dream.

I lean over, tug on the lamp cord, and soft lighting filters around the room. The last time I saw him, he was lying in his coffin, his skin pale, and he was wearing a suit, something he never would've worn while he was alive. Now, though, he resembles the Sawyer I knew with color in his cheeks, his shaggy brown hair hanging messily across his forehead, and his jeans and T-shirt wrinkled.

"It's been awhile since you've paid me a little visit in dreamland," I say, throwing the blanket off me.

"I know." He scratches his forehead, peering around my bedroom: the posters on the walls, my skateboard in the corner, and my computer on the floor. "You've made some changes since the last time I was here." He walks further into my room. "Where's your computer desk?"

"Mom sold it at a yard sale," I explain, lowering my feet to the floor. "She did a lot of that right after Dad vanished. Lately, though, she's toned it down."

He looks at me, strands of hair falling into his eyes. "Why's that?"

I shrug. "I don't know."

"Yes, you do," he encourages. "Come on, Mak; tell me. Let's talk like we used to."

I open my mouth to tell him that I think Mom is getting money from Don, but the words die on my tongue because this isn't real. None of this is real.

"I wish we could talk like we used to," I say instead. "But

things aren't like they used to be. Everything's different now. You're gone. Dad's gone. And Mom ... Well, I don't even know who she is anymore."

"You've changed, too." He carries my gaze, the darkness in his eyes conveying a warning. "The stuff you're doing ... The things you're getting into ... This isn't going to end well, Mak." He looks away from me, ashamed. "Trust me; I know. And I really think you should stop looking."

"I can't do that, not until I find out the truth."

"You should, just like Dad should have."

"I know."

He sighs. "Just be careful, please."

"I'll try." I rise to my feet and cross the room toward him. "What happened to you?" When he says nothing, I beg, "Please, Sawyer, just tell me if someone did something to you ... if your death ... if you didn't hurt yourself ... If someone else hurt you, you need to tell me so I can make them pay."

Sorrow fills his eyes as he looks at me. "You sound just like Dad."

"That's not a bad thing."

He arches a brow. "If that's true, then why isn't he here?"

"Wait. Do you know what happened to Dad?"

He frowns then walks out of the room. "I need to show you something."

My heart slams against my chest as I jog into the hallway after him. Maybe I'm being delusional, but a small part of me hopes he's about to show me an answer to what happened to our dad.

He leads me down the hallway to the final door on the right. Opening the door, he walks into his old bedroom. A layer of dust covers the made bed, the boxes stacked on the floor, and the light fixtures.

"You packed up my stuff?" he asks, peering around the room.

The pain in his voice makes my heart squeeze inside my chest.

"Not all of it. Mom thought ... Well, she thought it'd help us all heal more quickly if your stuff was out of sight, out of mind." I feel like an asshole for saying it aloud. He's dead. He doesn't need me reminding him of that. "I'm really sorry."

"For what?" he mutters, opening the closet door. "I'm the one who caused this mess."

Before I can ask him what he means by that, he steps inside the closet and vanishes into the darkness.

I follow after him, fearing he's going to leave me.

"Sawyer?" I whisper, feeling above my head until I find the cord to the light. With a soft tug, the lightbulb clicks on, and I sigh in relief at the sight of Sawyer standing at my side. "I was worried you left."

He shakes his head. "Not yet. Not until I show you." With a remorseful expression, he crouches down. "I'm really sorry about this, Mak."

"Sorry about what?"

"About what's back here ... I just want you to know that I never meant to get into things this deep. I just wanted some extra cash and to stop being picked on all the time. I

thought this would help, but once I got started, I couldn't stop."

I gulp. "What happened—"

He slips through the floor, his voice echoing, "Just please forgive me when you find it ..."

MY EYES POP OPEN, and I gasp for air, bolting upright in bed. My forehead is damp with sweat, and my soaring pulse makes me question if I'm having a heart attack.

Deep breath in. Deep breath out. In. Out.

After a minute or two, I manage to steady my heartbeat and breathing. I glance at the clock and shake my head. 4:30 in the morning. Man, this is too early to be up.

I lie down in bed and attempt to go back to sleep, but my dream replays in my mind, branded into my thoughts. Every step we took, every word we exchanged felt so real, like most of my dreams about Sawyer and my hallucinations. Then again, this dream felt different, too. He wasn't there to talk to me. He was trying to show me something.

Slipping out of bed, I tiptoe out of the room, being extra quiet to avoid waking up Kennedy who is passed out on the inflatable mattress on my floor. Once I get into the hallway, I hurry straight for my brother's closet and flip on the light. I don't even know what I'm looking for, especially since most of his belongings have been emptied out.

"What were you trying to show me?" I crouch down and

rest my palm on the closet floor, unsure what I'm even looking for or if I should be looking for anything. Maybe I'm just some crazy girl sitting in her dead brother's closet, hoping to find an answer that doesn't exist. "It's just carpet, Mak. What do you think you're going to find? It's not like we didn't clean out his room."

Still, I'm not ready to give up yet. Sawyer used to hide things in odd places: cigarettes under his mattress, beers beneath his bed, and my mom even once found a joint lying on his closet floor. Why he stupidly left the joint out in the open is a mystery other than maybe he was too stoned to realize.

Or maybe he was trying to hide it somewhere and got caught.

Hmmm ... I glance around and notice a torn spot of carpet in the far back corner of the closet. Not untypical for our house, but I peel back the corner, anyway. By the time the carpet catches, I have half the damn floor flipped back.

Scratching my head, I stare at what I've found. "A crawl space? Just how long has that been here? And why did it seem like Sawyer was trying to show it to me in my dream?"

I slip my fingers along the cracks, drag the piece of wood off the entrance, and a cold chill slithers down my spine. Does he want me to go inside? I shiver again at the thought, getting a really bad case of the heebie-jeebies. Then I think of Sawyer in that lake, drowning ... of him coming into my room that day and asking for my help ... of me letting him go without finding out what was wrong. I need to do this ... for Sawyer ... for my dad ... for myself.

You can do this, Mak. For him.

Holding my breath, I stick my hand into the dark hole and test how deep it goes. Instead of finding the bottom, my fingers graze what feels like paper. Grabbing it, I pull my arm back up to see what I found.

A large manila envelope.

My gut twists into tight knots. Somehow, I know whatever is inside the envelope isn't going to be good.

Opening the top flap, I dump out the contents: a small stack of hundred dollar bills; a tiny plastic bag filled with a white, powdery substance that I'm pretty sure is cocaine; a key; a newspaper clipping for a lawn care job; a necklace with a glass vile on the end, a thick leather bound book, and a small card with a circular symbol printed on it. It's the same symbol from the card I found in Lispy Larry's truck and the escorting site.

I fall back on my butt, staring at the contents in horror. "What did you get into, Sawyer?"

Tears sting my eyes as a single thought runs through my mind. One single thought that makes my body run cold with fear.

Is this why you're dead?

EIGHTEEN

LOCATION: MAK'S HOUSE
TIME: 7:11 AM
DATE: TUESDAY, MARCH 23RD

I wake up the next morning with a killer headache, probably because it took me over an hour to fall back asleep after I flushed Sawyer's stash of cocaine down the toilet. The rest of the stuff I held on to, though, the contents of the envelope currently tucked away in the secret nook in my dad's office. I have no idea what they're for—the key, the necklace, or the ancient looking book with pages of a language I couldn't recognize—but that doesn't mean they aren't clues.

I lie awake in bed for about half an hour, staring up at the ceiling, waiting for Kennedy to wake up. I can't stop thinking about everything I found and how I want to find more. I want to connect the dots, find out the truth.

"*You sound just like Dad,*" Sawyer said to me in my dream, and he was right. I do sound like Dad.

I don't know if that's a good thing, considering he went crazy then just disappeared. Regardless, I can't stop looking, not when I finally found the start of a trail.

Is this how my dad felt all the time? This overwhelming, desperate, addicting need to figure it all out, to get to the truth?

"Good morning," Kennedy says with a yawn as she sits up on the air mattress. She takes one look at me then frowns. "Why do you look worried?"

I climb out of bed. "Let's start getting ready for school, and then I'll tell you."

As we get dressed and do our hair, I give her a quick recap of what I found last night, minus the drugs. I plan on keeping that tidbit to myself. Maybe forever.

While I don't fully believe my brother's drug addiction led to his overdose, I still don't want any evidence out there that he was a drug addict. It makes me sad to think that my brother was struggling that hard before he died, that he was in such a dark place.

Maybe everyone's right. Maybe he did just kill himself.

Then why was my dad so strung out on proving Sawyer was murdered? And why did Lispy Larry imply he knew Sawyer didn't take his own life?

No, I'm not ready to accept my brother's death as a

suicide. I refuse to think anything else until I get to the truth.

"So, what do you think is up with all the help wanted ads?" Kennedy asks after I've finished telling her about what I found.

"I have a couple of theories, but they're a little out there." I take a seat on my bed and lean over to lace up my sneakers. "One, whoever is placing the ads in the newspaper, which I'm assuming is Lispy Larry since he's the only person I've seen hanging out at the ghost house, is sending secret messages through those ads."

She sets down the curling iron she's holding. "Secret messages, Mak? Really? Isn't that a little bit out there?"

"I'm not done yet." I stand up and slip on a dark green button-down jacket over my black tank top. "Another theory I have is that the person placing those ads—aka, Lispy Larry —is luring people into the house so he can kidnap them."

She tousles her hair with her fingers. "Why would Lispy Larry want to kidnap people? I know the guy's a total weirdo and everything, but kidnapping seems a bit extreme."

"Maybe because he's a sick, twisted freak." I sling the handle of my backpack over my shoulder. "Or maybe he's running a sex trafficking business along with his drug trafficking."

"That's a bit out there, too. Plus, you said your dad never proved he was drug trafficking."

"Yeah, but he didn't disprove it, either."

"You really think someone like Lispy Larry could be behind some huge ring of drug and sex trafficking?" she asks skeptically, shutting off the curling iron.

I head for my bedroom door. "I never said he was the only one behind it, just that he was in on running it."

She collects her purse and books from off my bed. "I know this is going to sound a bit strange coming from me, Miss Adventure Adventurous, but if you really believe Lispy Larry is doing all of this, then maybe you should go to the police."

"I can't yet. I don't have enough proof."

"You could always show them what you found."

"What, a few newspaper clippings and an escort site that we can't even log on to?" I grasp the doorknob, shaking my head. "Trust me; my dad had more proof than that about Sawyer's death, and the police still wouldn't do anything. Plus, this is the mayor's son we're talking about. If we're going to prove someone like him did actually kidnap people, we have to find some factual, hard evidence."

"How do we do that, exactly? We're not cops. We should really let them handle it."

Like they handled my brother's death, my dad's disappearance, and all those missing persons' cases.

"I need more proof before I do that. I'm hoping maybe Liam might know something about the site and the logo." As I pull open the door, the scent of bacon and eggs immediately engulfs my nostrils.

"I thought you said we were having Pop-Tarts,"

Kennedy says, exchanging a puzzled look with me. "Is your mom here?"

"She wasn't supposed to be, but ..." I walk down the hallway and into the kitchen where my mom is standing in front of the stove, dressed in her scrubs and apron, pans hissing from the stovetop.

Two things confuse me about the scene in front of me. For starters, my mom wasn't supposed to get off work until ten. Second, the last time my mom cooked breakfast was over a year ago, back when Sawyer was alive.

"Hey, honey," my mom says when she spies me lingering in the doorway. "I got off work early, so I thought I'd come home and make us some breakfast." She flips off the burner, sets down the fork she's holding, and opens the top cupboard. "I noticed Kennedy's car out front. Did she sleep-over last night?"

"Yeah. And thanks for letting me stay." Kennedy appears by my side, hugging her books to her chest. "Sorry I came over so late. My dad was just in a grumpy mood, and I needed a break."

"That's perfectly okay. You know you're always welcome here." She stacks three plates on the countertop. "I made more than enough eggs and bacon, so feel free to eat as much as you want." She begins shoveling eggs onto the plates.

Kennedy looks at me, as if waiting for my permission, but I don't budge.

"Why'd you get off work early?" I ask, leaning against the doorjamb with my arms crossed.

"I was tired." She grabs a plate of bacon and eggs then pulls out a chair at the table. "I've been working a lot of late shifts, trying to make sure we don't get behind on bills."

I press my lips together at the mention of bills, dying to ask her about the hefty deposit I noted in her checking account, but then I'd just be outing that I snooped.

She's about to dive into her eggs when she glances over at us. "Aren't you girls going to eat?"

"We don't have time. We need to be at the school early to work on a project for English." Not a complete lie. We do need to be at school early, but to meet up with Liam.

"Well, at least take some bacon with you." She pushes away from the table, tears a couple of paper towels off the roll, and places a few slices of bacon on each. "Here you go. I swear it's good. I didn't even burn it this time." She says it like she cooks all the time when she doesn't.

"Thanks." Kennedy smiles at her as she takes a paper towel full of bacon.

I take the offered bacon from my mom, eyeing her over, wondering over the real reason she's home early and why she cooked us breakfast. Because she was out all night with Don and feels guilty about it? Is cooking breakfast her way of trying to alleviate her guilt?

"Let's go," I say to Kennedy, turning for the front door.

I don't know what my mom's up to, but I've got bigger problems at the moment.

"Oh, wait, Mak. I forgot to ask you something," my mom calls out before we even make it to the front door.

The tension in her tone instantly makes me edgy.

I turn to Kennedy. "I'll be out in just a sec."

Kennedy nods, and then her heels click against the linoleum as she walks out the door.

I turn to my mom, adjusting the strap of my bag higher on my shoulder. "What's up?"

She leaves the kitchen, coming to stand in the foyer with me. "I was just wondering if you went anywhere last night." She fiddles with the tie on her apron. "Like, up by that turnoff near Kennedy's."

I hesitate, attempting to get a read on why she's asking, on how much she knows. "No. Why?"

"Oh, it's nothing." A mixture of relief and annoyance washes across her face. "A co-worker of mine thought he saw your car up there, but I figured it wasn't."

I want to ask her a thousand questions, but I doubt she'll divulge the truth and would likely get pissed off that I followed her around. I opt to keep my lips shut while she stares at me silently, and I do the exact same thing to her.

Look at us, mother and daughter, two little liars.

"I need to get going," I finally say, breaking the tension. "We're already running late."

"Hold on just a second," she says as I'm reaching for the front door. "I need to talk to you about Bria Brookenrose. Have you heard anything around school about her?"

My hand falls to my side as I slowly face her. "I heard that she died."

She chews nervously on her bottom lip. "Is that all you heard?"

I hesitate. "A couple of assholes were saying something about how she and Sawyer made a suicide pact, but I don't believe it."

"I heard that, too," she utters with wide eyes.

"Do you believe it?" I hold my breath, fearing her answer.

"I don't really know what to believe anymore." Her eyes begin to water, but she inhales deeply, sucking the tears back. "I spoke to Bria's mom when she came into the hospital to ... identify the body." She sucks in a tremulous breath, dabbing her tears away with her fingertips.

Worried she's about to lose it, I reach out and take her hand, and she holds on tightly.

"But, anyway, I really think we should go to the funeral to pay our respects."

"Okay," I say. "But, Mom, with the rumors going around ... are you sure the Brookenroses even want us there?"

She releases my hand. "No one believes those rumors, Mak. And the police already declared her death as an accidental drowning."

"Did they do a toxicology report on her?"

"Yes, but what does that matter?"

"Was there morphine in her system?" Like there was in Sawyer's system when he died.

"I have no idea." Her forehead furrows into a scowl. "I don't know what you're getting at, but I know your brother, and while he may have been struggling with his own personal demons, he would never talk another human being into taking their own life."

If she really did know him, why didn't she know about what was hidden underneath his closet floor?

"That's not what I'm getting at," I say. But the truth is, after what I found in my brother's bedroom last night, I feel like I have no clue who Sawyer is, and maybe I never did. Still, I can't help thinking about my dad's theory that Sawyer was murdered. What if he was and the killer killed Bria, too? What if they kill again? What if they're behind a lot of the deaths in Shadow Cove?

She folds her arms, her eyes remaining narrowed. "Then what are you getting at? Because you're really starting to sound like your dad."

"So what if I am? Maybe Dad was on to something."

"Like what? That the town is involved in some sort of murder conspiracy?" The ridicule in her tone makes my jaw tick.

No, Mom, that's not what I'm saying at all. I'm saying that, if someone killed Sawyer like Dad believed, then maybe they killed Bria, too. And the coroner's report could prove that.

"Nothing. Never mind. Forget I said anything." I yank open the door to leave.

"The funeral's on Saturday," she tells me as I step over the threshold. "We'll ride over together."

"Okay." I shut the door then trot down the front porch, breathing in the crisp morning air.

One of the main reasons my father believed Sawyer's death was not a suicide was because of the morphine in his system. Not only is morphine a pain in the ass to get ahold of, at least according to my dad's research notes, but he also mentioned it didn't make sense that Sawyer would go through all the trouble to get the morphine when he could've just raided my mom's stash of sleeping pills in the medicine cabinet. Plus, there were these strange scratches on his arms and legs, like tree branches clawed him. Or something else.

I want to know if Bria had morphine in her system and what her cause of death was listed as, if she had the scratches, too, and what the police believe the scratches were. I want to get my hands on the coroner's report. Find out all the details.

And I might know a way to do it.

NINETEEN

LOCATION: MAK'S CAR
TIME: 7:49 AM
DATE: TUESDAY, MARCH 23RD

Kennedy decides to ride with me to school and leave her car parked at my house. We pick up Embry and Ev on the way. During the ten-minute drive from Embry's house to the school, I tell them about the madness that happened yesterday, starting from when Kennedy and I tailed Liam all the way up to when I had an idea of how to get ahold of Bria's coroner's report. By the time I'm finished, we've made it to school, and Ev looks on the verge of yacking up her breakfast.

"Mak, I'm not sure if that's such a good idea," Ev says, as

pale as a vampire. "I mean, it's one thing to sneak in and look at the security footage of a school—which, just so you know, I had nightmares about—but tricking a coroner into giving us Bria's report ..." She shakes her head. "That's too illegal. I just can't do it."

"You're not going to do it. Embry and I are later today." I rotate around in my seat and stick out my fist to Embry. "Right, Em?"

She flips her newly dyed, pale purple hair off her shoulder and gives me a fist bump with zero hesitation. "I'm always down for a little rebellion. My parents have been on a real I-forgot-I-have-kids kick, anyway, so it's about time I remind them that they're completely wrong."

"But we're not going to get caught"—I check the time on the dashboard, noting that Liam should be here any minute —"so they probably won't ever find out."

"You can't be so sure you won't get caught. And if you do, you could go to jail." Ev blows out an exasperated breath. "Maybe you could just ask Bria's mom about whatever it is you need to know."

I get her point—I really do—but I can't let this go. I need to find out how Bria died, if her death was like Sawyer's, if there was anything suspicious about her death other than the fact that she died in the same place as my brother did. And asking Bria's parents will only cause drama and more than likely upset everyone. I'm nervous enough that we're even attending the funeral with the rumors floating around town about the suicide pact.

"We won't get caught. And even if we did, my dad was like this"—I hold up my crossed fingers—"with Legend."

Ev's brows dip. "Who's Legend?"

"The coroner," I say like *duh*.

"You say that like it's so obvious." Kennedy flips down the visor and leans close to the mirror as she applies yet another layer of face powder over her injured cheek. "Sorry, Mak. Love you to death and beyond, but you're the only one in this car twisted enough to know a guy who examines dead bodies for a living."

"That's not true. After today, Embry will, too."

"It'll be pretty interesting to meet him so I can see how my future's going to turn out," Embry says, digging out a stick of gum from her bag. She offers a piece to Ev, and Ev accepts, popping the gum in her mouth. "Because, according to everyone here"—she gestures around at the people loitering around the school parking lot—"that's what my career is going to be. Well, either that or a serial killer."

"People suck, Em; you should know that by now." Kennedy's hand drifts to her cheek. She may have caked on enough makeup to hide the mark, but it doesn't hide the anger in her voice as she says, "Just remember, one day, we're going to get out of Shadow Cove, and all this shit will be behind us. No one will hurt us anymore."

Embry and Ev look from Kennedy to me. I shrug, wanting to tell them about the mark on her cheek, but knowing Kennedy, she will lose her shit if I do.

"Are you okay?" Ev asks Kennedy worriedly. "Your hand's shaking."

Kennedy jerks her hand away and puts on a plastic smile. "Yeah. Sorry. I was just thinking about some stuff."

Embry places a hand on Kennedy's shoulder. "You want to talk about it?"

Kennedy shakes her head then shoves open the door. "There's Liam. He looks lost." She escapes the car and shuts the door before any of us can say anything else.

Embry stares at Kennedy through the window, watching her weave through the parked cars toward Liam. "What was that about?"

I shrug, fiddling with the air conditioner knob, though the car isn't on. "She spent the night at my house because her dad was being an ass again." *And her stepmom hit her.*

God, I want to tell them just so they can give me some advice on what to do, if nothing else. But last night when we were going to bed, Kennedy made me promise I wouldn't tell anyone. I don't feel right about making that promise. I really don't.

Maybe I should tell Embry and Ev and just deal with Kennedy's wrath that will follow.

I open my mouth to spill the beans, but the back door opens up, and Kennedy pokes her head in. "All right, Em, hop out. Liam wants to sit between you and Ev."

"I never said that," Liam gripes from behind her. "You told me I had to."

"I know." Kennedy smiles sweetly at him. "To keep you from trying to bail out."

Liam snorts a laugh. "I could get out if I wanted to."

"Oh, really?" Kennedy's gaze glides to Embry, who grins and cracks her knuckles.

Liam stuffs his hands in the pockets of his khakis, carrying Embry's gaze. "I'm not afraid of you, Embry. You may have the entire school believing you're a badass, but deep down, I know who you really are. You're a nice girl, and all that heavy eyeliner, dyed hair, and I'll-kick-your-ass attitude is just a façade."

"Aw, thanks for the psych analysis, Liam. And here's a little advice in return: don't become a psychology major because you seriously suck at it." She climbs out of the car, the chains on her boots jiggling. Then she steps aside and motions for Liam to get in. "Now, get in, or I'll make you get in."

Liam rolls his eyes, but he slips into the backseat beside Ev. Ev offers him a sheepish smile as Embry hops in, sitting unnecessarily close to Liam who, strangely enough, doesn't seem bothered by this. If anything, he inches closer.

Well, well, well, does Shadow Cove's golden boy have a crush on my little social outcast, Embry?

I dropkick the thought from my head. That's so beyond the point right now, especially when Liam may have ratted me out to Lispy Larry.

"Tell me something, Liam." I tap my fingers against the console, staring him down. "After you left that store last night, you didn't by chance call the owner and inform him that I was asking you questions about the place, did you?"

"No ... Why?" He pales. "Oh, God, do they know I'm talking to you?"

"I'm not sure. Maybe. But not because we told them." I study him, deliberating whether his pale, shocked reaction is legit. "Are you sure you didn't do anything stupid last night when you got home? Like, say ... make a call to Lispy Larry?"

A pucker forms at his brows. "Who's Lispy Larry?"

"Larry Motaling, the mayor's son." I watch him like a hawk, searching for any tells that give away if he's lying. "That is who's blackmailing you, right?"

His Adam's apple bobs as he swallows hard. "How did you find that out?"

"I'm perceptive." I tap my temple. "Nothing gets by me, so think about that while we're having this conversation 'cause, if you try to lie, I'll know. And remember the consequences for lying." I gesture at the people hanging out in the parking lot and in the quad. "They'll all find out that perfect, little Liam isn't so perfect after all."

"Maybe I don't want them to think I'm perfect anymore," he mumbles with a sour look on his face.

"Well, that's quite a change of heart from yesterday, but whatever." I turn all the way around in my seat then rest my hands on the headrest and my chin on my hands. "If you need some more motivation, then consider this: what will all your friends think when they find out you were the one who took their laptops?"

"I really don't care what they think. They were the ones stupid enough to take that video in the first place, all because of some stupid, ridiculous club." He slumps back in the seat and crosses his arms with his jaw set tight. "I'm so sick of paying for their stupid mistakes and so fucking sick of that goddamn club."

Kennedy and I trade an amused look, and Kennedy gets a wicked glint in her eyes, which means trouble is coming.

"Now, Liam, when you say club, just what kind of club are we talking about?" Kennedy wraps a tendril of hair around her finger. "Are we talking, like, tree houses, secret handshakes, and let's promises to be BFFs forever kind of club? Or is it something else?"

If looks could kill, Liam would've murdered Kennedy by now with his fuck-you gaze.

"No, Kennedy," he says flatly. "I don't mean a club like that. We're not children."

Kennedy shrugs innocently. "It sounds like kid stuff to me."

"Well, it's not." His loud, clipped tone causes all four of us to flinch. "Do you have any idea what kind of shit you're getting into by just talking to me about this? When they find out, they'll come after you."

"Who's *they*?" I ask. "Lispy Larry? Or your club?"

"No, I'm not talking about that house or stupid Lispy Larry or my club. All of those are separate from this," he explains with frustration. "I'm talking about the people who got me into this mess."

"You mean the people who took the video?" I ask. "Your friends from this club?"

"My friends from my club will be pissed off, but I can handle them." He swiftly shakes his head, his frustration escalating. "I'm talking about the people who found out my friends took the video."

"Okay." We're so getting off track here, but that doesn't mean he hasn't piqued my interest. "So, what was the video of? And who are these people who found out you took the video? And which one of your friends are in your little club."

"Will you quit saying club like that?" He pounds his trembling fist against his thigh. "This isn't a joke."

"Hey, you need to chill out," Embry warns, staring Liam straight in the eye. "No more hitting things, including yourself."

His chest rises and crashes with each breath he takes. "Sorry. I'm just a little freaked out that I'm having this conversation with you." He aims a finger at me. "Particularly her."

I frown. "What's that supposed to mean?"

"I know who your father is," Liam tells me bitterly. "He did a story on my family once that almost cost my father his company."

"You're lucky, then. Most people can't say *almost*," I say, causing him to glare daggers at me. "Look, I'm sorry my dad wrote a true story about your family, but I'm not going to do that. I don't even work for the paper ... and my dad's gone, so ..." My voice fades away to nothing.

Just like my dad.

The car grows unnervingly quiet, and pity fills my friends' eyes.

"But, anyway," I say, getting back to the subject at hand. "My point is that I'm not going to rat your friends out. All I want to know is, what the hell is going on in that store, house—whatever the heck that place is that you took the computer to." I count down on my fingers. "I want to know what exactly is on the inside: furniture, display cases, drugs, stolen merchandise, etc. Are there any strange logos on anything? And what was on that video you took that was so bad that Lispy Larry decided to blackmail you into getting it?"

"Nothing's on the inside of that house," he says, fiddling with a button on the cuff of his light blue button-down shirt, completely ignoring my last question.

"Nothing at all?" I ask with a raised brow. "Oh, Liam, I highly doubt that, so please stop toying with me and just answer the damn question before the tardy bell rings."

"You say that like you're a normal girl who just wants to make it to class on time, but you're not normal, Mak. Not at all. This isn't normal." He huffs out a drawn out sigh. "And I'm not toying with you. The house is empty except for the computers I brought to him, and there was a duffel bag there."

"Okay." Is this the same duffel bag Lispy Larry came out

of the bar with? Better yet, I wonder what's in the bag. "What about the bedrooms and the kitchen? Did you go in any of those?"

"The house is completely open inside. The living room attaches to the kitchen, and that's about it. I did notice a padlocked door in the kitchen by the fridge, but I never went in it." He yanks his fingers through his hair. "The house has a basement, and there has to be an entrance to it, so…" He trails off, shrugging.

"God, I hate basements," Embry mutters. "Everything creepy always happens in basements."

Liam's gaze bounces from Embry to me. "Can I go now? I answered all of your questions."

"No, you didn't." Ev speaks for the first time since Liam got into the car. "You purposefully evaded her question about what was on the video and about the logo."

"I didn't purposefully evade them," Liam tells her. "I just forgot she asked them."

"No, you moved to the question most convenient for you." Ev lifts her chin, looking him in the eye. "It's a technique often used by criminals when they're being interrogated by the police. They pick the question they find easiest and make the answer just long and detailed enough that the police get sidetracked. It's actually been studied. There's even a name for it, but I can't think of it off the top of my head."

"Go, Ev." Kennedy smirks, and Liam fires a death glare

at her. "So, Liam, what does the logo mean? And what was on the video?"

He rolls his tongue, as if biting back a scream. "I don't know what was on the video, exactly since my friends filmed it. I just know that whatever was on it would be enough to not only incriminate Larry, but also his father."

"Of what?" I ask, observing his reactions closely. "An illegal escort service?"

"Who knows? Probably a lot of things," he replies, lifting his shoulders. "That man is about as corrupt as they come."

I examine him, the way he holds my gaze, the evenness of his tone. "Okay, I believe you." I reach for my phone and open the photo of the card. "But now I need to know if you know what this logo means? It was on the box you were carrying."

Liam squints at the photo, and then stares at me like I'm an idiot. "That logo is everywhere, right? All of the finest businesses in Shadow Cove have a decal of it on their entrance doors."

"I don't often wander into Shadow Cove's finest businesses, Liam." I pat his arm, causing him to flinch. "Not all of us are as lucky as you to be graced with such an honor."

"I'm sure Kennedy's been in some of them," he says. "Her dad owns one of the businesses himself."

"Yeah, but we want to know what it means," Kennedy replies, her fingers wandering to her cheek. "Because I don't have a clue."

"Neither do I," he says way too quickly.

"You sure about that?" I question. "Because you seem awfully squirmy right now."

He shakes his head, his jaw ticking. "I'm not squirmy. I'm annoyed I'm here, having this conversation."

"And I'm annoyed you clearly know what that logo means but keep evading from directly answering," I quip. "So fess up, dude, and maybe we'll let you go."

He narrows his eyes at me. "Like you could keep me here if I tried to get away."

"Maybe not with my bare hands." I pat the glovebox. "But my lovely, little Taser friend might do the trick."

His expression deflates. "Fine, you want to know stuff, then I'll tell you what I know, but I promise you're going to regret ever asking."

I arch a brow. "Is that a threat?"

"Not from me," he states, carrying my gaze. "From the people who live by what that logo represents."

His words send a chill down my spine, but that doesn't mean I'm about to back down.

"You say that like the logo represents some secret saying or rules or something?" I speculate.

He shrugs. "It might. Honestly, I don't know the exact meaning of it. You have to be part of the secret society to know everything. And I'm not part of it ... yet."

I trade a curious glance with Kennedy, who looks a little worried, probably because Liam just dropped the words "secret society."

I offer her a you-can-handle-this glance before redirecting my attention to Liam. "But you *will* be in it?"

"Eventually," he grumbles. "Or, well, I was supposed to be. After the whole computer thing ... that might change."

"Why's that?" I ask.

He grits his teeth. "Because the video my friends took pissed them off."

"And yet you have no idea what's on the video?" I question with doubt.

"Nope, I don't," he says, pretty much lying through his teeth.

"You sure about that?" I ask. "Or do I need to remind you of what's on the line if you don't tell the truth?"

"I've told you a thousand times I don't know what's on it." He holds his ground, his arms crossed.

I try to think of a way to get him to fess up, but the only solution I arrive at is to Taser him, and I'm not sure I'm ready to go there just yet.

"Okay, so how do you know for sure that you'll be accepted into this secret society?" I ask, thinking about my dad's research. He'd mentioned a secret society. Was this the same one?

"Because of my last name," he explains, growing even more stiff. "It's how secret societies generally work. You have to come from the right bloodline to get in."

"And what constitutes the right bloodline?" I can pretty much guess the answer.

"You definitely wouldn't qualify," he says snobbishly. Then his gaze travels to Kennedy. "She would, though."

Kennedy's face twists with disdain. "So, are you saying my dad is in this creepy secret society thing?"

"I have no idea," Liam says with a shrug. "I don't really know much because I'm not in it yet. I do know that wherever that logo is, the business or business owner is either part of the secret society or works for it."

"Which means Lispy Larry does." I tap my finger against my lip. "And probably his father." Interesting, but I still don't know what this all means. What I am interested in doing, though, is wandering around the glitzy side of town to see how many places are connected to this secret society that also may run an escorting site and who apparently got caught on camera doing something bad enough that they went to blackmailing lengths to get the video back.

Liam jolts in his seat, startled by the sound of the first bell ringing. "Can I go now? I've told you everything I know, and I can't be late for class. I'll ruin my zero tardies record."

Embry covers her mouth with her hand, mocking shock. "Oh, no, we wouldn't want that."

Liam doesn't glare at her like he did with Kennedy, Ev, and me. He just stares at her with curiosity as he drags his finger across his lip.

"Did that hurt?" he asks. "The lip piercing, I mean."

Embry's pierced brow meticulously arches. "Why? You thinking of piercing that pretty boy face of yours?"

"I don't know ..." He bites down on his lip. "Maybe."

Embry's forehead creases, and Liam grins.

Kennedy catches my eye and shakes her head, mouthing, "*Oh, my God, that's so not happening.*"

I nod, completely agreeing. Not only would Embry never date a guy who wears slacks and button-down shirts, but there's no way in hell we'd feel safe with her dating Liam after what he just told us.

"Well, Liam, it's been a real pleasure." I signal for Embry to open the door and let him out. "You better get going. You wouldn't want that perfect tardy record to be tarnished." I push him toward the door. "If we have any more questions, we'll call you."

"Please don't," Liam pleads, sliding across the leather seat. "I'd really appreciate if this was the last time we ever spoke, at least about this."

"I'd love to make that promise. I really would"—I gather my bag from off the floor—"but until I can check out all of your answers, I just can't promise anything."

He blasts me with one final cold glare. Then he jumps out of the car and storms toward the school.

I also climb out to haul ass to class because, unlike Liam, my tardy record is veering toward the I'm-going-to-get-detention red zone.

"What did you guys think about what he said?" Kennedy asks, bumping her door shut.

I shrug, eyeballing Liam through the sea of people flocking toward the school. "For the most part, I think he was telling the truth."

Ev loops her arms through her backpack. "I don't know about that. I think he held back a few details, like that video thing. He knows what's on it."

"Aw." Kennedy presses her hand to her chest. "I think Ev just went over to the dark side. I'm so proud right now."

Ev shakes her head yet cracks a tiny smile. "Whatever, guys. What I said in there was true. He didn't want to tell us about the video." She chews on her thumbnail. "But what about the whole secret society thing? Do you think he was telling the truth about that?"

Shielding my eyes from the sun, I say, "I highly doubt he could make something like that up off the top of his head." Plus, my dad spoke of something similar before. Noting a few people around us are eavesdropping, I catch Kennedy's eye from over the roof. "I think we need to go off campus for lunch and talk about this some more when we're not out in the open."

"I completely agree." She nods for us to get going.

"Let's all meet up at my car, and we'll go to the café or something," I say as the four of us meet at the front of the car and trek toward the school.

I keep my eyes on Liam as he pushes his way through the crowd and to the front door. Right before he reaches the curb, he pats his pockets then whirls around and stomps back toward me.

"Give me back my phone." He thrusts his hand in my direction. "Now."

I roll my eyes. "Why the heck would I have your phone?"

"Because you pickpocketed me!" he shouts, his voice echoing across the parking lot.

People around us freeze and rubberneck at the scene.

Great, just what we need. An audience.

"Thanks for that. Now they can all add thief to the ever growing list of gossip topics about me," I say with my eyes narrowed at Liam. "But FYI, I didn't take your damn phone."

"Well, someone did." He balls his hands into fists as he lowers his arms to his sides. "I had it when I got into the car, and now it's gone."

I shrug. "Sorry, but I didn't take it."

"You're going to regret this." Shaking his head, he reels around and stalks off, people scurrying out of his way.

"All right, people, move along!" Kennedy shouts, flicking her wrist at the crowd. "There's nothing to see."

Once most of the crowd clears, Ev releases a shaky exhale. "He really has a temper, doesn't he?"

I drape an arm around her shoulder. "I think he's just having a bad day."

"That really isn't an excuse, though." Kennedy leans in toward me, lowering her voice. "So, did you jack his phone?"

I pluck strands of hair out of my face as the wind kicks up. "As much as I'd love to take credit for that, it wasn't me."

"Well, it wasn't me. And we know it wasn't Ev, so ..." Kennedy spins around toward Embry with an accusing smile on her face. "Embry, would you like to tell us something?"

Embry raises a shoulder. "It was sticking out of his pocket, and I saw an opportunity. Figured we could snoop around on it and see if he's hiding anything."

"And he didn't notice you feeling around in his pocket?" I ask, walking backward against the wind.

"Oh, I'm sure he felt it." Kennedy grins. "He probably just thought she was touching him and got all turned on. Did you see how he was looking at her? He so has the hots for our little Goth girl."

"He does not." Embry play-kicks at Kennedy. "And who're you calling little?"

Kennedy squeals as Embry's boot nearly grazes her leg, and she shuffles off toward the school. We start to hurry after her until I hear my name called out.

I turn around and spot Rylen jogging across the parking lot toward me. He's sporting sneakers, dark jeans, and a black hoodie. His hair is damp, and his cheeks are wind-kissed. Well, either that or he's blushing.

"Hey." He smiles when he reaches me. "Sorry about yelling your name like a psycho, but I have something for you, and I really wanted to give it to you before school."

"You have something for me?" I point at myself stupidly because, seriously, I'm so lost. Since when does Rylen give me stuff?

A somewhat amused, somewhat nervous laugh escapes him. "Yeah, for you."

"Okay ..."

He sticks his hand into his pocket to retrieve a small black box. "I saw this yesterday and thought of you."

He hands me the box, but instead of opening it, I stare at it. *What in the hell is this? Like, a present? Why is Rylen giving me a present? As, like, a friend? Because even Kennedy, Embry, and Ev don't give me random gifts.*

I might have stood there all day like an idiot if Kennedy didn't materialize out of nowhere like a freakin' ninja and nudge me in the side.

"I think he wants you to open it, Mak." She pokes her elbow into my ribs again.

"Ow. Will you stop that?" I rub my side a few times then lift the lid off the box.

Inside is a shiny new set of bearings, silver trimmed with sky blue. My heart does a stupid little flutter because, holy shit, a guy bought me bearings, which might not seem that cool to most people, but to me ... holy awesomeness.

"I saw them at the store yesterday and thought they'd match your board." His tone carries a hint of nervousness. "And I remembered you saying you needed them."

"I did—I do." I look up at him and smile. "Thanks. You really didn't have to do this, but they're really cool."

"I know I didn't have to. I wanted to." He inches closer, sticking his hands into his back pockets. "Logan kept telling me that I should get you pink ones, but I told him you weren't really a pink kind of girl."

"No, not at all. These are way better." *Way perfect.*

I graze my finger across the bearings, questioning why he gave them to me. Is Kennedy right? Does Rylen like me as more than a friendly rival? The thought makes me oddly uncomfortable, not because I don't like Rylen, but because … Well, because he's rich and perfect and friends with people like Dixon. And I'm … Well, I'm the complete opposite.

Not knowing what else to do, I crack a joke. "Aren't you kind of upping my game by giving me good equipment? I mean, what if these bearings improve my skills just enough that I start winning all the competitions?"

He smiles. "I highly doubt that, if you start winning, it'll be from the bearings. It'll be because you kick ass."

I point a finger at him. "You're not supposed to build up your rival's confidence. Hasn't anyone ever told you that?"

"I don't think of you as just my rival." He rocks back on his heels, growing nervous again. "And actually, I was kind of thinking that maybe we could practice together. Maybe Friday night, I could pick you up, and we could go hit up the ramps at the park?"

Um … I may be kind of clueless about the whole dating scene, but I'm pretty sure Rylen just asked me out. Rylen, a cute guy who's nice to me and shares my love of skating. And also a cute guy who is friends with Dixon.

I hesitate, unsure what the heck to do or say. On one hand, I want to go, but on the other, it feels wrong.

I trace my fingertip along the edge of the box. "Um … Sure … We can do that."

"Are you sure?" He chews on his bottom lip. "Because you kind of sound unsure."

God, what the hell am I doing? Kennedy was right. I'm completely clueless when it comes to guys.

Just make a damn decision, Mak. Decide if you want to get into this or not.

"No, I'm sure," I say, attempting to sound more confident. "I want to go."

"Good." He releases a relieved breath, pressing his hand to his chest. "You were making me a little nervous for a minute."

"Sorry." I put the lid back on the box. "I really do want to go. I promise."

"Okay, I hate to break up this beautiful, little moment here, but the hall monitor's going to make her rounds in, like, one minute!" Kennedy shouts, interrupting us. "And I really don't want to get detention again. And I'm pretty sure you don't, either, Mak."

"Yes, *Mom.*" I glance over my shoulder at where she is waiting by the door with a huge-ass grin on her face. She's so going to give me crap about Rylen asking me out. "Where'd Embry and Ev go?"

"To class," Kennedy replies, pointing at the entrance doors. "I would've gone in, too, but I wanted to see if you two would finally get the balls to stop flirting and actually admit you like each other."

My jaw drops, and my eyes narrow. *She so did not just say that!*

She grins, blows me a kiss, and then skips off toward the doors.

Shaking my head, I turn back around to Rylen. "Um, yeah, and on that note, I guess we should get to class."

"I'll walk with you," he says then chuckles. "Don't worry; my friends are kind of crazy, too."

I think about Liam. About Dixon. About this club Liam spoke of.

Yes, Rylen, they are. They really, really are.

"So, I'll pick you up around seven?" Rylen asks, holding the entrance door open for me.

"Yeah, that sounds good ..." I trail off as I step into the hallway and the intercom clicks on.

"*Makayla Evingston, report to the main office immediately,*" the secretary's voice crackles through the speakers.

I freeze. *Crap, crap, crapity crap. Please say they didn't find out I looked at the security footage.*

"Is everything okay?" Rylen asks, letting the door shut.

"Yeah ... I just don't know why they're calling me in. But I guess I'll find out. I'll see you later." I wave at him from over my shoulder as I start down the hallway. "And thanks for the present."

"Anytime," he calls out. "See you Friday."

I nod, hoping I'll still be able to go out Friday. After all, if the school did find out I looked at the security footage, I'll probably be grounded for a very long time.

We part ways, him heading left and me veering right. As I reach the turn, I glance back over my shoulder at Rylen, and a frown instantly curves at my lips. Dixon is walking alongside him as they head down the hallway, their heads lowered, as if whispering to each other. When Dixon glances back at me, his lips curl into a smile.

"*Trust no one*," Sawyer whispers.

I jerk around, startled by the clarity of the voice, as if the words weren't spoken in my mind, but aloud.

I barely get turned around when I crash against a solid surface. Thinking I ran into the wall, I stumble back, but a hand slaps across my mouth as fingers snag my hip.

Lispy Larry grins at me as he yanks me closer to him and out of view of the camera mounted on the wall.

"You just couldn't stop, could you?"

I don't know why he's here, but I'm guessing Liam might have something to do with it. He did tell me I was going to regret questioning him and taking his phone.

I'm so going to kick his ass for this.

I bring up my knee to kick Larry between the legs and unhinge my jaw to bite down on his hand, but a sharp stabbing pain in my hip causes me to misstep, and I end up stepping on his toe. Wooziness almost immediately swishes around in my brain as I stagger to the left and bump into the wall.

I clutch the side of my head as I sway right then left. "What's ... happening? Why do I ... feel ... so ... weird?" Through my blurred vision, I catch sight of the syringe in Lispy Larry's hand.

"Don't worry; it's just a bit of morphine," he says, his

tone carrying an underlying meaning. "Not enough to kill you. We're not at that point ... *yet.*"

I want to ask him if he killed my brother, but words won't leave my lips as the drug swims through my veins.

Zigzagging sideways, I collapse to my knees on the cold tile floor. My heart is pounding in my chest as my head bobs back, and I blink up at the camera.

Please ... someone see me. Please be working.

The silence in the hallway, though, makes me wonder if perhaps the security cameras "shorted out" again.

"They're off right now," Lispy Larry says as if reading my thoughts. "So it's just you and me ... all alone."

Until the hall monitor comes along.

Please hurry.

"I tried to warn you, but you just wouldn't listen." Lispy Larry crouches down in front of me. "If you so much as utter a word about this or about what you know, your body will be found floating in that lake."

"Are ... you ... threatening to ... kill ... me?" I choke out, bracing my hand against the floor.

He laughs quietly under his breath. "Man, I thought you'd figure out more than that. I guess you're not as bright as your brother or father were, huh? Newsflash, Mak. This is way bigger than you or me. The people who are part of this, they could destroy you with the snap of a finger. They did to half your family already. And they will end you, too, if you keep digging around in things that are none of your business. So do yourself a favor and let what lies in the darkness stay

in the darkness. Don't be stupid like your brother and dad."
A slow smile twists at his lips as his words sink in, and my
eyes widen.

I have no clue what the hell he's talking about or what
he's doing—what I'm doing. Everything is so blurry, so
distorted. My brain is foggy, and my body is going numb.

"*Don't worry, Mak,*" Sawyer says. "*You'll make it out of
this.*"

I swear I feel my brother's hand in mine, his skin ice
cold.

Or maybe the chill is from my own body as my heart
rate slows and I'm dragged into darkness.

TWENTY

LOCATION: SHADOW COVE LAKE
TIME: UNKNOWN
DATE: UNKNOWN

"Mak, wake up," the sweetest voice floats through my thoughts.

My eyes roll into the back of my head as I force my eyelids open. At first, I think I'm dreaming as I peer up at Sawyer's face, but then his face shifts into the clouds as I drift out of dreamland and slam back into reality.

I bolt upright and blink at my surroundings. Then my blood turns ice cold.

Shadow Cove Lake stretches out to the side of me, the rocky shore below me, and a high cliff side towers to my right. My lungs constrict, my heart pounds, and my breathing turns ragged. I'm so close to where my brother died. All I would have to do is stand up and walk ten steps, and my toes would be in the water where his body was found.

Vomit suddenly burns at the back of my throat. I don't know whether it's a side effect of the drugs or the stress of being here, but I lean over and empty out my stomach in the sand. Once I stop yacking my guts out, I rise to my feet and look around, hoping someone is nearby.

Not a single person or car is in sight, and the sky is cloudy, which means rain will soon come. My phone is in my backpack, and the last time I saw it was back in the hallway at school.

Shaking my head, I stare out at the dirt road. It's about three miles back to town. Seeing no other alternative, I start walking.

One foot in front of the other, Mak. You can do this.

I feel lightheaded, dizzy, and sick to my stomach, completely beaten down, but beneath the pain and worry lies determination.

He threatened to kill me and practically admitted he knew what happened to my brother and father. I swallow hard at the memory of when Lispy Larry implied my dad was dead.

No! I won't accept that answer until I know for sure.

Inhaling and exhaling, I try to calm down as I make my way around the lake. As the wind kicks up, blowing the salty air past me, I stuff my hands into the pockets of my jeans, trying to stay warm.

When my fingers brush a piece of paper, my brows knit as I pull it out. On the front is that stupid circular symbol traced by a pattern of Greek letters. I nearly ball the paper up and chuck it into the water, but when I flip it over, I grind to a halt.

You want answers about what really happened to your brother and father? Meet me at the following location on March 26th at eleven p.m. on the dot. And make sure to come alone, Mak. No one can follow you in any way, shape, or form. Tell no one about the meeting. It's a matter of life and death. Because if they find out about this, then we both could end up dead.

PS: Your car is parked in the trees.

Scratching my head, I tentatively make my way toward the trees with the card clutched in my hand. I don't recognize the address listed, and I have no idea where the card came from. My first assumption is Lispy Larry, but why would he leave something like this after going through all the trouble to make sure I don't go looking for answers?

One thing I'm fairly certain of, though, is that the "they" referred to in the note is the secret society. I just wish I knew all of the names of the members.

I thrum my fingers against the sides of my legs as I walk, debating what to do. I know it's risky, but I can't walk away from a potential lead, even if it means risking my life. It's not in my character to walk away. I can pretend all I want that

I'm only thinking about going, or I can accept what is and make sure to have a really good plan on how to keep the meet-up a secret. And protect my ass if the meet-up ends badly, which it probably will. At least, that's what I think until I spot my car parked in the trees, just like the note said.

When I climb in and spot not only the keys in the ignition, but Dixon's computer on the back seat, I start to wonder if the note person was sent from heaven. Then I hesitate as a thought occurs to me about my so-called guardian angel.

I mean, first off, I haven't told anyone—except my friends—that I was looking for Dixon's computer. And why on earth would someone leave my car and the computer, yet let me lie out on the shore? It makes no sense unless ...

"This is all some sort of bribe or way to keep me quiet until ..." Well, I'm not really sure what follows the until part. But I will find out, no matter what it takes, because like I mentioned earlier, I'm not about to walk away from this. Not when I feel like I finally have a starting point toward a path that will lead me to Sawyer's killer.

"Are you sure you want to do this, Mak?" Sawyer whispers. *"It would be better if you just walked away."*

I stare out at the lake in front of me that stretches for as far as my eyes can see. I picture Sawyer's body floating in the waves and my dad's body hidden at the bottom. I think about Bria and the other bodies found in the lake. All the deaths were reported accidental, but what if they weren't? What if my dad was right, and this is a cover up? What if someone else I love ends up dead? What if this secret society is connected to the deaths somehow?

"Yeah, Sawyer, I'm sure I want to do this," I say, starting the engine.

Then you need to put the necklace on; or else they'll be able to get you.

"What necklace?" I ask. "The one I found in your closet?"

He doesn't respond. I don't know if that means I've finally reached sanity again or if Sawyer just thinks I'm crazy. It doesn't matter. I made my decision already. I'm going to find out what's going on in this town and find out who killed my brother.

TWENTY-ONE

LOCATION: MAK'S CAR
TIME: 2:29 PM
DATE: TUESDAY, MARCH 23RD

I'm parked in front of the police station, thrumming my fingers on the steering wheel as I debate my next move—whether I have the courage to go inside or not. I haven't gone home to take a shower, so I reek of lake water and forest. Dirt stains my pants and shirt, and my hair has a few flakes of mud in it. I should go home. I really should. I need to take a shower, clean up, and wash this horrible day off me. But I can't bring myself to do so just yet.

After driving away from the lake about half an hour ago, I drove to the police station. As I passed the town marquee that flashed the date and time, I became painfully aware that the morphine Lispy Larry had injected into me had knocked me out for about six hours, which means I missed the entire day of school. My mom should've received a call about my absence by now.

I haven't ditched before, but I'm guessing she'll probably think I did. Sawyer used to do it all the time, at least when he started getting depressed. And whenever he did, he got grounded.

I can't get grounded right now, not if I ever plan on seeing my friends again and figuring out what's going on in this town. I also need to meet up with the person who left the note in my pocket.

I pick up the note from out of the console and reread it.

You want answers about what really happened to your brother and father? Meet me at the following location on March 26th at eleven p.m. on the dot. And make sure to come alone, Mak. No one can follow you in any way, shape, or form. Tell no one about the meeting. It's a matter of life and death. If anyone finds out about this, then we both could end up dead.

PS: Your car is parked in the trees.

The address listed at the bottom isn't one I recognize, but I can do a search for that later.

March 26th is three days away, giving me three days to figure out who sent the note so I can decide if they're a legitimate source or not.

Three days isn't a lot of time, especially when I have so many other things to do, like get the reward money from Dixon in exchange for the computer, enter the skate competition, report Lispy Larry's attack on me, and sneak a look at the coroner's report for Bria Brookenrose, my brother's girlfriend when he was alive, who mysteriously died a few days ago in the same place my brother did—up by the lake.

From the way my mom acted when she told me about Bria's death, Bria had morphine in her system, just like Sawyer. My brother also had these weird scratches on his body, which is the main reason I want to see the coroner's report on Bria—to find out if she had those scratches, too, even if I have no clue what could've caused them. I'll worry about that later.

"One step at a time, Mak," I whisper to myself, trying not to fall apart.

I've always been great at holding myself together, but right now, I feel as though I'm veering toward a breakdown. If I start thinking about what happened too much—what Lispy Larry did to me—I know I'm going to. Instead, I focus on the task at hand—working up the courage to go into the police station and report the attack.

I shouldn't be so nervous, but Shadow Cove police have never been kind to my family, particularly my dad. According to some of my dad's theories, the mayor donates a large amount of money to the police station every year. And since the mayor is Lispy Larry's father ... yeah, let's just say I'm not too optimistic about reporting this. The only thing I have in my favor is that the attack happened at school, so the cameras may have caught what happened. Lispy Larry told me they were off, but I'm not about to take his word for it.

Still, I can't help being uneasy, fearing I'll be attacked for trying to go to the police.

Lispy Larry did attack me at school. Who's to say he won't do it again if I try to report the incident? Or maybe he's already here, watching me.

I peer around, searching for his beady little eyes, but all I see are shops and restaurants, and the wealthy people traveling into and from them.

My knuckles turn white as my grip on the steering wheel constricts. *Woman up, Mak. You can't back down. Not from this,* I mentally tell myself. *You have to report this.*

Summoning a shaky breath, I climb out of the car and cross the street toward the station.

Don't do this yet, Mak, Sawyer's voice rises into my mind. *Put on the necklace.*

This is the second time he's mentioned the necklace in the last half hour, and while he's never specified what it is, I'm assuming it's this glass vial attached to a string that I found in his closet the other day. Why he thinks it'll protect me is beyond me. The idea just seems crazy.

Then again, I'm hearing the voice of my dead older brother, so ... yeah.

My legs shake as I hike toward the police station's entrance, hugging my arms around myself. People wander up and down the sidewalks, heading either into or out of the shops.

As I pass by each of the fancy shops, I note a circular symbol traced by a pattern of Greek-like letters on at least half the doors. The same symbol I found on the card in Lispy Larry's truck and the same one on the secret escorting site I discovered online.

Liam wasn't lying. The symbol is on almost every single one of Shadow Cove's finest businesses. And when I say "finest," I mean they carry overly priced items, services, or food, and have the snobbiest customer service you can possibly imagine. And, according to Liam, every owner is either part of some secret society in Shadow Cove or works for it.

"I can't believe this. There are so many ..." I trail off as I reach the entrance of the police station, seeing the symbol on the upper right section of the door. It's smaller than on the other businesses, only about the size of a fingernail. It's still there, though, like a warning, indicating that, if what Liam said is true, the police either work for or are a part of the secret society.

I stand in front of the door, contemplating what to do next. Lispy Larry can't get away with what he did to me. Then again, my father was always adamant about the police in this town being corrupt. Now they have the symbol on their door, or maybe it has always been there and I never noticed, never thought to look.

I may not know much about the secret society yet, but Liam warned me they were dangerous. Then, only minutes after his warning, Lispy Larry injected me with morphine and threatened to kill me if I didn't stop digging around in things that weren't my business.

I'm guessing Lispy Larry is part of the secret society and they were behind my attack. This is all based on assumption, though. As of now, I have no hardcore proof, other than maybe the school's security cameras recording the attack.

"I need to find out if they did. That way, I have some proof."

I start to turn back toward my car. I need to meet up with my friends, fill them in on what happened, and see if we can work our magic a second time by getting ahold of the footage from the school's security cameras.

Mid-turn, though, I halt as the door to the police station swings open and out walks the mayor himself and none other than Don Jennings.

Here's all I know about Don Jennings:

Place of Work: Owner of every car dealership in Shadow Cove.

Hobbies: Sexism, bragging about his wealth, running for mayor, and raising children who are beyond snobby.

Wealth Status: One of the wealthiest businessmen in town.

Relationship Status: Married, but may be having an affair with my mom.

Not too impressive if you ask me. And the mayor isn't any better.

Mayor's status:

Full Name: Walter Greinegone.

Hobbies: Bailing his son out of trouble and making his criminal record disappear.

Wealth Status: Not nearly as wealthy as Don Jennings, but has the support of many wealthy business owners in town.

Relationship Status: Married, although hardly anyone has seen his wife in person and some speculate she doesn't exist.

Honestly, I don't have much information about either man. Maybe that should change. Right now, though, the last thing I want is to run into the man who's the father of the man who doped me up. Nor do I want to run into the man who may be having an affair with my mom. So, as they exit the police station, I sidestep out of the way and turn my head, letting my long, brown hair shield my face.

"Thanks for meeting me here today," Don Jennings says to the mayor. "I thought this would be the best place to discuss our little business agreement."

"Not a problem," the mayor replies as they stroll down the sidewalk past me. "Out of all the places in town, the station has the least eyes and ears around. Makes things easier for us to have a private conversation that not even *they* can hear."

"Yes, it does," Don agrees with a nod. "We should probably get together and do lunch before we announce the agreement. It'll make our partnership less out of the blue."

"How about Friday evening?" the mayor suggests. "We could meet up at Lana's in the backroom."

"Sounds good to me," Don says with another nod.

When they reach the street corner, they shake hands then part ways in opposite directions.

A shaky exhale flees my lips as they disappear.

The two of them being in cahoots with each other can't be good, but what's really got me squirrelly is the mention of eyes and ears. That usually means one of two things: either there are spies in the area or hidden cameras.

Without lifting my head, I peek around the streets and buildings, then at the people nearby. Nothing appears out of the ordinary, but that's how things usually are in Shadow Cove. On the outside, the town is sparkling with wealth with its fancy shops and businesses, expensive cars driving up and down the streets, and almost everyone is wearing designer clothes. Across the railroad tracks, though, where I live, it's an entirely different story.

Hardly anyone talks about the lower- and middle-class, focusing instead on the wealthy and pleasant side of town. Stories of disappearances and deaths are rarely spoken of, at least not publicly. Cover-ups, conspiracy theories, secret societies—my father thought all this existed. I always wondered: how?

How is the darker part of life in Shadow Cove being swept under the rug? Is it possible that perhaps the town is being watched? By whom? The secret society? Why?

So many questions. Questions I need to get answers to.

Be careful, Mak. Everyone is being watched. Go home and put the necklace on. That's the only way to stay safe.

Why, though? Just tell me, please.

Silence is my only response.

Sighing in frustration, I push away from the wall and hurry across the street to my car.

As much as I love being able to hear from my dead brother—well, either that or I'm hallucinating—his cryptic messages are starting to drive me crazy. Apparently, that's become the theme of my life.

TWENTY-TWO

LOCATION: MAK'S HOUSE
TIME: 2:47 PM
DATE: TUESDAY, MARCH 23RD

On my way home, I make a pit stop at the hospital where my mom works, but her car isn't in the parking lot, and since I don't have my phone with me, I can't call her.

My frustration builds as I leave the hospital and drive home, only to find that my mom isn't there, either. I'm not too surprised. She's rarely home.

I used to believe her constant MIA behavior was because of the long hours she put in at the hospital. After some snooping around, though, I found that isn't the case. She also spends time up at a local teenage party area, hanging out in a luxury car, doing who knows what with who knows who. All evidence so far points to Don Jennings.

Just thinking about what they could be doing behind those tinted windows makes me want to yack up the four Pop-Tarts I just devoured.

Apparently, getting doped up on morphine makes me as hungry as a Pop-Tart loving hippo.

Since school releases in about twenty minutes, I need to hurry my ass up so I can be there when the bell rings to meet up with Kennedy, Embry, and Everleigh, aka Ev, and see if they're down for more snooping around in the school's security footage—we're going to need a new plan from last time. They are probably freaking out right now over the sudden Houdini act I pulled.

Plus, I need to find my backpack and phone. I would've driven straight to the school after I left the hospital parking lot, but I decided I needed to find this necklace Sawyer keeps whispering about.

Dusting the crumbs off my fingers, I go to my father's office and slip into the secret nook located behind the bookshelf. Then I pull out the pile of stuff I found in Sawyer's closet last night, which consists of a key, a newspaper clipping for a lawn care job, a glass vial hanging on a piece of string, a thick leather-bound book, and a small card with a circular symbol printed on it. It's the same symbol from the card I found in Lispy Larry's truck and the escorting site. There was also a small bag of cocaine, but I dumped that down the toilet.

So far, I haven't had time to explore the items or figure out why Sawyer was hiding them in the floor of his closet. I make a mental note to look into it some more, then examine the key. There's a spot filed down where I'm assuming a name or digit was, but what on earth could it go to? Stuffing it into my pocket, I collect the card and the glass vial attached to the string.

I give the vial a shake, unsure what I expect to happen. With how obsessed Sawyer is with it, I wonder if something crazy will occur, but the glass simply reflects against the sunlight filtering in through the window.

"This is what you want me to wear?" I ask quietly, being extra careful no one hears me. Sure, no one is home right now, but if anyone ever does realize I'm talking to Sawyer, they'll think I'm as insane as the town did about my father. And my mom will probably want to put me back on the meds I was taking for hallucinations after Sawyer died and also when my father disappeared.

Back then, I thought I was losing my mind. Now, well, I'm either veering toward crazy land again or I was never hallucinating to begin with. If that's true, that leaves me with yet another unanswered question: why can I hear and talk to the dead?

I dig a pen and notebook out of the top drawer of my dad's desk and quickly jot down a list of questions that need answers.

1. What does the key go to?

2. What's the deal with the necklace?

3. Are there spies or bugs in Shadow Cove? If so, who put them there?

4. Who is in this secret society? And what is its purpose?

5. What is Lispy Larry hiding in that strange store located in the ghost house?

6. Did Bria die in the same manner as Sawyer?

7. Who put the note in my pocket at the lake?

8. How is all this linked to the illegal escorting site?

9. What happened to my father?

10. What was the real reason behind Sawyer's death?

And the question I'd really like to know:

11. Am I really hearing Sawyer from beyond the grave? If so, why?

There are probably more questions than even those. I can add as I go.

Setting the list down, I pick up the leather-bound book and flip through the pages. The book is penned in a different language, and so far, I haven't had time to decipher it. I make a note on my list to research it online, then make another note to burn the damn piece of paper after I transfer the questions to my computer, which has so many passcodes and security no one should be able to hack it. Well, except Ev since she set it all up for me.

The last thing I need is for the wrong person to discover what I'm up to, including my mom. Not only will she freak out if she finds out I'm following in my father's footsteps, but Lispy Larry warned me not to dig around in this anymore. I could just walk away and let it go—it'd be a lot less dangerous if I did—but walking away isn't who I am, especially if this search could lead me to my brother's killer and give me answers to what happened to my father.

I'm going to have to be careful about my every move, which means the number one item on my list needs to be finding out if the town is bugged or has spies, and if so, where or who they are and who put them there. That way, I can plan accordingly.

Noting the time, I rush out of the office. Since I want to remain inconspicuous and am currently covered in dirt, I run to my room to change out my clothes, pulling on a black T-shirt, jeans, and a pair of lace-up boots. I quickly brush out my hair, call it good, and jog out to my car, ready to hit the road.

As I'm climbing in, the sunlight reflects against the glass vial hanging around my neck. The reflection briefly creates the strangest green glow and heats warmly against my skin.

Put your guard up. Now. They're around.

Swallowing hard, I cup the necklace and cast a discreet glance around the neighborhood crammed with rundown homes similar to mine. Other than a few dogs, a bird, and an older man sitting out on his porch in a rocking chair, no one is around.

I'm about to arrive at the conclusion that dead Sawyer is as crazy as me, when the man on the porch locks eyes with me. He stares at me for a beat or two, then his gaze zeroes in on the necklace.

Feeling super uncomfortable, I end up looking away and

ducking into the car. Then I start up the engine, lock the doors, and tuck the necklace inside my shirt collar.

"What was that about?" I ask Sawyer as I fasten my seatbelt and shift the car into drive.

Like usual, he doesn't answer.

Sighing, I drive forward, more than aware the man is still watching me and the necklace is glowing brightly.

It only dims when I exit the neighborhood and the man slips from my view.

TWENTY-THREE

I pull into the school parking lot three minutes before the bell rings. Then I remain there until the final bell rings to avoid running into the hall monitor who will for sure write me up for ditching, even though I didn't technically ditch. But, giving her the old excuse that the mayor's son injected morphine into me and dumped me on the shore of the lake isn't going to fly.

As I sit and wait for the bell to ring, I fiddle with the glass vial, trying to replicate the strange glowing color that emitted from it earlier. No matter how I angle it, shake it, or flip it, the glass remains plain, old, and non-glowy.

"Maybe I just hallucinated it?" I murmur. "Maybe I've

hallucinated everything over the last couple days?"

If that's so, then it means you can't really hear me. Do you want that, Mak? Not to hear from me ever again?

I let the glass vial fall against the hollow of my neck. "No, not really. But I also don't want to be crazy, either."

No one ever does.

"Maybe it'd help if you told me some more. Like, why can I hear you at all? What does this necklace do? What the hell is going on in this town? And while we're at it, can you tell me where Dad is, because he's the only person I know who would understand what I'm going through ...? And I really miss him." I suck in a deep breath as tears sting my eyes.

I wait for Sawyer to respond, but he doesn't. I wonder why. Why does his voice come and go?

Before I can analyze the question, the bell rings. Shoving my door open, I hop out, lock Dixon's computer in the trunk, and start across the parking lot. By the time I reach the sidewalk in front of the school, students are pouring out from the entrance.

More than a handful of people glance in my direction. Nothing new about that—they were doing that to me yesterday after the rumor spread around school that Bria and Sawyer had made a suicide pact. It didn't bother me as much yesterday, but after talking to Liam about secret societies, the morphine incident with Lispy Larry, and overhearing Don Jennings and the mayor whispering about eyes and ears everywhere, I'm a bit on edge. Still, having come from a family who's been ridiculed for years now, I'm a pro at holding my head up high and pretending to be more chillaxed than I am.

Yep, that's me, Makayla "Mak" Evingston, badass detective, eavesdropping extraordinaire, and pro badass pretender.

When I enter the school, I head down the hallway toward the main office so I can sneak into the lost and found room and look for my backpack. If the wrong person, like say, Dixon or Liam stumbled across it and realized it was my bag, it more than likely is at the bottom of a dumpster by now, along with my phone that I can't afford to replace.

Speak of the devil ...

"Hey, Mak, missed you in English today," Dixon sneers as he walks by.

He has on designer jeans, a button-down vest, and a watch that probably cost more than my car. And, as usual, he's sporting his infamous my-shit-don't-stink smirk that some girls consider sexy. Personally, I think it makes him look constipated, but I'm probably biased.

I continue onward, not wanting to get into it with him ... yet.

Unfortunately, Dixon thrives on getting under my skin and reels around to follow me.

"I was worried you were sick or something." He strides alongside me. "No one would blame you if you were. I mean, first your brother offs himself, then your father abandons you, and then your mother turns into a whore. Then this whole suicide pact with Bria happens." He smirks. "It really sucks. For Bria, anyway. She was a helpless victim in your family's crazy."

I slam on the brakes, unable to keep my lips zipped any longer. "The bathroom's that way." I point in the opposite direction.

His brows slightly dip. "Yeah, so what?"

"Well, I figured, since you look like you're constipated, you probably need to try to go." I gesture at him. "I mean, that's what that tense, contorted look on you face means, right? Or is that just how your face always looks?"

His eyes narrow into slits. "You think I give a shit about anything you say? You're just a waste of space. Nothing more."

"If that's true, then why are you here, standing beside me, talking to me?" I raise my brows.

His eyes darken as he leans in and lowers his voice. "To remind you of where your place is in this town."

Two things happen simultaneously in that moment. 1.) I catch the strangest, overwhelming scent of lake water. And 2.) The glass vial begins to warm against my skin again. Since it's tucked beneath the collar of my shirt, I can't tell if it glows green again. And I'm not about to look down my shirt and check while I'm in front of Dixon.

"Thanks for the reminder." I battle to keep my voice as even as I can, while inside, I'm a nervous wreck.

Dixon smells like lake water? Does that mean he was up by the lake? Did he help Lispy Larry haul me up there? If so, then maybe Dixon is part of the secret society. Liam did say people with the right last name are part of it, which basically means you have to be wealthy and popular. Dixon and his family definitely fall into that category. Then again, Liam also said he and his friends are part of a club that pissed the secret society off, and Dixon is in his circle of friends.

"Take care, Mak." Dixon backs away from me, his smirk returning. "I'd say see you around, but I'm going to be pretty busy preparing for the skate competition. You know, the one you can't afford to enter because your father bailed on your family and left your mom to take care of everything."

I bite down on my tongue, resisting the urge to declare I will be competing. Until I get the reward money from him for his computer and actually register for the Shadow Cove's Skate Charity Event, it's too risky. Plus, it ruins the surprise of telling him that it was his money that paid my entry fee. Still, when he throws me a wink, I want to declare it to the world right then and there.

With him gone, I start for the office again.

As I round the corner, I run into Kennedy and Embry.

Kennedy's eyes widen. "Oh, my God, what the hell happened to you today?" she hisses as she strides toward me, her heels clicking against the floor. "First, you blow us off for lunch, and then you don't answer any of our texts or calls ..." She drifts off as she reaches me, her forehead creasing. "What's wrong? You look upset."

Guess I'm not as good at pretending as I thought.

"Something happened to me today." I glance around the hallway at the few lingering students and teachers. "I can't talk about it out here in the open. Meet me in my car in, like, ten minutes?"

She exchanges a worried glance with Embry then looks back at me. "Sure, but where are you going?"

"To get my bag and phone from the lost and found," I tell her. "Well, that is, if it's there."

"You lost your bag?" Embry tucks a strand of her blazing red hair behind her ear as her brows furrow. "That doesn't sound like you. You never lose shit."

"I didn't lose it. I dropped it. I'll explain in the car." I swing past them, calling over my shoulder, "Text Ev and see if she can meet us there, too."

I take off, crossing my fingers that my bag is at the lost and found, and that I can get in without being spotted. Otherwise, I'm going to get accused of ditching and get afterschool detention, something I don't need right now.

When I reach the office, the door is closed. I peer through the window. Ms. Finkleson is at her desk, leaning back in her chair and laughing at something on her phone. The lost and found room is across from her desk on the opposite side of the room. It dawns on me that, right before I was doped up and hauled off, she had called me down to the office over the intercom, more than likely because they found out I snooped through the school's security footage. Another reason remaining unnoticed is a good idea. So, how am I going to get in there without being seen?

"Mak?"

I whirl around, my heart hammering inside my chest. Then I relax a drop at the sight of Rylen standing behind me with a hint of worry in his eyes.

Let me stress the *drop* part, since the last time I saw Rylen was right before Lispy Larry injected morphine into my system. Rylen had just asked me out on a date and gave me the most awesome bearings, which are also currently inside my backpack. Then he walked me into school, only to part ways to meet up with Dixon. The two of them then whispered something to each other before Dixon looked back at me and sneered.

I don't want to believe Rylen has any part of what's going on, but as of now, I need to be cautious.

"Hey," I say, forcing a smile.

"Hey."

He's wearing a grey-knitted cap over his chin-length black hair, his jeans are faded but in an intentional way, and his sneakers have a bit of paint on the toe. He's also sporting an immense amount of confusion as he stares at me.

"Am I going crazy or were you not here for school today? I know you were here this morning when you"—a tentative smile touches his lips—"agreed to go out with me, but then I didn't see you in any of our classes together or in the hallway or at lunch."

"Yeah, I had to go home for the day. My mom couldn't reach me on the phone and needed me to come home ASAP. That's why I got called to the office." I hate that I have to lie to him, especially if it turns out he isn't involved, but I don't see any other choice right now.

"Is everything okay?" he asks worriedly.

"Yeah, everything's cool. My mom just found out about Bria and wanted to talk and make sure I was okay." Man, Everleigh was right. I am a chillingly good liar.

The crease between his brows deepens. "Are you doing okay with that? And with the rumors going around?" He swiftly shakes his head. "You know what; forget I asked that. The last thing you probably want is for me to bring it up."

"You're fine. I'm the one who brought it up. And I'm fine, I promise. I'm actually sort of a champ when it comes to dealing with rumors."

"You shouldn't have to be. This school sometimes ..." He shakes his head then sighs. "You know you're awesome, right?"

I smile for reals this time. "Oh, I completely know that. It's cool you finally caught on, though."

He smiles sincerely. "I didn't just catch on. I've known for a long time. Since middle school, actually, when I first saw you at the skate park."

"Really?" Shock whips through me. I didn't even know Rylen was aware I existed back then.

The first time we spoke to each other was at the beginning of freshman year at the very first skate competition I went to. I took third place, and he took first. He congratulated me, something none of the other competitors did.

"Yes, really. I remember you showed up and completely schooled everyone at the park, and everyone spent the entire day bitching and complaining over getting their asses handed to them by the newbie. Personally, I thought it was pretty badass ... Thought *you* were pretty badass." His cheeks flush a little.

So do mine.

"But, yeah, anyway." He nervously clears his throat. "You still are."

"Thanks." My cheeks warm even more. Jeez, I'm so not good with guys. Well, guys giving me compliments and what I'm pretty sure is flirting with me. Where is Kennedy when I need her? "So are you."

His smile conveys his nervousness. "It's nice to hear you say that. When I asked you out earlier, I wasn't sure if you were really into it or not."

"I am." Am I, though, after the exchange I witnessed between him and Dixon earlier? "I've just never been asked out before, so it kind of surprised me."

His brows spring upward. "No one's ever asked you out?"

I shrug. "People in this town aren't a huge fan of me or my family. It's cool, though. Between school, work, and skating, I don't have a lot of free time anyway."

"I guess I must be pretty lucky then, if you're making time to go out with me," he teases with a grin.

I mirror his grin. "Oh, you definitely should."

We stand there, stupidly grinning at each other for probably way too long. Then Everleigh comes rushing up and ruins the moment.

"You need to hurry up," she says, shifting the handle of her bag higher onto her shoulder. "Kennedy needs to get home before four-thirty today."

A total lie, but I catch on to what she's doing—getting me to hurry my butt up before Kennedy has a meltdown.

"Sorry, I was distracting her," Rylen apologizes, backing away. "I'll see you tomorrow, Mak." He pauses. "Or maybe at the skate park later today?"

I waver. "I might not make it down there today. There's just too much going on right now."

He starts to frown, but then shakes off the look. "All right, then. I'll see you tomorrow."

I throw him a wave then turn to Ev. I wait until Rylen has vanished down the hallway before I say, "Sorry. He just started talking to me, and then I got distracted with the conversation."

"It's fine," Ev says. "Kennedy's just worried, and you know how she gets when she's like that."

"Yep, like a caged Gremlin baby."

Ev slightly smiles, but then frowns. "Why weren't you in school today?"

"I'll get to that as soon as we get to the car." I peer into the office window again and grimace. "Just as soon as I figure out a way to get into the office and ..." I glance back at Ev, realizing a much easier solution. "Can you go into the lost and found and see if my backpack's in there so I don't have to explain to Ms. Finkleson why I wasn't in school today?" Why didn't I do that to begin with? I think the morphine must have left my brain a bit groggy or something.

Ev nods then slides her backpack off and hands it to me. "Hold this so I can just say it's mine and avoid getting drilled with questions."

I take her backpack, slip it on, and then step aside. "Thanks, Ev. I totally owe you one."

She offers me a small, nervous smile before drawing open the door and stepping inside. I don't dare peek through the window while she's in there, worried Ms. Finkleson will spot me. Deep down, I realize facing my punishment for not being here today and maybe breaking into the security footage is inevitable. However, if I play my cards correctly, I could get my mom to phone in my absence. That is, if I tell her the truth about what happened to me. That just leaves the problem with being busted for going through the security footage, if that's the reason I was called to the office this morning.

Don't tell Mom, Mak. I hate to say this, but she can't be trusted, Sawyer whispers through my thoughts.

I tense. *What are you talking about?*

No response.

Come on, Sawyer; you have to give me some answers. I start to pace the vacant hallway, unable to stand still any longer.

"Be careful, Mak. Things are about to get dangerous."

I nearly jump out of my skin as Sawyer's voice, as clear

as mine and Dixon's hatred for each other, floats up from down the hallway.

"Sawyer?" I whisper as I creep up the hallway. "Are you …? Are you here?" As soon as I ask that, I become hyper-aware of how insane I sound.

Sawyer isn't here.

Sawyer is gone.

Has been gone for a while now.

Then, who's mimicking his voice and pretending to be him?

As soon as the question crosses my thoughts, the glass vial illuminates from underneath the collar of my shirt.

My gaze skims the hallway as I place my hand over the base of my neck, covering up the glow. No one is around, except Trysten Wellbroking, a guy in my grade who runs in the same circle as Liam and Dixon. Nothing too strange about that, other than he seemingly appeared out of nowhere and is leaning against a locker a ways down the hallway with his gaze fixed on me.

Don't understand why that's odd? Take a look at what I know about Trysten:

Full Name: Trysten Wellbroking.

Age: Seventeen.

School Status: A senior at Shadow Cove.

Current GPA: 3.0.

Extracurricular Activities: None that I know of.

Titles: Again, none that I know of.

Parents' Occupations: Owners of several housing developments in Shadow Cove.

Means of Transportation: 1969 GTO that he's currently restoring himself.

Times We've Spoken: Once when we were assigned to work on a group project.

Trysten isn't your typical rich douchebag like most of Dixon's friends. He sort of reminds me of Rylen in a way—more quiet and reserved—only Rylen participates in a lot more extracurricular activities and rarely sticks around after school lets out. Plus, Trysten hardly ever notes my presence.

"Makayla," he says as I make my way past him.

My nervousness doubles. What if he's a spy for Lispy Larry or something?

"Yeah?"

He pushes himself off the lockers and strolls beside me. "You weren't in school today."

"Yeah, I had to go home for a bit. Family emergency. Just came back to grab some stuff." I'm the epitome of chill, but inside, I'm a confused mess.

Trysten and I don't know each other very well, so why is he suddenly noticing my absence?

He bobs his head up and down with a contemplative look on his face. "That makes sense."

As the necklace glows warmer against my skin, my pulse quickens.

"Be careful, Mak," Trysten whispers softly under his breath. "They're watching you." With that, he swings around in front of me and wraps his arms around me.

What the actual hell?

My knee instinctively lifts upward toward his manly goodies as I move to shove him away. But as quickly as he … hugged me, I guess, he steps back.

"I'll see you around." The corner of his lips kicks up into a small smile, and then he walks off, leaving me standing alone in the hallway with my jaw hanging to my knees.

I'm not sure how long I remain frozen in a state of stupor, but Ev eventually exits the office and tears me out of my trance.

"Got your bag," she announces as she hurries toward me. "Ms. Finkleson did ask where you were. Said she called you to the office this morning, but you didn't show up."

I blink at her. "What'd you say?"

"That you went home sick." Her forehead creases. "What's wrong? You look sick."

"I think I'm going to be," I mumble as vomit burns up the back of my throat. "I'll be right back."

I sprint to the bathroom, rush into an empty stall, collapse to my knees, and spend the next five minutes puking my guts out. I question if I'm sick, or just stressed out. Or maybe this is a side effect from the morphine.

I'm not sure.

I'm not sure about anything anymore.

A first for me.

I have to say, I'm not a fan.

Time to bring up your game and get to the bottom of this mystery, Mak, before things get even stranger.

TWENTY-FOUR

LOCATION: MAK'S CAR
TIME: 3:39 PM
DATE: TUESDAY, MARCH 23RD

After I finish barfing, Ev and I hurry out to the parking lot.

After a quick glance around to make sure no one is watching, I grab Dixon's computer from out of the trunk of my car before I climb in.

"All right, spill your guts," Kennedy demands as I shut the door.

Ev scoots into the back seat with Embry. "Go easy on her, Kennedy. She just threw up."

Kennedy relaxes a smidgeon. "Is that why you took off from school? Because you're sick?"

I shake my head, strands of hair falling into my face as I stare out the window. While I rarely keep anything from my friends, other than the fact that I can hear Sawyer some-times and that he occasionally visits me in my dreams, I hesitate to utter today's events aloud. Once I do, everything will become real. Too real. And then I'll have to deal with it, something I'm pretty sure I haven't done yet.

Then again, shying away from fear has never been my thing, so I open my mouth and let the words spill out. I tell them about how I was called to the office this morning. How, when I was heading there, Lispy Larry attacked me. How I woke up by the lake with a note in my pocket and Dixon's computer in the back seat of my car. I recap my brief journey to the police station and what I overheard between Don and the mayor. I even tell them about how Trysten hugged me in the hallway. The only details I really omit are the ones about Sawyer and the necklace.

By the time I'm finished, their eyes are wide and glazed over with fear.

"Holy shit, you have to go to the police." Kennedy shakes her head, anger flaring in her eyes. "You have to report what Larry did to you."

"You should've already." Ev hugs her backpack to her chest. "I know the police here aren't always great, but what Larry did was a crime. A huge crime that you have proof of, so you should be able to press charges."

"Yeah, but do I even have proof? Unless the security cameras in the school were working at the time—which according to Larry, they weren't—it's pretty much his word against mine." I lower my head to the steering wheel and take a deep breath as my head begins to pulsate. "I've seen Larry's criminal record; he always gets acquitted no matter what he's charged for, probably because of his father. How he does it, I have no idea, but I wouldn't be surprised if he was paying off the officers and judges around here. And that's just the crimes that make it to court. Most of them get dropped before things get that far."

"You should at least try," Kennedy insists. "He can't just get away with this. It's not right."

"And you need to go to the hospital and get checked out," Ev adds. "Morphine can have some unpleasant side effects, if that was even what he injected you with. For all we know, he could've been lying."

"Whatever it was, it made me black out for six hours." I shudder at the thought of being unconscious for that long. Other than the brief nausea, my body doesn't feel strange, so I'm fairly sure nothing bad was physically done to me. Still, being unconscious like that and vulnerable ...

I shiver again, rubbing my hands up and down my arms, as reality catches up with me. I question if perhaps I was in shock earlier, because everything suddenly feels twice as severe as it did moments ago.

"Maybe you're right," I admit. "I should get checked out by a doctor just to make sure I'm okay."

"You should go to your mom," Ev says. "That way, you can also tell her what happened."

Don't do it, Mak. Don't utter a word to Mom.

"I can't tell my mom yet." I lean back in the seat.

Kennedy tilts her head to the side. "Why not?"

"I'm not sure," I mutter. "But I have a feeling I shouldn't tell her about any of this just yet."

"Mak, someone doped you up with the same drug that killed your brother." Embry slants forward and rests her arms on the console with a stern look on her face. "You have to take this seriously."

"I am taking this seriously." Sighing, I reach for my backpack to get my phone. "I'll call her."

Don't do it, Mak. It's too dangerous.

I have to, Sawyer. This shit is becoming too dangerous.

I'm begging you, don't.

I won't if you'll tell me why. Why can't I trust Mom?

When he stays silent, I make the decision and push her contact number. After four rings, it goes to her voicemail. I then send her a text, but after a couple minutes, she still doesn't respond.

"She's not answering," I tell them as I open the app to track her phone.

"Maybe she's at work," Ev suggests. "We can stop by the hospital and see."

"I already drove by there earlier. Her car wasn't there." I type in the login information. "I'm going to track her phone and see where she's at."

"You can do that to your mom's phone?" Embry asks, impressed.

"I added it to my phone when I first got it and put her on it, as well, just in case anything happened." Like her disappearing like my dad did. I wish I'd thought to do it with my father, too, but I guess it wouldn't have really mattered anyway since, when he vanished, he left his phone behind. "She doesn't know I did it. In fact, I'm pretty sure she doesn't know I know her login info to her phone's account."

"You're such a little snoop." Embry raises her hand for a high-five. "But I like it."

I tap my palm to hers then redirect my attention back to my phone to see if the app has tracked her location yet.

"Crap. It says it's untraceable."

"Maybe her battery's dead," Kennedy suggests as she digs out a pack of gum from her purse.

I shake my head. "If it was, it would've gone straight to voicemail when I called."

"Then why can't the app track her phone?" Embry wonders, fiddling with one of the many piercings in her ears.

"Probably because either her phone is broken, the data is shut off, or she's in some sort of dead zone where she can't get a signal." I thrum my fingers on top of the steering wheel. "As far as I know, the only dead zones in Shadow Cove are up in the mountains."

"You think your mom went on a hike?" Kennedy asks, popping a piece of gum into her mouth.

"Maybe, except she's not much of a hiker." I chew on my bottom lip. "She could also be out of Shadow Cove and her phone is just out of signal. I don't think she planned on leaving town." That doesn't mean she didn't.

From snooping around through her bank records, I've

seen that she's gone on vacations she's never told me about. Still, I can't help worrying she'll end up like my dad. That she'll vanish and never return.

The idea makes my stomach ache even more.

"Everything will be okay," Ev tries to reassure me. "I'm sure she's just out of signal."

"Yeah, probably." I don't believe it. Not even a bit. But the only way to find out is to look into it, not freak out. So, sucking in a breath, I open my contacts. "I'm going to call a friend of my mom's. She's a doctor who might know where she is. Plus, I can see if she will give me a checkup. I'm not going to tell her what's wrong with me."

"We already discussed this. You have to report what Larry did to you," Ev scolds, wagging her finger. "You can't just let this go."

"I'm not going to just let this go. I'm going to call Scarlett, my mom's friend; talk to her and see if she can see me now. Then I'm going to sneak into the school's office after they close and look through the security footage to see if there's any evidence of the attack. And while I'm at it, I'm going to look up my record and find out why the heck they called me down to the office today. Then, after all that's taken care of, I want to go down to the coroner's office and look at Bria's autopsy report. I'm not going to just let this go. It's not in my DNA to let things go just because it's starting to look a bit scary." I release a deafening breath. "But I totally get if you guys want to bail on this. In fact, I think you should."

Embry rolls her heavily lined eyes. "Hello, I'm the definition of scary." She holds out her fist. "You know I always have your back."

"Thanks." When I tap my fist against hers, Kennedy holds out her fist.

"You know how much I love trouble." She bumps her knuckles against mine. "Count me in, too."

"You guys are crazy," Ev murmurs from the back seat. "This is crossing a line. I mean, you're not just hacking into the school's security footage. You're breaking and entering. Plus, you're going to get caught—there are cameras everywhere."

"Not everywhere." I twist around in my seat to look at her. "I noticed this morning when Lispy Larry grabbed me that he dragged me into a corner, out of the camera's view. There are places like that all over the school. I just have to make sure to stay in those places."

"But, if Larry dragged you out of the camera's view, then what's the point of getting the footage?" Kennedy asks, applying a layer of lip gloss.

"If the cameras were working, him grabbing me was definitely caught," I explain. "Plus, he had to get me out of the school, and unless he was super careful, he probably got spotted by the cameras at least once or twice."

"If that's the case, then isn't there a chance you'll get caught?" Worry crosses Ev's face. "The school has an alarm system."

"Yeah, I know." I drum my finger against my bottom lip.

"There are a couple of ways around the passcode problem. I can call a guy who was a friend of my dad's. He works at the alarm company. See if maybe he can do me a favor. Or I can black light the passcode buttons."

"Black light the passcode buttons?" Embry's face contorts in confusion. "What the hell is that?"

"Using a black light to see which buttons have the most grime on." Ev adjusts her glasses. "The buttons that do are the ones that probably are used the most frequently." Her frown deepens. "But, more than likely, it'll be a six-digit code and the grime residue level isn't going to show you which order to push them." She shakes her head "I don't know, Mak. There are a lot of unreliable steps in your plan."

"I know. I'm still working those out." I heave a sigh. "Look, you guys don't have to be part of this. In fact, you probably shouldn't. It's risky and dangerous and who knows what else. I'm not even positive what we're dealing with yet. And if this was a normal town, I'd just go to the police. But we're not in a normal town. And the police ... they could be part of ... well, whatever this is." I tuck a strand of hair behind my ear and square my shoulders. "But I can't just let this go. Not when these people could've killed my brother and countless others." I swallow a lump in my throat. "From some of the stuff Lispy Larry said, whoever he works for, may have even killed my dad." As tears pool in my eyes, I rotate back around in the seat and start up the engine. This is wrong. I shouldn't bring them into this mess. I need to handle this on my own. "Ev, I'm going to take you home.

You shouldn't be part of this. And Kennedy and Embry ... you guys should do the same." I set my phone on my lap and reach for the shifter.

Kennedy places a hand over mine to stop me. "Well, tough shit. We're in this with you, whether you like it or not."

"My dad may have *died* trying to figure this out," I stress. "You guys do realize that, right?"

"You don't know that for sure. And it's our choice, not yours." She cracks her knuckles. "Besides, you're going to need muscle in case something bad does happen again."

A drop of relief ripples through the sea of guilt stirring around inside me. "Are you sure you're sure? Because, I wouldn't think any less of you if you bailed."

"We're positive," Embry assures me, and Kennedy nods in agreement. "We'll always have your back, Mak. And besides, if what you're saying about this town is true—if there are spies or bugs and murder cover-ups—then this affects us, too." She motions at my phone on my lap. "Now, call this doctor friend and let's get this plan in motion."

I start to open my mouth to say I will as soon as I drive Ev home, but Ev speaks first.

"I'm in," she informs us quietly.

I trade a glance with Kennedy, who gives a quick shake of her head and mouths, "*I think she feels forced.*"

Agreeing, I tell Ev, "I don't think that's such a good idea. Things could get really dangerous, and we could get into a ton of trouble."

"Well, I don't care what you think." Her voice quivers with her nerves, but she straightens with confidence. "Embry's right; if what you're saying is true, then it affects all of us and our families." She crosses her arms and stares out the window. "My family may have fallen to pieces when my mom died, but I can't handle losing any of those pieces ... or you guys."

I want to argue, but after what she said, I'm not sure it would be right. Still ...

"Okay. But if you change your mind at *any* time, let me know, and we'll get you out, okay?" I wait until she nods before removing my hand from the shifter. Then I pick up the phone and dial Scarlett's number. She must be off duty because she answers after two rings.

"Hey, Makayla, I haven't heard from you in a while," she greets me cheerfully. "Is everything okay?"

"Yeah, everything's fine." I give a short pause. "Actually, I need a favor. I'm going to be participating in this skate competition that requires me to get a physical. I'd just go to the doctor, but my mom doesn't want me entering the competition because she thinks I spend too much of my free time skating. But the competition is a really big deal, and if I win, I could even get a sponsor, so I was wondering if you'd mind doing the physical on me, then signing the slip? I can even pay you." I cross my fingers that I won't have to pay since my cash funds are currently under ten dollars.

"I don't know, Makayla." She hesitates. "If your mom doesn't want you to enter, maybe you shouldn't."

"Please," I beg. "Haven't you ever wanted to do something that not everyone thought you could? That's what this competition is to me. There's even this guy who's been talking shit to me for the past week, saying all this stuff about how girls don't belong on the ramps."

Scarlett is a huge feminist, so if that doesn't persuade her, I don't know what will.

Silence ticks by. I start to sweat, but that might be another side effect of the morphine kicking in.

"Oh, all right," she gives in. "But instead of paying me, I want you to make sure you kick this boy's butt in the competition."

"Oh, I fully plan on doing so." My gaze skates to Dixon's computer sitting on the back seat. "Trust me."

"Good," she says. "Meet me at my office at seven o'clock, and we'll get this taken care of."

"Sounds good." I scratch at the spot where Lispy Larry stabbed me with a needle, hoping nothing is wrong with me. "One more question really quickly. You haven't heard from my mom today, have you? I've been trying to get ahold of her, but I think her phone is out of signal."

"Sorry, hon, but I haven't heard from her for almost a week," she tells me apologetically. "I've been working back-to-back shifts. This is actually my first day off in over two weeks."

I feel bad for making her go to her office on her day off, but my friends are right. I need to get checked out to make sure the morphine—or whatever drug Lispy Larry injected into me—hasn't affected me physically or mentally. It's either go to Scarlett or wait until my mom shows up. Considering I sometimes don't see my mom for days on end, Scarlett is my best option at the moment.

"Okay, well, if you hear from her, will you tell her to call me?" I reach for the shifter.

"Of course. See you in a couple hours. And don't forget to bring the papers for the physical for me to sign."

"I won't." I hang up and drive forward.

"So ...?" Kennedy reaches to put on her seatbelt while giving me an expectant look.

I pull out onto the street. "I'm supposed to meet her at her office at seven."

"Where are we headed now?" Ev asks as she fastens her seatbelt.

"To my house to print up a form for the physical." I slip on my sunglasses as sunlight peeks through the clouds.

Embry snorts a laugh. "You know, I know this has been said before, but it's cool as shit how easily you can come up with lies."

"Cool?" Ev gapes at her. "Try frightening."

"Nah." Embry dismisses her with a wave. "Everyone has to have their talents. Mine's kicking ass. Yours is computers. Mak's is cleverness and thinking on her feet. And Kennedy's is clothes."

"*Clothes?*" Kennedy glares at her. "Seriously? That's what you're giving me?"

"If you want, I can call it"—she makes air quotes—" 'fashion.' But honestly, it's all pretty much the same to me."

"Yeah, clearly." She purposefully eyes over Embry's all-black outfit and leather choker.

Embry simply shrugs. "Like I care if I'm not some fashionista."

"Whatever." Kennedy faces forward and crosses her arms. "But my thing isn't fashion. In fact, I'm the one who started this whole thing to begin with when I came up with a plan to get back at Dixon."

"She has a point," I intervene before their argument gets too heated.

Sure, I was looking into the mysterious deaths happening in Shadow Cove long before Kennedy suggested we get Dixon back for all the times he's made my life miserable. But if I hadn't followed Liam that day, I never would've found out about Lispy Larry, the escorting site, and the secret society and their connection to my brother's death and possibly my dad's. I wouldn't have overheard that the town may have spies or be bugged. Honestly, more than likely, I'd still be sitting in my dad's nook, staring at the wall of newspaper clippings, wondering how on earth that trail could lead to anything.

"Speaking of Dixon," Embry thankfully gets sidetracked. "How are we going to collect the money for his computer? Because, if one of us does it, he probably won't hand over the cash."

"Do we even want to do that still?" Ev asks. "I find it a

little strange Mak finds the computer just sitting in her back seat after she woke up at the lake. It kind of sounds like a setup."

"I've thought that, too." I catch her gaze in the rearview mirror, noting a dark blue car riding my tail. My nerves ascend a notch, but I don't freak out ... yet. "But a setup for what? I can't come up with an answer for that. At least, not a rational one."

"Is any of this really rational?" Kennedy questions. "I mean, look at everything going on. If someone else had told me any of this, I'd think they belonged in a nuthouse."

Which proves my point as to why I can't tell them I sometimes hear Sawyer's voice.

"I don't know if I agree with you." Embry props her knees against the back of Kennedy's seat. "I've always been a firm believer in the weird. Ghosts, aliens, conspiracy theories—all that shit is real, no matter what all you normal people say."

"Hey, I believe in ghosts, too," Ev protests, hurt ringing in her tone. "In fact, I'm pretty sure that ... that I've seen my mom once or twice."

Kennedy and I glance over our shoulders at her and simultaneously say, "*Really?*"

Holy crap, I *so* didn't expect that to come out of her mouth.

"Yes." She pushes her glasses up the brim of her nose and raises her chin. "Don't look at me like I'm crazy. There's been scientific proof that ghosts do exist, though most scientists refer to them as *entities*."

"No one's looking at you like you're crazy," Kennedy vows. "I think we're all just surprised because you're Ev and you're so ..."

"Super smart and by the book," I help Kennedy out as I steer the car over the railroad tracks and toward my neighborhood. "And ghosts aren't usually by-the-book sort of stuff."

"By the book or not, I know what I saw." Ev inhales and exhales shakily. "It happened a couple months after my mom died. She appeared in my room and told me I needed to make sure I took care of my dad and brother." She pauses. "It's sort of why I took on the role as mom." She grows quiet for a few beats. "Do you guys think I'm crazy?"

"Not at all." I hesitate, unsure how far I want to reassure her. Will she think I'm nuts?

You can trust her, Mak. Listen to the necklace.

Listen, as in, it can talk? Or, as in, that glowing, warm thing is how it communicates?

Nothing. Of course.

I grimace, but pay attention to the necklace. Currently, the glass vial is cool against my skin; has been since Trysten walked away from me.

Is that what it was doing? Warning me that I couldn't trust Trysten? It also glowed when my neighbor was sitting on his porch. Yet it didn't glow around Dixon, who I know I can't trust.

What is this thing, Sawyer? Just tell me!

Silence.

After deliberating my options, I arrive at a decision. I can either go at this alone, like my dad did, and possibly end up disappearing without so much as a drop of evidence as to where I went. Or, I can clue in my friends, hope I can trust them, and tell them the entire truth about what's going on with me.

Taking a deep breath, I blurt out, "I sometimes hear Sawyer's voice in my head."

I hold my breath, waiting for them to say something, but the car remains chillingly silent.

Great.

Psych ward, here I come.

TWENTY-FIVE

It takes my friends a whole minute before they assert their feelings about my declaration of ghost hearing abilities. One entire minute that somehow manages to feel like an eternity.

"Maybe you and Ev have psychic powers or something," Embry states with a crinkle at her brow. "Or, what's that thing called when someone can communicate with the dead …?" She snaps her fingers. "I think it's called necromancy."

"I thought that was the ability to communicate with dead bodies," Kennedy says, slipping off her shoes and tossing them onto the floor.

Embry stares incredulously at her. "Since when do you know anything about this sort of stuff?"

She shrugs, fishing her phone out of her bag. "I told you I'm not just about fashion." She taps the screen of her phone then clicks on a few buttons. "Hmmm ... Online, it doesn't necessarily mention that necromancy is communicating with dead bodies. It just mentions the dead. It also suggests that most necromancers communicate with the dead to find out about the future." Her gaze glides to me. "Does Sawyer tell you anything about the future?"

"He maybe has a couple of times, but like, two seconds before something happens."

I flick a glance in the mirror to check on the car again. It's still there, but then it turns onto a side road a few seconds later. I let a breath ease from my lips. I need to keep my guard up, but not be completely paranoid. That's what started getting my dad into serious trouble.

"He mostly just tells me vague, ominous warnings without explaining the details." I scratch at my neck where the necklace is hidden underneath my shirt. I want to tell them about it, but since I'm still unsure if they believe I can hear Sawyer or if they're just trying to be supportive, I'm conflicted if I should. "Don't you guys think that makes me sound a bit insane?"

"If it does, then I guess I'm insane, too," Ev says, fiddling with the elastic at the end of her braid.

"Neither of you are crazy." Embry retrieves her phone from the pocket of her leather jacket. "There's even an entire underground society dedicated to this stuff."

"Society?" I cock my brow as I park in front of my house.

My mom's car isn't in the driveway, which makes my worry for her double. Dammit, I was hoping she'd be home. "Like the same sort of society Liam was talking about?"

"Hell no." Embry hands me her phone. "Check that out."

I glance at the website on the screen. "SC Shadow of the Undead Inc."

"SC stands for Shadow Cove," Embry clarifies, propping her boot onto her knee. "It's basically a place where people go and chat about their strange, otherworldly encounters. You do run into some crazies every once in a while, but there are some regulars who I think are pretty sound of mind. There's even a place where they meet up every month. I don't know the location, but I've never really had a reason to ask."

Kennedy turns around in her seat to look at Embry, her brows lifted. "Why were you ever on this site at all?"

"I've always been pretty curious about ghosts and the undead." Embry gives an indifferent shrug. "I stumbled across the site while I was searching out some information on ghostly sightings. I sometimes go on it before bed to read people's stories."

"So, these are your bedtime stories?" Kennedy flicks Embry's phone that's in my hand.

Embry rolls her eyes. "It's not that weird."

"I wouldn't go that far," Kennedy rotates around in her seat. "But you're our little weirdo, so I guess it's cool."

Embry rolls her eyes again. "Glad I have your approval."

"Glad you realize you need my approval," Kennedy quips, flashing her a sassy smirk.

"Guys," I interrupt, angling the phone toward Embry. "What language is this on the header?"

Embry lifts a shoulder. "I have no idea. Why?"

"Because"—I gulp—"the other day, I found this book hidden in the floor of Sawyer's closet and it was filled with words from a language I don't recognize. But this"—I point at the symbols on the top of the screen—"this is the language."

"Wait, why did your brother even have a book hidden in the floor of his closet?" Kennedy questions.

"I'm not sure. There was other stuff in there, too, like a key, a newspaper clipping for a help wanted ad, a necklace, the book, and ..." I lower my voice to a mutter, "a bag of what I think was cocaine." As their eyes widen, I hurriedly add, "Don't worry; I flushed it down the toilet."

"Are you sure you got all of it?" Ev asks as she chews on her fingernail. "He didn't hide anymore anywhere else in his room, did he?"

"I don't think so." I hand Embry back her phone. "We can go search his room a bit better. I was planning on doing it anyway. Then I'll show you guys this book, print out the physical form, and head over to Scarlett's." I slip the keys out of the ignition and peer around the neighborhood, tuning in with my necklace. The vial isn't blasting heat against my skin, so I'm assuming—well, hoping—that means we're safe. "We need to be discreet about all this. No one can know we're looking into it. If we need to question someone, we'll have to be super careful about our choice of words or do it anonymously through a call or email. We should probably keep the questioning to a minimum."

"We can do all that, but I want to stress that, no matter how safe we are"—Ev reaches for the door handle—"snooping around usually leads to getting caught." She holds up her hands in front of her as Kennedy's lips part. "I'm still in, so don't even ask." She starts to climb out of the car.

"Wait," I hiss as I spot the dark blue car with the tinted windows slowly driving up the street.

Ev freezes, her gaze darting to me. "What's wrong?"

"Get back in the car." As the necklace heats against my skin, I reach for my phone.

Concern creases Ev's forehead as she sits back down and closes the door.

"What's going on?" Kennedy asks as I swipe my finger across the screen.

"This car coming up the road ..." I watch the car from the side mirror. "Earlier it was riding my tail, and I was worried it was following us. But then it turned off the road, so I figured I was being paranoid. But now it's here, right by my house."

Ev peers over her shoulder at the back window. "Maybe the owner lives around here."

The necklace increases in temperature, scalding my skin. "No. Whoever is in that car, they can't be trusted."

Kennedy stares at me with her brows elevated. "What?"

I shrug. "It's true."

"Mak, you're really freaking me out right now," Ev utters as she clutches her phone. "Should we call the police?"

"No," Kennedy, Embry, and I snap at the same time.

Ev winces, then hurt floods her eyes. "It was just a suggestion."

"Sorry, Ev. I think everyone is just a little on edge," I tell her as I tap open my camera app on my phone.

"It's fine," she says softly. "What do you plan on doing?"

"I'm going to take a photo of the car and the license plate number," I answer with my gaze fixed on the side mirror. "And then I'm going to find out who the owner is."

"Dude, remind me never to get on Mak's bad side," Embry jokes edgily. "Then again, being on *my* bad side's not that great, either."

"Guess we'll all have to remain besties forever." I start to smile, but then frown when the car drives closer.

We grow quiet as the car practically crawls beside mine. I pretend to be engulfed with my phone while sneaking a sidelong glance out the window. Doesn't do any good since the car's windows are too tinted.

I wait until it passes before raising my phone and snapping several photos of the rear end. Once I'm satisfied I got what I needed, I put the phone in my pocket, only to realize how hot the necklace has gotten. Scorching hot.

I peek down the front of my shirt and frown at the red marks covering the skin beneath my collarbone.

"Um, Mak? Why are you checking out your tatas?" Kennedy asks, breaking the silence that took over the car.

"Making sure they're still there?" Embry snorts a laugh.

Rolling my eyes, I release my collar. "No."

When they wait expectantly for an explanation, I sigh.

"Let's go inside, and I'll try to explain."

TWENTY-SIX

After we raid the cupboards for some snacks, I grab the stuff I found in Sawyer's room. Then we go into my bedroom and lock the door.

"This is everything I found in Sawyer's closet floor," I tell them as I toss the newspaper clipping, book, and card onto the bed. I also retrieve the key from my pocket and add it to the pile. Then I reach for my neck. "This was also in there." I remove the glass vial out from underneath the collar of my shirt.

"A necklace?" Embry remarks as she begins sifting through the pile.

Kennedy squints at the vial. "I hate to say this, Mak, but Sawyer had awful taste in jewelry." She picks up the vial to examine it, forcing me to lean closer to her. "Do you think he was planning on giving this to Bria or something?"

"I honestly have no idea, but ..." I dither, sinking my teeth into my bottom lip.

"But ...?" Kennedy encourages.

I release my lip with a heavy sigh. "I have to tell you guys something. I need you to swear you won't think I'm nuts."

"I thought we already established that," Embry mutters as she skims over the newspaper clipping. "Why on earth would your brother hide a help wanted ad for a lawn care job?"

"I have no idea, but I definitely want to look into it." I tap the bottom of the newspaper clipping. "There's a phone number listed. I was thinking about calling it."

"The ad's, like, two years old," Ev points out as she picks it up. "There's no way the job is still available."

"I'm not going to call about the job," I clarify. "I want to ask the owner of the phone number a couple questions. I'll look up the number before I do that to see who it belongs to."

"Um, hello?" Kennedy lets go of the necklace. "You guys are getting sidetracked." She turns to me with her arms crossed. "What were you going to say before Embry so rudely interrupted?"

Embry flips her the middle finger, but Kennedy just smirks.

I sink down onto the bed and hug my knees to my chest. "This necklace that I'm wearing ... well, the only reason I have it on is because ... is because Sawyer told me to."

"Before he died?" Kennedy asks, and I slowly shake my head. Her expression remains uncomfortably neutral. "So, after he died?"

I nod warily. "I told you guys I hear his voice inside my head sometimes. Well, after I woke up at the lake, he told me I needed to put the necklace on; that it'd let me know who I can trust. Honestly, I thought I was going crazy, but with everything that happened, I put it on anyway." I reach for my shirt collar. "I figured it was just a necklace until the vial started glowing and heating up. The first time it happened, I was outside, about to get in my car. The only person around was my neighbor, and he was staring at the necklace. It also heated up and glowed when I was around Trysten, and when that car just drove by." I tug the collar down just enough to see the burns. "That time it got so hot it burned my skin."

"Holy crazy, weird balls," Kennedy whispers as she examines the red marks branding my skin. "Ew, it's blistering."

Embry's gaze dances from my face to the burns to my face again. Her brows dip. "What would cause it to do that?" She drifts to her feet and skims her thumb along the vial. "Is it just made of glass or something else?"

"Maybe it's made of a foreign material that Mak's allergic to," Ev offers as she retrieves her phone from her backpack. "Is there anything strange about the surface? Like, does it have a rough texture or a tinge to it?" Her fingers are poised and ready to type information into a search engine.

"It's smooth," Embry sketches her thumb along the vial. "And it has a bit of a green tint to it."

"Which makes sense," I say. "Since it glows green."

Nodding, Ev taps her fingers along the screen. She sinks into silence as she scrolls through the information the search pulled up.

Embry begins to get fidgety and releases the vial, allowing it to fall against the hollow of my neck again. Kennedy seems to grow restless, too, stepping back and crossing her arms while she stares out the window and taps her foot.

The silence is maddening. Perhaps telling them about the necklace wasn't my most brilliant idea.

Then Kennedy says, "If what you're saying is true—if that necklace has some sort of magical powers or whatever—then everything we've ever known could be a lie."

"Don't be overdramatic, Ken." Embry hoists herself up to sit on the dresser, letting her legs hang over the edge. "Not everything was a lie. There's just more to life than what we thought."

"But, what if our families knew that and never told us?" Kennedy glances over her shoulder at Embry and cocks her brow. "What if our parents have been lying to us? Because, according to Liam, my dad's part of this secret society."

"We don't really know if the secret society has anything to do with this necklace," I say. "Sawyer's the one who had it and who told me to put it on, but I don't think he was ever part of the society."

"Yeah, but they might be the reason he's not here," Kennedy stresses with a hint of guilt. "Which means my father could be partly responsible for that."

"We don't know that for sure. And even if we did, what your father does isn't your fault." I grasp the vial. "What I do know is that, if this necklace is some sort of trustworthy warning device, it hasn't warned me of you guys, which means I can trust you. I already knew that. That's why I'm telling you all this, because I know you're good people and I can trust you."

"Of course you can." Kennedy turns and leans against the wall behind her. "I just want to say that, if it turns out my father is part of this, he's going to pay."

I lower my hand to my side. "I'm totally on board with that."

"I'd say same goes for my parents," Embry says, "but considering the credentials required to get into this society, I'm betting my parents aren't going to qualify."

"That's a good thing," Kennedy stresses. "Trust me."

"I know." Embry nods. "I was just sort of thinking aloud."

"Um, guys, I think I found something," Ev interrupts with a trace of worry on her expression.

"What's up?" Kennedy crosses the room and plops down on the bed beside her.

Ev tucks a stray strand of hair behind her ear. "Well, I did some searching on green minerals and rocks, and there is a lot. So, I searched green minerals and rocks in Shadow Cove, and apparently, the mountains are filled with jade."

"Jade?" I assess the vial closely. "This doesn't look like jade."

"Yeah, but the glass could be laced with jade," Ev explains. "That would explain the greenish tint."

"But it doesn't explain why it burned the shit out of Mak's neck when that car drove by." Kennedy rests back on her hands with her thinking face on. "None of this makes sense. If jade is all over the Shadow Cove mountains, wouldn't people be mining it by now?"

"Honestly, it shouldn't be in this area, yet it is," Ev informs. "But you're right; it doesn't make any sense why no one is mining it."

I sit down on the bed beside Ev. "Where'd you find that info?"

When she shows me the screen, I lean forward to get a better look, only to have the breath knocked out of me.

"The *Shadow Cove Daily News*?" I blink up at her. "The paper my dad wrote for?"

She nods. "It's the only place jade is mentioned along with Shadow Cove. And the sentence is brief, just a little mention of how the wealthy town of Shadow Cove is built inside a precious stone of jade. The article was written over five years ago, too, and nothing about jade was ever mentioned again."

"Strange," I mumble, wondering if my dad knew about this. Wondering why, if jade is so common here, no one is digging it up. Wondering if jade has any strange side effects. Wondering a lot of things.

"I wonder if jade has any powers," Embry absentmindedly says, crossing her legs.

"Powers?" Ev lifts her brows. "As in, magical powers?"

Embry shrugs. "Whether that vial is laced with jade or not is beside the point. Mak was burned by that damn thing. Something odd had to have caused it, because glass doesn't just randomly heat up. And as far as I know, neither does jade."

"Are you allergic to jade?" Ev asks me. "If you are, that could explain why it burned you."

"Not that I know of. Then again, I haven't been around a lot of jade, either." I pause. "Well, I guess technically I have if the whole damn mountain is full of it."

"She's probably not allergic to it, or else symptoms would be more consistent," Kennedy puts in her two cents. "I had this sweater once that was made out of some fancy fabric my mom had sent from overseas. It was really pretty and everything, but the first day I wore it, I broke out in hives. Turns out, I was allergic to the fabric. It took almost three days for my skin to go back to normal."

"I don't know why you're acting like magic can't exist," Embry tells Ev. "Especially after you just said you basically believe in ghosts."

"Entities," Ev corrects. "And believing in ghost isn't that out there. Magic on the other hand ... I've never seen any hardcore, factual proof that it could exist."

"Except for the fact that Mak's necklace, or whatever the hell that vial is, just burned the shit out of her neck for no logical reason." Embry hops of the dresser and crosses her arms. "Not everything is fact and fiction, Ev. There's stuff in life—grey areas—that don't necessarily make sense, yet somehow exists."

"I know, but ... magic?" Ev shakes her head. "I'm not sure I can believe in that."

"We're not even sure if it's magic yet," I say, slipping the necklace off.

Mak, don't do it. Put that back on.

I will in a bit, I tell him mentally. *Right now, I need Ev to wear it so she'll see. I need my friends to be on my side, Sawyer. I can't do this alone like you and Dad did.*

I didn't do this alone, he whispers, causing me to tense.

Was Bria part of this, too?

Silence.

Sawyer, please answer me.

A beat of silence ticks by, and then he utters, *Yes.*

A tremulous breath slips from my lips. *Is that why she died?*

Nothing but silence. He doesn't need to answer, though.

Not this time. I have a way of finding out the answer myself. By getting ahold of the coroner's report.

"Wear this for a while," I tell Ev as I slip the necklace over her head.

"I'm not sure if that's a good idea." Ev moves to take the necklace off.

I place a hand over hers. "You want proof that the necklace heats and glows when an untrustworthy person is around, right?" I ask, and she nods. "Well, what better way to get your truth than to experience it firsthand?" I withdraw my hand.

She reaches up and folds her finger around the vial. "All right, I'll wear it for a bit."

"Good." I rise to my feet, cross the room, and grab a notebook and pen from the closet. "Now, how about we plan our next steps, starting with what I'm going to do if Scarlett finds something strange about me while doing the checkup?" I flop down on the bed.

"You might have to tell her the truth"—Ev reclines against the footboard—"so she can treat you properly."

I chew on the end of the pen. "What if she's not trustworthy? I mean, I think she is, but still ... I'm honestly not sure who I can trust anymore. Not even my mom."

"You don't trust your mom?" Ev asks, her brows raising to her hairline.

"She might be having an affair with Don Jennings, who's definitely connected to this secret society. She's taken money from him for God knows what." I let out a trapped breath. "I don't want to think it, but for all I know, she could be connected to the society. Or, at least, working for them." Tears threaten to pour out of my eyes, but I suck them back.

Crying won't do any good, and it won't help me solve any of this. Still, I can't help feeling a bit heartbroken over the idea that my mom might be mixed up with the people who could've possibly killed Sawyer and perhaps even my dad.

"Mak …" Kennedy starts with pity in her tone.

I hold up a hand. "I'm fine, I promise. I just need to make a plan and focus on that for a bit."

Smashing her lips together, she nods then drops down on the bed beside me. Embry moves around the foot of the bed and takes a seat there, tearing open a bag of chips.

"Okay, so the first step in our plan is to figure out what to tell Scarlett if my test results come back a little wonky," I say, stealing a handful of chips from the bag.

"I think you should wear the necklace during your checkup," Kennedy says. "That way, you'll know if you can trust her."

I shake my head. "Let Ev wear it. She can tell me whether or not to keep my trap shut around Scarlett."

"Sure," Ev says, doubt weighing on her expression, revealing she's not totally buying into this magical necklace theory. That's okay. Once she feels the vial heat up and glow, she'll realize the truth.

"Good. And if she is untrustworthy and my test results

come back weird, I pretend like I have no clue why," I say as I write the first step to my plan.

"You think that'll work?" Embry's voice rings with skepticism.

I shrug. "My dad always said that, when you can't think of a reasonable lie to tell someone, the best thing to do is play dumb. It stops you from creating a lie that sounds too out there, and it eliminates any slipups."

"Your dad taught you the best way to lie?" Kennedy asks with a grin. "That's actually kind of cool. Strange, but cool."

A smile rises at my lips. "My dad was a pretty cool guy."

Was, Mak? Are you so convinced he's dead?

I'm not sure anymore …

I clear the congestion from my throat. "So, I think the next step is to break into the school tonight. I'll go alone on this one since it's so risky."

Kennedy promptly shakes her head. "Hell no."

"Um, yeah, I think I'm going to agree with Kennedy on this one." Embry stretches her legs out. "At least one of us should go with you so we can keep an eye out. And I think it should be me."

Kennedy's lips part in protest. "No way. I'm way more useful than you."

Embry's pierced eyebrow meticulously arches. "Have you ever broken into anything in your entire life?"

Kennedy shakes her head. "No, but if we get caught, my dad is a hotshot lawyer who can get us out of trouble."

"If your stepmom doesn't tell him not to. Plus, he probably won't help Mak." Embry sticks her hand into the bag of chips, giving Kennedy a remorseful look. "Sorry to be a bitch, but the truth is, your dad's kind of a dick."

Kennedy sighs in defeat. "Yeah, I know." She crosses her arms, sulking. "I still want to be the one to go with Mak. I think I'd be really good at this whole breaking and entering thing."

Embry and I subtly exchange an amused look. Kennedy is our best friend, and we totally love her, but we both know Kennedy will be the worse person for me to bring when I break into the school. Not only does she get bored easily, but she tends to talk when she gets bored. She also hasn't ever broken into a place before, unlike Embry and myself. However, if I tell her I want to take Embry instead, she's going to get upset.

"I think you should wait until tomorrow to do this," Ev chimes in, popping the tab of a soda. "That will give us time to scope out the school, maybe even get the blueprints, and figure out the best way to get inside without being seen. Plus, it'll give Mak time to get ahold of her dad's friend at the alarm company. I really don't like the idea of relying on the black light for this."

"I can't wait until tomorrow. I need to find out tonight why the hell I got called into the office so I can figure out a way out of it." I stuff a handful of chips into my mouth.

Ev nervously picks at the soda tab. "I guess I could do that part for you, just as long as you promise to wait until tomorrow to break into the school."

"Are you talking about hacking into my school records?" I question, wiping my greasy fingers on the sides of my jeans. "I don't want you to risk getting into trouble just to help me out."

"I'm not going to do it," she explains. "I'm going to have a friend of mine do it."

"What friend?" I wonder, reaching for the nightstand to grab my soda.

"Well, he's not really a friend, per se." Her cheeks pinken. "I talk to him in this chatroom sometimes. He hacks into computers for a living."

"You were in a hacker chatroom?" Embry stares at Ev as if she barely knows her. "Who the hell are you?"

"It's not really a big deal." She lowers her head. "I mostly just went on there because of my interest in computers."

Kennedy, Embry, and I trade a baffled look.

"Holy mother of effin' aliens," I tease. "Ev has a secret life. A secret *criminal* life. Who would've ever guessed?"

She raises her head and scowls at me. "I so do not. I've never even hacked into anything. I just know how."

"Relax, I'm just messing with you." I pat her knee. "I feel like I should welcome you to the dark side or something."

Ev blows out an exasperated sigh. "Are you going to wait until tomorrow to break in or not?"

I deliberate, but not for very long. "Yeah, I'll wait until tomorrow."

I just hope all this trouble will be worth it. That in the end, there will be evidence of Lispy Larry attacking me. Otherwise, I feel like I'm going to have to constantly look over my shoulder.

Then again, with the way things are going, Lispy Larry might be one problem in a sea of many.

TWENTY-SEVEN

LOCATION: MAK'S CAR
TIME: 6:51 PM
DATE: TUESDAY, MARCH 23RD

After we settle on breaking into the school tomorrow night, I go online to do a search on the dark blue car's plate number. But the site is temporarily down.

"Is that normal?" Kennedy asks when I inform my friends the search will have to wait until later.

I waver. "It's not too unusual for a site to be inaccessible for maintenance. I'll just try again later tonight."

We spend the next couple hours going over the details of the rest of the plan. Tomorrow afternoon, we'll go to the coroner's office to talk to Legend—aka, the coroner—and see if I can sneak a look at Bria's report. Tonight, Embry is going to do more research on speaking to ghosts and see if she can get someone from SC Shadow of the Undead Inc. to translate the book for us. She's also going to look into the possibility of jade having some sort of magical powers. While she does all that, Kennedy is going to drive around town and find out which buildings have symbols on them so we have a better idea of who's involved in the secret society. She also mentioned searching through her dad's files to see if perhaps he has any information that will give us more insight into the society and the illegal escorting site online, if he's ever handled a case on it.

Ev's part involves her friend hacking into my records so I know whether it's safe to go to school tomorrow or not, and if he can find out if there's a high number of security cameras in Shadow Cove. If there are, then we know the eyes and ears Don and the mayor were yammering about were more than likely cameras. After that, she'll work on gaining access to Liam's phone that Embry jacked from his pocket yesterday morning.

And me? I'll be the one breaking into the school, trying to figure out who left that note in my pocket at the lake, attempting to solve what the key I found in Sawyer's closet goes to, running the plate number, and I'll be calling the phone number on the help wanted ad. On top of that, I need to find out what Lispy Larry is hiding in that ghost house of his. I thought about just breaking in, but Ev and Kennedy had a shit-fit, saying it was too dangerous. Embry seemed down for it, so I might return to that idea later, after I find out if there are spies or cameras around town.

So, yeah, that's pretty much the gist of our plan. Individually, it doesn't seem too bad, but when I think of everything as a whole, I have a hard time wrapping my head around the possibility that we're going to pull this off *and* without getting caught. That was the main thing I stressed before we parted ways—if anyone wants to bail at any time, just do it. Do not hesitate.

"Have you heard from your mom at all?" Ev asks as I pull into the mostly vacant parking lot in front of Scarlett's practice.

She came with me mainly so she can test out the necklace. Although, if Scarlett is trustworthy, then Ev's skepticism in the necklace having magical powers will deepen further.

I shake my head as I park the car and click off the headlights. "I tried to track her phone again before we left, but it's still saying her location is untraceable."

"I'm sure she's fine," she says as she unfastens her seatbelt. "Maybe she just lost her phone or turned the data off."

"Why the heck would she turn off her data?"

"Maybe she found out you have access to the account and didn't want you tracking her."

"Maybe. That still leaves me wondering why she wouldn't want me tracking her."

"I was mostly kidding."

We climb out of the car and meet around the front.

"Kidding or not, you could be right," I tell her as we make our way up the sidewalk to the front entrance.

All the businesses in the area are closed, the lights all off. With only a handful of lampposts around and the moon and stars out, darkness blankets the area. The air is eerily quiet, too, but that might just be me being paranoid.

"It's chilly tonight," I remark as goosebumps sprout across my arms.

"It feels kind of hot to me." A crease forms between her brows as she looks at me. "Are you really that cold?"

I shiver. "Um, yeah. Isn't it obvious?" When she presses lips together, I lightly nudge her in the side. "What's up?"

"It's nothing." Seeming distracted, she shrugs. "I'm just wondering if getting the chills could be a side effect of the morphine."

"Do you really think I'd still be experiencing side effects?"

"Um, yeah. Morphine is a pretty intense drug, Mak. Plus"—she fiddles with the necklace around her neck—"it might not have been morphine that was injected into you."

"Yeah, you already told me that." I exhale a stressed breath as we arrive at the door. The lights aren't on in the waiting room, but light illuminates from the back hallway where the examining rooms are. "I guess we're about to find out." I tug on the door, but it's locked, so I give a few good knocks.

After knocking for several minutes, Scarlett still doesn't come to let us in. Giving up, I send her a text. When she doesn't respond, I dial her number. Again, no response.

"This is so weird," I mumble. "Scarlett isn't the sort of

person to just blow me off."

"Maybe she's running late."

"Then why isn't she answering her phone?"

When Ev has no answer for this, I scan the parking lot for Scarlett's car, but it's nowhere in sight. She usually parks in the back, so I motion for Ev to follow me as I head around the building.

"There's her car." Relief washes over me as I spot it out back, making me realize how nervous I was.

Get ahold of yourself, Mak. You can't breakdown yet, I tell myself.

"Now the question is: where is she?" I tap my finger against my bottom lip as I approach the back door of the office then tug on it. "Jackpot," I say when the door creaks open.

"Is it okay for us to go in this way?" Ev whispers as I step inside.

I nod, motioning for her to follow. "My mom and I have used this way a couple times when we met up with Scarlett on her lunch break." Knowing she'll grow even more nervous, I don't bother mentioning that Scarlett usually lets us in; that the back door is normally locked.

After Ev steps inside, we close the door then head down the hallway, past the medical supply room and Scarlett's private office. We're nearing the front entrance when one of the examining room doors swings open and out walks ...

"Trysten?" The word falls off my tongue in surprise.

He's wearing the same outfit from earlier and aims the

same unfamiliar smile at me. "Hey, Mak. Wait. Is it okay for me to call you Mak? I know only your friends call you that."

"Um, sure, it's fine." I flick a puzzled look in Ev's direction. Her face practically mirrors how I feel inside.

"Good. I'm glad you think of me as a friend." He gives my shoulder a soft squeeze. "And if you need anything at all, let me know. Especially with cars." He winks at me. "I'm excellent at fixing mechanical problems."

"Okay." I fake a smile, trying not to squirm at the intense look he's giving me.

"In fact, I should probably give you my number, just in case." He sticks out his hand expectantly.

"Sure." I've never been more confused in my life, which is saying a lot.

Fishing my phone from my pocket, I unlock the screen, but make no move to hand him the phone, because *hello*, there's too much private stuff on that phone and Trysten is seriously about one step away from being as creepy as Larry.

"Just tell me what it is, and I'll—"

My heart jumps as he snatches my phone from my hand, then irritation simmers through me.

"All right, dude, I played it cool when you hugged me in the hallway, even though we barely know each other, but taking my phone without my permission is where I draw the line." I reach to steal it back from him, but he chuckles and sidesteps out of my way.

Crap, where's Embry when you need her? 'Cause he so needs an ass-kicking.

"Relax, Mak." He hurriedly types something onto my phone then returns it to me. "I'm not here to hurt you. I'm here to help."

What an odd thing to say.

I clutch my phone. "Why are you even here, at the doctor's office? It's supposed to be closed."

"I could ask you the same thing." He winks at me again then strolls down the hallway toward the back door. "See you around, Mak. And don't forget to give me a call when you have some car trouble."

We nervously watch him walk away, waiting for him to push out the back door before either of us speaks again.

"Okay, that was strange," Ev breathes out.

"I know. And his last words were super ominous." I glance down at my phone. "I swear, if I go out to my car and it doesn't start, I'm going to blame ..." I trail off as I open Trysten's contact and see the note he left beside his number.

Have you checked your pocket yet? I left something inside there for you earlier today. Oh yeah, and make sure to delete this message when you're done. Keep my number, though. You never know when you might need it.

"What's on there?" Ev asks, and I show her the message. "What on earth ...?" She glances up at me. "Is there anything in your pockets?"

"I don't think so." I check the back, and then the front pockets of my jeans. When my finger grazes the edge of a piece of paper, my thoughts drift back to when Trysten gave me that weird hug in the hallway.

Is that what he was doing? Sticking whatever this is into my pocket.

I pull the paper—no, card—out. The front side is blank, but on the back, scribbled in black ink is: *BOX 1005.*

Ev leans over my shoulder to get a better look. "Is that a post office box?"

I shrug. "I have no idea, but I'm pretty sure I've seen this handwriting before."

"On what?"

"On that note I found in my pocket after I woke up at the lake. I mean, I'm not positive, but I can check when I get home."

"Then, does that mean Trysten left you the note?"

"Either that or he knows who wrote it."

Ev scratches her head, looking as lost as I feel. "Why does it feel like someone's playing a game with you?"

"Because I think they are." I swallow hard. "I just wish I knew what sort of game, who the players are, and what the hell is at the end of all this."

Ev's lips part to say who knows what, when Scarlett exits the room Trysten walked out of, removing a pair of latex gloves from her hands. When she sees us, her eyes widen in surprise.

"Makayla, I didn't hear you come in." She glances at her watch. "Oh, my word, I completely lost track of time."

I want to ask her why Trysten was here, but I know she'll just feed me a line about patient confidentiality. "It's fine. We were a few minutes early."

She leans back in the room to toss the gloves into the trashcan. "Still, I'm sorry I made you wait." When she straightens, lines crease her forehead. "How did you get in? I thought the front door was locked."

"The back door was unlocked." I hitch my finger over my shoulder. "I tried to call and text, but you didn't answer."

She pats her pockets, frowning. "Dang it, I must've left my phone on my desk." She holds up a finger and gives me the most plastic smile I've ever seen. "Go ahead and go into the room. I'll be right back." She hurries down the hallway.

"Is she always that scatterbrained?" Ev asks as we wander into the examining room.

I shake my head. "No, not really. In fact, she's usually pretty organized." I roam around the room, peeking in the cupboards and drawers. "Her smile isn't usually so creepy clown-ish, either."

"Yeah, it looked a bit odd to me, too—wait, what are you doing?" Ev hisses, quickly shutting the door. "You can't just go through her stuff like that."

"I'm trying to figure out why she was seeing Trysten." I peer inside the last of the drawers then move over to the computer and wiggle the mouse around. The screen lights up and ... "Jackpot. I'm sort of glad she's scatterbrained tonight."

Ev moves up behind me and adjusts her glasses as she squints at the computer screen. "Is that Trysten's chart?"

I move the cursor over Trysten's full name at the top of the page. "Yep, sure is."

Most of what's listed is written in medical terms that I don't fully understand. But at the bottom, she's listed Trysten's current symptoms, which include hallucinations of his dead parents, hearing voices, and …

"Jade poisoning?" Ev and I say at the same time.

"I didn't even know that was a thing." I scratch my head, turning toward Ev. "Have you ever heard of it?"

Ev shakes her head as she pulls out her phone. "Let me look it up."

"It's creepy that his symptoms include hallucinations of his dead parents and hearing voices, kind of like me and you," I mutter as I continue to search through Trysten's chart.

He just started seeing Scarlett, too. Tonight was his first visit.

"Yeah, I know." Ev lets out a shaky breath then sits down on a chair and begins typing away on her phone, the necklace falling out from the collar of her shirt.

"Hey, did you by chance feel any heat coming from the necklace when Trysten was around?" I ask, recalling how hot the necklace got when he gave me a hug in the hallway.

She shakes her head. "I haven't felt anything yet."

"Oh." I return my attention to the computer, questioning if the necklace only works for me.

Well, either that or there was someone else in the school hallway earlier today. If so, where and why were they hiding?

TWENTY-EIGHT

LOCATION: AN EXAMINING ROOM AT THE
SHADOW COVE DOWNTOWN CLINIC
TIME: 7:59 PM
DATE: TUESDAY, MARCH 23RD

I don't find anything else of interest on Trysten's chart, but I make a mental note to find out how his parents died. Not because I have a morbid interest in it. I'm just curious if there were any strange circumstances surrounding their deaths, like Sawyer's and Bria's.

Luckily, Ev has better luck than I do and discovers that jade can be mildly poisonous.

"That still doesn't explain how it poisoned him," I say as I hoist myself up onto the examining table with my legs dangling over the side.

"Unless he was walking around in the mountains where

there are high levels of it," Ev says. "But it'd have to be really, really high levels. And if that's the case, I think we would've heard about that risk by now."

My brow curves upward. "Like we heard about jade being up in the mountains?"

"I guess I see your point." She sets her phone on her lap. "I know you've mentioned before that you believe Shadow Cove covers up a lot of the unpleasant news stories. I think I'm starting to understand what you're talking about."

"About time you realized I'm always right." I grip the edge of the table as a smile spreads across my face. The smile then falters as my fingers touch something sticky.

Mak, Sawyer's voice briefly flashes through my mind then fades away.

"What the hell?" I lift my hand and gag at the sight of green, gooey substance coating the tips of my fingers. "Ew, what the hell is this? Alien shit or something?" Panicking, I jump up and rush for the sinks while Ev hurries over to the table and crouches down to look underneath it.

I flip the faucet on then coat my hand with as much soap as possible. "Do you know what it is?"

"No. There are a few droplets under here, and they look like they're glowing." She pushes to her feet, pulls open a drawer, and grabs a swab kit.

"You gonna steal a sample?" I ask as I practically scrub my hands raw.

Nodding, she squats back down in front of the table and swipes the cotton across a droplet of green goo. "I have a friend at the university in Mayfield who studies foreign minerals and substances. He could run some tests on this and find out what it is."

"Maybe it's just slime," I suggest with hope because, seriously, the last thing I want is to have stuck my hand in a foreign, gooey, glowy, green substance. "You know, like the stuff you can buy at toy stores."

"Maybe." She sounds doubtful. "It smells funny." She sniffs the swab before dropping it into a small, plastic envelope. "Like fish and moldy water."

"Can I smell it?" I ask as I dry off my hands with a paper towel.

"Yeah." She stands up and hands me the envelope.

Forcing back a dry heave, I put my nose up to it and sniff. "It smells like lake water."

She snaps her fingers. "That's exactly what it smells like, doesn't it?" Her expression immediately plummets. "That's not a good thing, is it?"

"I don't know yet. What I do know is that, only hours ago, I was left close to the lake after I was doped up. I also know that Sawyer's body was found near the lake, and Bria's."

"Have you ever seen anything like that at the lake before?" She points at the envelope.

I shake my head. "But I've only been up there a couple times and haven't endeavored farther than the shore."

"You think maybe we should go look around?"

"Quite possibly." Although, the idea of going back up there is giving me the heebie-jeebies.

Before we can discuss anything further, the door starts to open.

Ev snatches the envelope from me, tucks it into her pocket, then hurries back to the chair while I hop back up onto the table, avoiding the area where the slime is.

A moment later, Scarlett walks in to the room. Then she claps her hands together and grins. "All right, Mak, let's get this physical done."

If only things were that simple. Unfortunately, they never are.

I smile at her, pretending to be as cool as a person who didn't just stick their hand in questionable alien shit. My smile falters, though, when I glance at Ev.

Her eyes are wide, and she's clutching the bottom of the chair, her knuckles turning white.

"Ev," I whisper when Scarlett's back is turned.

Her gaze slides to mine, and she moves her hand toward her neck.

That's when I know what's going on. She can feel the heat from the necklace, too. That means, not only am I not going crazy, at least with that, but it also means Scarlett can't be trusted.

TWENTY-NINE

"Maybe you could ask her what jade poisoning is?" Ev suggest as we sit in the dark waiting room about an hour later.

Scarlett finished my exam about fifteen minutes ago, but told me to wait out here while she ran some tests on some blood she drew from me. She said some illnesses have been going around and she wanted to make sure I wasn't infected. Honestly, the whole thing felt very end-of-the-world-zombie-apocalypse to me, but that's probably due to the fact that I've spent the day being burned by a necklace, ran into what I can only assume is a doppelganger of Trysten, stuck my hand in what seriously looked like alien diarrhea, and found out my mom's lifetime friend might be working for the dark side.

Yep, I've had a pretty eventful day.

Scarlett was acting really strange during the entire exam. Forgetting things and saying the wrong names. Not to mention she kept giving me that overly cheerful, robotic smile.

"I can't," I whisper under my breath to Ev. "It'll seem too suspicious. Plus, the necklace went off around her, which means she can't be trusted."

"Yeah, you're probably right." Sighing, her hand falls to her lap. "Sorry, I'm not thinking clearly. All this is just a lot to take in. My brain is still trying to process."

"That's understandable." I keep my voice low enough that not even security cameras should be able to hear me. "The stuff we're dealing with is really out there."

She bobs her head up and down. "I had a hard time wrapping my mind around the fact that I spoke to my mom's entity. Now this happens, and I feel like my whole structured world is spinning out of control."

"You want out? Because I'd totally understand."

"No way. Now that I know this sort of stuff exists, I want to find out more."

I hold out my fist for a fist bump. "That's the knowledge seeker I know and love."

Chuckling, we tap fists. Then Ev's smile erases as Scarlett emerges from the hallway. She winces, pressing her hand to her chest.

Crap. That probably means the necklace is burning her fairly badly.

"Well, I have great news." A smile breaks out across Scarlett's face. "Your tests all came back negative. And you passed the physical with flying colors." She hands me the physical form. "Here's your slip for the competition. You'll have to let me know when it is. I'd really love to see you compete."

A drop of relief douses through me, though her potential untrustworthiness makes me question if I can trust the results. "It's next weekend. I'm not sure what time, but I will message you when I find out."

"Sounds great." She's alarmingly cheery, her smile all teeth. "There was one small thing, though." She reaches into the pocket of her white overcoat. "You were a little low on vitamin B, so I'd like you to work a supplement into your diet." She hands me a yellow and green bottle. "Take two of these in the morning with food."

I take the bottle from her and fake a smile. "Okay." *Yeah, not okay.*

There is no way in hell I'm taking anything she recommends unless I know what it is. In fact, if Ev's up for it, I'd like to have her hacker friend hack into my files so I can see the test results for myself.

"Thanks for doing this." I rise to my feet, fold up the paper, and tuck it into my pocket. "I owe you big time."

"I might just take you up on that one day." She offers me another toothy smile.

Lovely, her smile is going to give me nightmares for a week.

"Sounds good." Looping my arm through Ev's, I steer us toward the door, but pause before we walk out. "Hey, Scarlett?" I call out, turning around, only to find her watching us.

"Yeah?" she asks, sticking her hands into her pockets.

My body tenses. I'm not even sure why. "Have you heard from my mom yet?"

She shakes her head, her smile fading. "I'm sorry, hon. I'm sure she'll turn up, though."

I don't like her use of "turn up," as if my mom is already missing.

As if she knows my mom is missing.

I give her one last fake smile before ushering Ev out the door and across the parking lot.

"Oh, my gosh. Oh, my gosh," Ev chants after we hop into my car. "That was by far the most terrifying experience I've ever ... well, experienced." She peers underneath the collar of her shirt. "The necklace got so hot I thought I was going to have third-degree burns."

"Are you okay?" I ask, slipping the keys into the ignition.

She nods, pushing her shirt back into place. "I'm sorry. I'm panicking, and I don't even know why."

"You're fine," I assure her. "You don't have to be collected all the time, Ev."

"But I feel like I do," she divulges, staring down at her

hands. "Ever since my mom died, it's been my job to keep things together and be the rational, responsible one."

My heart hurts for her. "Maybe that's how you feel you have to be with your family, but not with me, Kennedy, and Embry."

She laughs softly. "Someone has to be the responsible one when you guys decide to do something that could potentially land you in jail."

"Hey, we're always responsible about the crimes we commit," I joke. "Well, almost always."

She glances up at me with a surprising smile on her face. "I just can't believe this is all happening. I feel like we are nowhere near close to finding out exactly what all this is."

"Yeah, I don't think so either." I grip the keys, ready to start the engine. "What I do know is the Scarlett in there isn't the Scarlett who went to my first skate competition to cheer me on. She was too smiley and kept forgetting things. She even called me McKenzie once, and she's known me since I was three!"

"Why do you think she was like that?" Ev asks, unclasping the necklace from around her neck.

"I'm not sure, but I don't like how she acts as if my mom is already missing. I saw her just this morning." For some reason, my gaze travels to the missing person's flyers taped to the lampposts. There are flyers like that all over town. Hardly anyone ever gets found, yet no one acts alarmed by this, except for my father.

My father who is now also missing. Just like my mom might be.

No, I'm not going to go there yet. Scarlett may have acted like my mom was gone, but she also acted like she was auditioning for a role in a horror movie.

"We should get going. We both have a ton of stuff to do tonight." I hold up my crossed fingers. "Fingers crossed this damn thing starts up. If it doesn't, I'm totally blaming Trysten."

She holds her breath as I twist the key. I was so convinced Trysten had done something to the car that the rumbling of the engine starting actually startles me.

"Guess I was wrong about that one," I breathe in relief.

I drive out the parking lot, hoping I'm wrong about some of my other theories, as well.

THIRTY

LOCATION: MAK'S HOUSE
TIME: 10:38 PM
DATE: WEDNESDAY, MARCH 24th

Before I drop Ev off, I ask if she can also have her hacker friend look at my doctor records. Normally, she'd give me a lecture about how illegal that is, but all she does is nod and get out of the car.

I'm worried about her. She's usually so put together, all about order and structure, but now she seems a little out of it. I hope what's happening doesn't break her.

I need to keep an eye on her, I vow to myself as I make the short drive to my house. *Make sure she doesn't fall apart.*

By the time I make it to the house, it's well past ten. None of the lights are on inside and my mom's car still isn't in the driveway.

I immediately rush inside, lock the door, and try to text and call her. When she doesn't answer, I call her work. Apparently, she took the week off, which is news to me.

In my last effort, I try to track her phone again, to no avail.

My stomach churns with uneasiness as I recall the days after my dad vanished, how I felt the same worry I do now. My mom didn't report him missing until several days later, insisting he'd show up. Legally, she could've reported his disappearance twenty-four hours after we'd last seen him, if we had reason to believe something bad had happened.

Eighteen hours have passed since I last saw my mom, so I have another six before I can even phone the police and report my concern. I know the drill. I'll have to triple-check with her work to make sure she hasn't been coming in and any other places she might be. Even if I do end up having to report her missing, I doubt the police will put a lot of effort into searching for her, just like they didn't with my dad.

"Crap." I swivel from side to side in the chair as I sit in front of the computer, staring at the map on the screen that shows my mom's phone's current location as untraceable.

On a whim, I decide to call the customer service number listed on the site to see if perhaps the system is having issues. After giving the customer service representative our account info, she puts me on hold.

A few minutes later, she gets back on the phone.

"I'm sorry, but we're currently having technical issues in our Shadow Cove area," she tells me. "If you want, I can send this information down to tech and they can try to manually check the location of the phone. It might take a couple days."

"Do you know when the technical issues will be resolved?"

"I'm sorry, but unfortunately, I don't."

"Do you know what's causing the issues?"

"Unfortunately, I don't know that, either. But Shadow Cove is listed as an area for high technical outages, which means issues like this are quite common there."

That's news to me. Then again, the security systems in the school power out every other day ...

Sighing, I tell her, "Okay, yeah, if you could send this down to tech, that would be great."

"Great," she says. "You'll receive a callback from us probably by Friday. Now, is there anything else I can help you with?"

Yeah, you could figure out what's going on in my town. That would be great.

"No, you've been very helpful," I say routinely. "Thank you."

"You're very welcome," she says cheerfully. "Goodbye."

"Bye." I hang up and return my focus to the computer, opening the search engine. My plan is to call the number on the help wanted ad Sawyer left in his closet floor so I can talk to the person who placed it, but before I do that in the morning, I want to find out who is the owner of the number; see if it'll pull up online.

I quickly type the info in and *holy jackpot*, the number pops up on dozens of sites. As I start to scroll through them, I note a very common occurrence—the number is listed on several wanted ads. Ads for a dog walker, a groomer, a fashion consultant, a butler, a chauffeur. There are also puppies for sale, cars, designer shoes. The list goes on and on. Seriously, either the owner of the phone number has an obsession for wanted ads or the ads aren't legit. What else could they be? Codes? A secret form of communication? I've heard of stuff like that before ...

"Wait ..." I jump from the computer chair, dash to the nook in my father's office, and skim over the notes and ads tacked to his wall, aka what my father referred to as his "trail."

"Holy shit," I whisper as I note the phone number listed.

It's the same number listed on the one Sawyer had in his office. On a couple of them, there's also another number listed, and my dad has circled that one several times.

Running back to the computer, I type in that number, as well. The same thing happens—countless help wanted ads pop up, along with an address. I'm about to give myself a high-five until I actually pay attention to the address

"Lispy Larry's alleged store," I mutter to myself. "The freakin' ghost house. You have got to be shitting me." I open and flex my hands, thinking about how many missing people in Shadow Cove vanished close to that house. "I need to get inside it somehow."

My gaze travels to the window. Outside, the starry night

sky stretches toward the mountains. Most of Shadow Cove's citizens are probably nestled away in their beds. I could go now. Sneak over and at least take a peek in the windows. One thing holds me back, though—the town may be bugged or have spies roaming around. I wish I knew a way to figure out if there was, but that's the one problem I can't figure out how to find an answer.

"Sawyer," I whisper aloud. "Want to help me out here?"

Only silence.

He's been pretty quiet for the last few hours, ever since I stuck my hand in that goo. Could that be causing Sawyer's silence? He had shouted at me right before I touched it, like a warning.

I lift my hand in front of me and examine my fingers. My skin looks fine. I feel fine. The only thing strange is the quietness inside my head. I may have thought I was going insane when I first heard his voice, but now ... well, I want him to come back. The house is too quiet. Everything is too quiet.

"Sawyer, are you there?" I practically beg. "Come on, please."

A dog howling outside is my only answer.

Getting up from the chair, I take a quick shower to make sure I'm one-hundred percent clean of any creepy, potentially ghost silencing goo. Afterward, I return to my computer to do one final search before I crash for the night, and that's for the dark blue car's plate number.

After I type it in, I cross my fingers and hit enter. "Please don't let the site be down. Please, please, please—"

The results ping through.

The car is registered to an Alexander Garyinford, and the address listed is up on the wealthier side of town where Kennedy lives. Strange, since the car was nothing fancy. And double strange because I've never heard of the guy before. That doesn't mean I'm not going to go check it out.

I jot the address down then set my alarm for a couple hours earlier than usual so I can scope out the place before school starts and find out who this Alexander is. Then I climb into bed and try to fall asleep. But after tossing and turning, I give up, grab my skateboard, my tools, and the bearings Rylen gave me, and work on changing those until I finally doze off.

DRESSED *in my pajama shorts and a thin T-shirt, I walk up the side of the mountain, heading to who knows where. The sky is cloudy above me, and the dirt is moist against my bare feet. The air is chilly, too chilly for me to be walking up the side of a mountain while practically wearing nothing.*

"Where are we going?" I shout to the figure in front of me.

When he looks over his shoulder, I realize it's Sawyer.

"To a place where I can show you."

I rub my hands up and down my arms. "Show me what?"

He just offers me a sad smile and continues up the mountain. "I won't be able to talk to you for a while, unless you're asleep."

"Why not?" I call out as the wind picks up.

"I think you already know why."

"Because I stuck my hand in that green stuff?" When he doesn't respond, I add, "What was it?"

He stops as he reaches the top of the mountain and waits for me to catch up.

"I can't tell you everything, Mak," he whispers softly as he stares out at the lake below. "If I could, I would've been able to help Dad."

I swallow the lump in my throat. "You talked to Dad?"

He bobs his head up and down. "I did."

Goosebumps break out across my arms. "Did? As in, past tense?"

"I haven't spoken to Dad in a while," he utters sadly. "I wish I could. I miss him."

"I miss him, too," I whisper as my body begins to tremble. "Sawyer, is he ...? Do you know...?" I suck in an inhale. "Is he dead?"

When he gradually shakes his head from side to side, a rush of air escapes my lips.

I turn toward him. "Do you know where he is?"

He shakes his head again.

My chest tightens. "What about you?"

He doesn't look at me. "What about me?"

"Are you ...? Are you dead?"

"I think you already know the answer to that, Mak."

Deep down, I think I do. Unlike my dad, my brother was found in the very lake that's below us now.

Tears burn my eyes, but I suck them back. "I'm sorry, Sawyer. I'm sorry this happened to you. I'm sorry that I was mean to you the last time we spoke to each other. Well, in real life."

"You don't need to be sorry. What happened to me isn't your fault. It was my own fault ... and theirs." Anger flashes in his eyes as bright as the lightning snapping across the clouds.

I jump at the sound of thunder. "Who's they?"

Closing his eyes, he lifts his hand and points at the lake. "Do you see it?"

"The lake? Yeah, I see it," I say in confusion.

"No, you don't." He points firmly at the lake again. "Look closer."

Exhaling, I step to the ledge and peer down at the water. The longer I stare, the more the water begins to ripple, the surface changing, shifting, turning a slimy green—

Beep. Beep. Beep.

My alarm sirens off, yanking me from the dream.

I sit up, feeling disoriented and groggy as I hit the snooze button. My head is pounding, my heart is racing, and I have the worst taste in my mouth, like I ate a bunch of rotten eggs.

The dream is vivid in my mind, just like the dream I had when Sawyer led me to his closet.

"What are you trying to tell me, Sawyer?" I stare up at

the ceiling. "That you want me to climb up the mountain and look at the lake? That Dad isn't dead? If that's true, then where the hell is he?"

He doesn't answer, but he did mention in the dream that he couldn't talk to me for a while unless I'm asleep. I shut my eyes and try to drift back to dreamland, but my alarm goes off again. Just like that, I'm wide awake.

Throwing the covers off, I drag my ass out of bed, and go into my mom's room. Like when I peeked in last night, the bed is made, the floor is covered in clothes, and the closet light is on. From what I can tell, she hasn't been home.

After I shower and get dressed in a holey pair of jeans, a grey shirt with a plaid overshirt, my favorite pair of sneakers, and the necklace, I go through the ritual of trying to track down my mom again. No luck.

I check the time and sigh. I can report her missing, but I want to give myself twenty-four more hours to find her myself, since I'd rather not get the police involved.

Grabbing my bag, my skateboard, and a couple of granola bars, I head out of the house. This early in the morning, the sun isn't even up yet. The sky is a deep grey.

Once I toss my board and bag into the trunk of my car, I slide into the driver's seat and dig my phone out of my pocket to see if any of my friends have messaged me yet. None of them have, so I send out a thread.

Me: Call me when you guys wake up. I found out a couple of things last night.

I then punch Alexander Garyinford's address in the

GPS of my phone and drive forward, double-checking in my rearview mirror that I'm not being followed.

Surprisingly, the streets are empty, the neighborhood quiet, not a single car or person in sight. Everything is so still.

Perhaps a little too still. As if the town is just a ghost.

THIRTY-ONE

LOCATION: OUTSIDE OF THE GATE OF
ALEXANDER GARYINFORD'S MANSION
TIME: 6:26 AM
DATE: WEDNESDAY, MARCH 24th

Alexander's place is similar to Kennedy's—a couple of stories, with a large columned entryway and a massive iron gate in front of the driveway. Pulling up to the house is impossible unless I'm buzzed in, and parking out front isn't an option unless I want to park in the street. Instead, I drive up the road to a hill that overlooks the five acres of land just behind the house. The area is a local hotspot for runners, so it's not too strange for me to be up here—well, maybe not for the people who actually know me and understand how much I hate running.

The shitty part is I can't see the front door, though the

garage is in plain sight. When he pulls out, I should be able to see. Then I can tail him until I get a clear view of who this dude is that made the necklace scald my skin so badly it left blisters.

I've been parked for about ten minutes and have made it halfway through my coffee when my phone buzzes from the console with an incoming call from Kennedy.

"Yo, yo, yo, what's up?" she greets me cheerfully after I answer.

"Not much," I say. "Just parked up on a hill a few miles from your house, staking out the house of Alexander Garyinford."

"Who the heck is that?"

"The guy who owns that blue car that I'm pretty sure was following us yesterday."

"Really?" She sounds intrigued. "What's the address? Maybe I know who he is."

After I prattle off the address, she grows unnervingly quiet.

"What's up?" I ask. "I can tell something is."

"Well," she hesitantly starts, "I don't know who this Alexander dude is, but I do know who owns that house. And so do you."

I'm about to ask her who it is when one of the garage doors open and out walks Rylen.

"You have got to be kidding me. My eyes have got to be shitting me or something."

Nope. The longer I stare at him, the more I realize my

eyes are indeed not shitting me. Rylen is right there. This is his house.

He's wearing a pair of black jeans, a grey T-shirt, and leather bands cover his wrists. When I zoom in on him with my camera phone, I notice his hair is wet, as if he just got out of the shower.

"*Rylen?* This is *Rylen's* house?"

I shouldn't be so surprised. He's friends with Dixon, after all. But sadly, I am. Shocked. Disappointed. And shamefully, a bit hurt, too.

"Yeah," Kennedy says apologetically. "His family actually owns two houses in Shadow Cove, but I think Rylen mostly lives in the one you're staking out right now."

"But Garyinford isn't his last name."

"Yeah, I know. I've never heard of it before."

"So then, why is that car linked to this address?"

"Maybe it's like their butler's car or something? Or their maid's? Ours live in the guesthouse out back, but they use the same address as us."

"That could be it." As Rylen gets in his SUV, I start up my engine. "I think I'm going to tail him."

"You're gonna tail Rylen?"

"Yep."

"Why?"

"Call it a hunch."

"A hunch for what?"

"I have no idea." I back up, steer out onto the road, and speed around the curving road toward the front gate of

Rylen's house. "But the best way to find out what a person is truly up to is to follow them."

"Where'd you hear that?"

I slip on my sunglasses. "I just made it up, actually."

"Well, let me know how that turns out. Twenty bucks says he drives by your house."

My fingers tighten on the steering wheel as I zoom past the mansions that make up the neighborhood. "So, you do think he's the one driving the blue car and following us around?"

"No, I think he's a guy who has a major crush on you. And you're going to end up breaking his heart when you accuse him of stalking us."

"Who says I'm going to do that?"

"Were you not planning on it?" she challenges with skepticism.

"Nope."

"Liar."

"All right, maybe I've already thought about doing it, but it doesn't mean I'm going to." I slow down as I near the front gates to Rylen's place and pull over to the curb near a large tree. "It all really depends on what I find out about him."

She sighs. "Oh, Mak, not everyone is out to get you."

"You can still say that after what happened yesterday?" I hunker down in the seat as Rylen pulls his SUV out of the driveway.

"Yeah, I can. Things might seem a little crazy right now,

but if I went around not trusting anyone, I'd be super lonely."

I wait a beat or two before steering back onto the road, keeping a safe distance from Rylen to avoid being spotted, but not enough distance that I'll lose him if he makes a turn.

"I trust you, Ev, and Embry," I point out, then put my phone on speaker and set it in the console. "Besides, right now, we need to be careful of who we trust. At least until we figure some things out. Speaking of which, did you find anything out last night?"

"A couple of things, actually," she says over the sound of keys clanking. "Over half the stores and businesses in Shadow Cove have that mark on them, including my father's."

"Shit, that's a lot," I say, then add apologetically, "Sorry about your dad."

"No worries. We already kind of knew that anyway." She aims for a cheerful tone, but I know her well enough that I can tell it's fake. "I also found out that my dad does a lot of work for the businesses in Shadow Cove. And I'm not talking about court cases, either."

"Then, what's he doing for them?"

"I couldn't find anything specific, but he has all these receipts and forms documenting the work he did for them. It never states the details. I'm thinking he might be doing work for this secret society, but I can't document it."

"That could be it." As Rylen makes a turn off the main

road, I flip on my blinker. "The main goal of secret societies is to keep everything a secret."

"I just wish we knew what the point of this secret society was. What they're up to. If they're linked to all the murders and disappearances around here. And what the hell any of this has to do with you and that bizarre necklace."

"Yeah, I'd like to know all that, too."

"Do you still think the secret society has something to do with human trafficking?"

"Honestly, I'm not so sure anymore." Then I begin to tell her what happened to Ev and me last night while I was getting a checkup. I'm almost finished when Rylen reaches his final destination—the Shadow Cove Skate Park.

"So not where I was expecting him to go," I mumble as I slowly steer up to the entrance.

"What's wrong?" Kennedy asks.

I park toward the back and silence the engine. "I just found out where Rylen was heading to this morning."

"And ...?"

"The skate park."

She snickers. "See, I was totally right."

I down the last droplets of my coffee. "About what?"

"About Rylen having nothing to do with this."

I toss the empty cup aside. "That's not what you said at all."

"Yes, I did. You just weren't listening."

"Okay, maybe. Still, it doesn't mean I'm convinced

Rylen isn't part of this society thing. I mean, let's look at the facts. One"—I raise my finger, though she can't see—"according to Liam, you have to have the right last name to be in the society. A last name that's connected to wealth and power. Collinforton is a name that more than qualifies. Plus, Rylen's father owns, like, twenty-five percent of the stores in Shadow Cove *and* two houses. Rylen hangs out with Dixon, who I know has to be connected to the society via his douchebag father. And Rylen hangs out with Liam, who's already admitted he's part of some club that pissed off the society. So, Rylen could be part of this club or the society itself. A society that, just yesterday morning, doped me up with morphine and tossed me out by the lake as a warning."

"Or, he could simply be a guy who's completely unaware that the town he lives in is connected to some creepy-ass society who roughs up teenage girls to scare them," she says matter-of-factly. "Maybe he's just the sweet guy you've always known, who loves to skate and who is crushing on my awesome, albeit slightly neurotic, best friend. Seriously, Mak, how much coffee have you had this morning? I can feel your damn jitteriness through the phone."

I glance down at the two empty coffee cups on the passenger seat. "I don't know. A couple of cups."

"Well, you need to chill on the caffeine for a bit. And you need to chill out about Rylen, and accept that maybe he is just a guy who likes you."

"I'll accept that when I have proof. It's just the way I

am, Ken. And with everything going on ... I can't just trust people."

"Mak—"

"I have to go check on something," I cut her off. "Do me a favor; call Ev and see if she found out if I'm good to go to school today. Call you in a bit." I hang up before she can scold me further. Then I tuck my phone and car keys into my pocket, hop out of the car, and grab my iPod and skateboard.

I haven't skated in a couple of days, so my heart bursts with eagerness as I approach the ramps. But being here isn't about skating.

Well, okay, that might be a lie, but it's not the main reason I'm here.

No, the main reason is because of the necklace.

Yesterday when I talked to Rylen in school, it didn't get all blistering hot while I was near him, but it did a few moments after he allegedly left. What if the vial hadn't heated in the hallway because of Trysten, but because Rylen was still lingering around? What if he was the person driving the blue car?

There's only one way to find out.

THIRTY-TWO

I'm not sure I've ever been to the skate park this early. Boy, oh boy, is it crowded. Mostly with guys, although there is a girl a few years older than me hitting up the half-pipe. I've seen her here before. Don't know her name, but she has some pretty wicked moves. Enough to draw attention. Good, that'll keep me out of the spotlight for a bit, because I'm not here to show off. I'm here to find answers.

Tucking the vial underneath the neckline of my shirt, I pop in my earbuds, yet don't crank up the music. I just want to give off the illusion that I'm not paying attention. That way, people won't be cautious with what they say around me.

After I kick off, I skate toward the farthest ramp away from almost everyone, pretending I'm in the zone. I do a couple of tail stalls, a few rock to fakies, and a 360, highly aware Rylen keeps glancing in my direction. He hasn't been on the ramps since I rolled up, just standing over on the side, chatting with a couple of his friends.

I've about convinced myself to skate over there, to chat with him for a bit and see if I can get this currently dormant necklace to go all glowworm on me, when Dixon strolls up to Rylen.

The two of them exchange a couple of words, then Dixon throws me a smirk from over his shoulder. My lip twitches in irritation as I skate up the side of the ramp. When I reach the top, I flip around, delivering an almost perfect 720. After I land it, I flip Dixon the middle finger then skate off toward the other side. Once I reach the back of the ramp, I kick my board up into my hands then creep back toward where Dixon and Rylen are standing. The ramp is high enough and at the right angle that I can easily get close to them without being seen. I keep my earbuds in to appear as if I'm not eavesdropping, highly aware that the necklace is cool against my sweaty skin.

"Why do you always have to be such a dick to her?" Rylen is saying as I tuck my skateboard underneath my arm and strain my ears to listen.

"Why not?" Dixon replies in an arrogant tone.

"That's the stupidest reason I've ever heard," Rylen

mutters. "Honestly, if I didn't know better, I'd swear you had a thing for her or something."

"It's a good thing you do know better then," Dixon replies coldly.

"Still, it would be better if you lay off her," Rylen says. "Now that they're targeting her, we need to be more careful around her. She can't know anything's up yet, or they'll end up knowing."

"If I was nice to her, she'd think something *was* up," Dixon stresses. "Mak and I have been going at it for years now. It's what we do."

"Sometimes you act like you get off on pissing her off," Rylen states with disgust.

"So what if I do?" Dixon responds indifferently. "It's better than following her around like a lovesick puppy. A puppy she's going to kick to the curb once she finds out the truth."

I lean closer, ready to hear more, when someone taps me on the shoulder.

I jolt, raising my fist for reasons I can barely comprehend.

"It's just me." Kennedy stands in front of me with her hands up. Her blonde hair is in a braid, her eyeshadow is as sparkly as her shoes, and her pink dress matches her lip gloss. Underneath the glitz and makeup, though, a large, gnarly, very fresh welt marks her cheek.

"Holy crap, is that new?" I hiss with wide eyes as I grab

her arm and steer her away from Dixon and Rylen before they realize I was eavesdropping.

Her fingers float to her cheek as she trots in her heels to keep up with me. "Yeah, I hit it on the top of the car door when I was opening it."

I narrow my eyes at her as I tug the earbuds out. "Bullshit. Your stepmom hit you again, didn't she?"

Strands of her hair puff from her face as she blows out an exasperated breath. "Look, I don't want to talk about it right now."

I shake my head as I steer us toward the parking lot. "Nope, that's what you said the other night. I'm not letting you off the hook twice."

"Let me off the hook?" She arches her brow. "Since when are you the boss of me?"

"Since forever," I quip. "Now fess up."

She sighs in defeat. "Look, I'll talk to you about it later. I promise." Her gaze flicks to the parking lot. "When we're alone, okay?" Her skin pales as she swallows hard. "The less people who know about what happened, the better."

"You know Embry and Ev will understand, right? It's not your fault. It's your stepmom's and your dad's for allowing this to happen."

"I know, but right now"—her eyes travel around the skaters cramming up the area—"I'm not ready for anyone to find out about this."

"Tonight, you and I will talk about it," I stress as I

quicken my pace. "And I'm not taking any excuses. We're going to talk and figure out a way to get her to stop."

"Fine." She appears distracted, distant as she dazes off over her shoulder then looks back at me. "What were you just doing back there, hiding out behind the ramp?"

I more than notice her obvious subject change, but we will return to the conversation because there's no way in hell I'm going to continue to allow her stepmom to hit her.

"Listening to Rylen and Dixon chat about Dixon's fetish with tormenting me, and how I'm going to be pissed off when I find out the truth about them. And how they're setting me up for something."

When we make it to my car, I see Kennedy's is parked beside mine, and sitting inside is Embry and Ev.

"Awesome, everyone's here." I quicken my pace. "Now we can chat before school starts, and find out if I can even go to school without getting into major trouble."

"Oh yeah, Ev said you're good to go on that."

"Really?"

She nods. "She said there was nothing listed in your files about why you were called into the office yesterday, so she called up one of her friends who is an assistant or something in the office. They said they overheard the principal telling the secretary to buzz you into the office for a college counseling meeting."

I open the door to the back seat of her car. "That's weird. They just had me do one of those a couple weeks ago."

She peers over the roof with her brows knit. "That's a little strange."

"Yeah, especially since, if I hadn't been called to the office, I never would've gone down the hallway where Lispy Larry was waiting for me," I whisper lowly, the revelation causing my stomach to ravel in knots.

Why haven't I thought about that before? That maybe someone from the office is in the society and helped him out?

Because I was too fixated on thinking I got caught snooping through the security cameras. Rookie mistake, Mak, rookie mistake.

Kennedy's eyes cram with worry as she ducks into the car.

I slide into the back beside Ev, my stomach twisting into tighter knots.

"So, you think someone in the school office is part of the society and set you up to get caught by Larry?" Kennedy asks the second we get the doors shut.

"What?" Ev gapes, her eyes huge behind her glasses.

"I'm not positive." I set my board down on the floor beside my feet and wrap the cord of the earbuds around my iPod. "But I've already had my college counseling meeting, so unless there's a logical reason as to why I need two, then whoever called me to the office yesterday morning could've been trying to get me into the perfect location for Lispy Larry to dope me up." I flip back in the seat. "He said it himself when he injected me. He said we were out of view of the cameras. Maybe that's because he planned it out with someone in the main office. They'd know better than anyone which spots of the school are out of view. Or, better yet, they could power down the cameras altogether." I brush my hair out of my eyes as another revelation smacks me square in the gut. "If that's the case, then my attack *wasn't* captured on camera ... I'm still going to look. If by chance anything was caught, I'll have proof of Lispy Larry's attack."

Ev fidgets nervously with a band of bracelets she's wearing. "After what I found out this morning ... I think maybe you should consider going to Mayfield to make the report."

"What'd you find out?" I ask, leaning forward.

She picks at her fingernails. "I messaged my hacker friend to ask him to look into your school records, medical records, and to see if he can find out if there is a high number of security cameras in town. Your records came back clean, Mak—both the school's and the medical. Although, you should know that nowhere in your medical records did it suggest you have a vitamin B deficiency, so I wouldn't take those vitamins Scarlett gave you."

"What vitamins?" Embry interrupts, the chains on her plaid pants jiggling as she scoots forward.

"We'll fill you in, in a sec," I tell her then look back at Ev. "I wasn't planning on it, but I was thinking that maybe we could get the vitamins tested and see what they are."

"I think that's a good idea," Ev agrees. "That way, we can at least have an idea of what Scarlett's motives are for lying to you."

"I can look online and see if I can figure it out." I pull out my phone from my pocket. "They have this number on them and this really strange aquamarine coloring. That should be enough information."

"If they're legal pills," Embry points out. "Illegal ones aren't going to be easy to track down. I'd be able to help you more if you told me what the hell is going on."

I open my mouth to start giving details about last night's doctor office events, but Ev talks over me.

"No, you guys need to hear what Porter found out—"

"Porter?" Kennedy starts up the engine to crank up the heat. "Who the hell is Porter?"

"My hacker connection," Ev says. When Kennedy frowns, probably because we know a Porter who runs in the same circle as Liam and Dixon, Ev tacks on, "Don't worry; he doesn't even live in this country and has absolutely no connection to Shadow Cove." She shakes her head. "Guys, give me a bit of credit, will you?"

"Sorry." Kennedy collects her coffee cup from the console. "I just heard Porter and started freaking out. I should've known better than to think you would do something like that."

Ev offers her a small smile before turning toward me. "Anyway, I had Porter look into security camera systems installed in Shadow Cove. At first, he couldn't find any, which I thought was odd, considering the median home value in Shadow Cove is way higher than most towns. After

I told him this, he started digging deeper. And I'm talking black market deeper."

"There's a black market for security cameras?" Kennedy asks as she fiddles with the temperature.

"There's a black market for everything." I stuff my iPod into my pocket. "It's actually pretty crazy when you start digging into it."

"Like what, exactly?" Kennedy asks curiously.

"Guys, stop getting off track," Ev exclaims, startling the shit out of us.

"Ev, calm down." Kennedy's eyes are wide with shock.

Her shock is understandable. Ev rarely flips out, let alone on us, which proves my theory that she's not handling this very well.

"How can I calm down when our town is wired with over five thousand security cameras?" She breathes raggedly. "Considering our population, that's, like, a camera per home. But I know my house doesn't have one, and Mak's doesn't, and Embry's, and I'm sure that's the case for all of the homes in our neighborhoods, so where are all these cameras, guys? Huh? Do you have an answer? Because I sure don't."

"Ev, breathe." I place a hand on her arm. "Nothing bad has happened. There's just security cameras around town; that's all."

"Yeah, but for what?" Her voice is all squeaky and high, and her eyes are huge with panic. "Porter also was able to find out these cameras were all bought by the same person or company."

Blood roars in my eardrums. Someone in Shadow Cove purchased five thousand security cameras? I think I may have just found out my answer to what the eyes and ears are in this town. The question is: where are these cameras installed and how the hell did they install them without the townspeople being aware?

"Was he able to find out who this person or group is?" I ask, gripping my phone.

She wipes her palms on the front of her pants. "No. The buyer wanted to remain anonymous."

"Dammit," I mutter. "Honestly, I'd say it was either the mayor or Don Jennings since they seem to know about the cameras, but the way they were acting yesterday ... When they brought up the eyes and ears thing, they mentioned needing to have their meeting at the station so that"—I make air quotes—" 'they' couldn't hear them." My hands fall to my lap. "They made it sound like someone was watching them, not them watching someone." I turn to Kennedy. "Did Dixon's dad's car lots have symbols on them?"

Kennedy nods firmly. "Every single one."

"Then that more than likely means the society didn't bug the town," I say. "Well, either that or whoever's in charge likes to keep a close eye on their members."

Kennedy rubs her hand across her forehead. "This is seriously giving me a migraine." With an exhale, she lowers her hand. "What about you, Em? You find anything out on that book?"

Embry shakes her head. "Not yet, but I emailed a guy who supposedly knows the language. Hopefully, I'll hear back from him later tonight. As for jade having magical powers, I seriously couldn't find a lot of information, other than it's valuable and extremely old." She sweeps her fiery red hair to the side. "Although, I did find a small connection between jade and speaking to ghosts, but the information was limited."

"What exactly was the connection?" I ask, thinking of Trysten and how he has jade poisoning and can talk to ghosts. Maybe the one coincides with the other?

"That sometimes certain doses of jade can give a person sight," she says. "But sight doesn't necessarily mean you have necromancy or can speak to ghosts. It just means a connection to the supernatural."

"But I've been speaking to Sawyer for a couple weeks and only put the necklace on yesterday," I point out. "So, I highly doubt it's doing it."

She gives me an intense, pressing look. "Yeah, but according to that article, the mountains are full of it. And the mountains completely surround the town."

I drum my fingers on top of my leg, contemplating. "But, if that's what's causing mine and Ev's little spirit chatting abilities, then wouldn't the entire town be having conversations with the dead?"

She lifts a shoulder. "Some people are more sensitive to

supernatural abilities. Maybe that's why. Honestly, I need to look into it more. I ran out of time last night."

"Speaking of time ..." Kennedy glances at the clock on the dash. "We need to get to school before we're late."

I reach for the door to get out. "I still need to tell you guys what I just overheard Dixon and Rylen say and what I found out about the blue car."

"And about the slime," Ev adds, seeming extremely distracted.

"Slime?" Kennedy and Embry's eyes bulge.

Then Kennedy raises her hands in front of her. "Okay, this crap is getting too strange for me."

"You want out?" I ask as I wrap my fingers around the door handle.

Kennedy shakes her head. "Not a chance. I was just pointing that out."

Nodding, I glance from Embry to Ev. "What about you two? You still in, or are you out?"

"I'm in," Kennedy says after a second ticks by.

Ev is far more reluctant to answer. "I'm still in."

"Are you sure?" I double-check. "I don't want you making yourself sick over this."

She nods. "I'm fine." She faces forward. "It's not like I can just forget everything that's happened. Walking away ... it's not possible anymore."

I understand how she feels, but that doesn't mean I want her making herself ill over this.

"Well, it's always an option." I shove open the door. "Anyone want to ride with me to school?"

"Just leave your car here and ride with us," Kennedy suggests as she checks her messages on her phone. "That way, you guys can tell us about this"—she trades a skeptical look with Embry—"slime thing."

"It sounds very *Ghostbusters* to me," Embry remarks as she adjusts the leather bands on her wrists.

"I honestly don't know what it is. But yeah, let me grab my bag, and I'll ride with you." Leaving my skateboard in the car, I hope out and grab my backpack from the trunk of my car.

"You know, I don't know why you don't just haul that thing to the dump," Dixon's annoying voice sails over my shoulder.

My gaze flicks to his computer sitting in my trunk, and I casually drop my bag onto it before turning around. "What, you mean you?" I tap my finger against my lips. "Yeah, I thought about it, but figured you'd have Daddy get me in trouble."

His lip curls. "Daddy, huh? Is that what your mom calls him when she's whoring herself out to him?"

My jaw ticks. "You say that like it makes my mom a terrible person. But, if that's true, then your dad's equally as bad. You know, since he pays to have sex with my mom. Well, bad enough that he has to pay someone to have sex with him."

His eyes narrow into slits. "You know, one of these days

you're going to look back at these little moments between us and regret ever opening your mouth."

My pulse sprints and my skin dampens, but I battle to keep my tone even. "Is that a threat?"

"No, a warning." His lips start to tug upward, but the smile falters when his gaze travels to something over my shoulder.

I peer behind me and spot Rylen walking toward us with his board tucked under his arm.

"Hey," he greets me with a warm smile.

"Hey," I greet him back, but my smile is much more forced.

He must notice, too, because he fumbles to maintain his cheerful demeanor.

"Everything okay?" He stops in front of me, his gaze bouncing between Dixon and me.

I nod. "Yep. Everything's fantastic."

He continues to smile, but I can tell he's struggling. "I've never noticed you here this early before. Did you get up early?"

I nod, watching him closely. "Yeah, I had a couple errands to run and had a little time leftover, so I thought I'd hang out here for a bit. Get some extra practice in."

He bobs his head up and down. "I was going to come over and say hi when I saw you skate up, but you looked really into it, and I didn't want to bother you."

I assess him closely, his kind smile, his warm eyes, and then I note the lack of heat against my neck. I don't understand any of it. Rylen has always seemed like a good guy, and the necklace seems convinced of the same thing, yet the facts point in the opposite direction. And with Dixon right behind me.

Maybe I'm wrong about what the necklace can do.

Sawyer, now would be a fantastic time to chime in.

I internally sigh when his voice doesn't appear.

"Yeah, I was—"

Kennedy honks her horn while shouting out her window, "Mak, we gotta go!"

"Where's the love, Kennedy?" Dixon shouts back at her with a grin.

She flips him the middle finger then rolls up the window.

I turn to Rylen and plaster on a fake, apologetic smile. "Sorry, but the boss says it's time to go."

Rylen stuffs his hand into his pocket. "I'll see you at school today, right? You'll be there?"

"Yeah, I will." Well, that is, unless someone attacks me again.

A chill crawls up my spine. Would they come after me again? I've still been digging around into things, but not so out in the open. However, if there are cameras around ... Wait, could there be a camera in my house?

I shiver at the thought and make a mental note to inspect the house thoroughly when I get home today. And to have Kennedy, Embry, and Ev do the same to theirs.

"See you later, Mak." Rylen waves as he starts for his car.

As he brushes past me, I swear I hear him whisper in the faintest voice, "Be careful." When I glance at him, though, he simply smiles and walks off, leaving me to wonder if I heard him correctly or not.

I need to be careful around him.

I wait until Dixon and Rylen are in their cars before picking up my backpack. Then I discreetly stuff Dixon's computer inside my bag and scoot back into Kennedy's car before pulling out Dixon's computer again.

"What're you doing?" Embry asks as I open the laptop.

"Looking through his shit really quick before I turn this thing in for the reward money." I hold down the power button, but the battery is dead. "Anyone got a power adapter?"

Ev nods as she picks up her backpack from off her floor and digs through it. "See if this fits." She hands me a cord.

I plug it in and smile. "Yep, we're good to go." I crack my knuckles. "Now, if I can just figure out his login password, I might be able to get some answers as to what the hell is going on—"

Ding. Ding. Ding. Ding.

Mine, Embry, Ev, and Kennedy's phones go off simultaneously.

With puzzled expressions, we all dig out our phones and check the incoming text.

Message from Shadow Cove High: Dear students, due to the recent thefts and security camera outages, school will be canceled Wednesday, March 24th to Friday, March 26th. Students will return to school on Monday, March 29th after we install a new camera system and update our security. Thank you for your cooperation.

Embry lifts her gaze to mine. "Canceling school for security camera maintenance? Is that a real thing?"

"It seems like something they could do while school is going on," Ev says after she finishes reading the message.

"Unless they're putting in new cameras for a new system," I say. "Like the same system that's apparently all over Shadow Cove. And they don't want anyone to know about it."

Ev's face slightly pales. "You could be right." She gulps. "So, what do we do now?"

I shrug. "Take the next couple days to figure out what the hell is going on in Shadow Cove." I hand her Dixon's computer. "Starting with you breaking Dixon's passcode."

She rubs her lips together then nods with a lot less reluctance than I expected. "I can do that. I'm still working on Liam's phone, too. But I can work on both for a bit."

"Awesome." I turn toward Embry. "Are you ready to hit up the coroner's office?"

She grins deviously. "I thought you'd never ask."

THIRTY-THREE

LOCATION: KENNEDY'S CAR
TIME: 7:48 AM
DATE: WEDNESDAY, MARCH 24th

During the drive to the coroner's office, I tell the three of them what I overheard Dixon and Rylen say. Then I give Kennedy and Embry a recap of what happened at the doctor's office with both the slime, Scarlett, and Trysten. I also give them the details I found out about the ads and the dark blue car. By the time I'm finished, everyone looks a bit ill.

"So, you think someone is using the wanted ads to lure people into ... well, into what exactly?" Ev asks after I'm finished.

"I'm not sure. The other night, I thought maybe for human trafficking. I mean, there is that escorting site linked to the logo of the society." I recline on my seat and cross my arms. "But I can't figure out the connection to the cameras and to the deaths."

"Maybe there isn't a connection," Kennedy suggests. "Maybe they're two separate things. I mean, you did say Don and the mayor acted as if they were being watched, too, and they're probably part of the society."

"Maybe, but then, who's watching the society?" I think aloud. "I really doubt it's the police. Not only because I'm almost positive they're connected, but because police don't generally hotwire an entire town with security cameras."

"Maybe there are so many people in the society that they have to." Embry takes a swig from a water bottle. "Maybe, in order to find evidence, they have to look every-where because almost everyone is covering it up."

"That could be a theory," I agree with a nod. "But, for some reason, I have a feeling that all of this is connected. From my brother's death, to the tons of disappearances in town, to Ev and I being able to talk to the dead, to how strange Scarlett was acting."

"Even the slime?" Kennedy asks, making a turn down the side road that leads to the coroner's office.

"I was thinking about that last night. The slime could've been from Scarlett's supplies, though that wouldn't explain why it smelled like lake water." Ev types a couple of buttons on the keyboard of Dixon's laptop, trying to break through his passcode. "We'll know for sure in about a week or so after I hear back from my friend at the university."

"A week?" I frown. "That's how long this will take?"

She double-clicks the mouse. "I had to mail it in this morning, and even with express shipping, it won't arrive there for two days. The tests could take anywhere from a couple hours to a handful of days, depending on how rare the substance is."

"Crap, I was hoping it'd be quicker." While Ev may think the slime is unrelated to what's going on, I'm not so sure I agree. After the dream I had ... how the lake fleetingly looked the same color green ... Sure, it could've just been the day's events leaking into my dream. Or it could've been something else.

"I still think it might be unrelated," Ev says, clicking some more keys and causing the computer screen to flash.

"Maybe." I absentmindedly spin one of my skateboard wheels. "Has anyone ever noticed if the lake ever gets a green tint to it?"

Embry looks up from her phone with her forehead creased. "No, but I'm really damn curious why you asked that."

I give a shrug. "I had this dream last night. Sawyer was in it, which wasn't too strange, but what was is that he made me hike to the top of a mountain and look down at the lake. When I did, the water briefly tinted the same color green as the slime. It was really weird."

"It might have happened because we found the slime only a couple hours before you went to bed," Kennedy throws the idea out there. "I think that sometimes happens with dreams, right?"

"Yeah, but ..." I pick at a loose thread on my jeans. "The other night, I had a dream where Sawyer told me to look in his room for something—something important. When I awoke, I found all that stuff hidden in his closet floor." I fiddle with the vial hanging around my neck, dragging it back and forth across the string. "Maybe it was a coincidence, but honestly, it feels like I'm actually talking to him whenever it happens."

An unnerving silence settles between us, making me regret opening my mouth.

"I believe you," Embry speaks first. "Stories like that are actually common on SC Shadow of the Undead Inc. It's crazy how many different ways people can communicate with the dead."

"We could go look at the lake water?" Kennedy proposes. "See if it is tinted green. Although, I'd rather not climb up a mountain to do it."

"Yeah, I think we should. After we talk to Legend, we can drive out there. To the *shore*," I emphasize when Kennedy frowns. "See if we can see what I saw in the dream."

Kennedy and Embry agree, while Ev has a bit more reservations, but in the end, she agrees.

THIRTY-FOUR

When we pull up to the coroner's office, the parking lot is mostly vacant, except for a couple of cars parked out back. As an extra bonus, the building doesn't have the symbol on it. Both are good signs. Now, hopefully, Legend won't be busy, and I can ask him a few questions without the worry of being overheard. Unless, of course, one of the security cameras is inside.

I frown at the thought. Man, I'm going to have to be extra careful about what I say and keep a low profile while we're here.

"Hey, Ken, how about you drop us off, and then go park somewhere else?" I slip on my jacket.

"Why?" Kennedy asks as she pulls up to the front entrance of the small brick building.

"I just want to make sure we're careful." I zip up my jacket and pull the hood over my head. "You never know who is watching."

Nodding, she leaves the engine running as she parks beside the curb.

Noting my lame-ass, desperate-times-call-for-desperate-measures disguise, Embry follows my lead and pulls her hood over her head, as well.

"Hopefully, by the time you guys get out, I'll have gained access to Dixon's computer." Ev picks up her coffee mug from the cupholder and takes a sip.

"How intense is his security?" I pat my pockets to make sure I have my phone and can of pepper spray, just in case this plan takes a turn for the worse. Not that I don't trust Legend. I'm just really starting to not trust this town.

"He has some pretty state of the art security software on it." Ev sets her coffee mug back down. "But nothing I can't handle. Although, it makes me wonder what he has on here to have such high security access programs."

"Hopefully, we'll find out soon." I push open the door.

"Wait. What should I do while you're in there?" Kennedy asks as I start to get out.

I stick my hand into my pocket, grab the bottle of vita-mins, and hand them to her. "See if you can figure out what these are."

Nodding, she takes the bottle from me, and then I hop out of the car.

"I'll call you when we're done so you can swing back by and pick us up." I start to close the door as I say, "Be careful."

"You, too," she calls out.

Nodding, I close the door, round the back of the car, and meet Embry on the sidewalk. I wait until Kennedy drives away before I approach the entrance.

"So, what's our game plan?" Embry whispers.

"Well, I'm going to chat with Legend for a few minutes and see if he'll just answer my questions about Bria's death. If he refuses or seems like he might be lying, you distract him while I excuse myself to the bathroom so I can sneak into his office and break into his files."

"What should I talk to him about? Like, dead bodies and stuff?"

"Talk to him about that SC Shadow of the Undead Inc. I think he's into that stuff. And you never know; maybe you'll learn something new from him."

"All right, that's doable." She slips her hands into the pocket of her black jacket that's embellished with silver buckles. "Is he a cool guy, then? This Legend dude, I mean?"

"Yeah, I met him a handful of times when I was working with my dad." I yank open the door. "He's pretty chill, so I think we'll be fine, even if we get caught."

She gives me a pressing look. "Unless he's working for the society."

"Doubtful," I say as I step inside. "And there's no mark on the door."

Embry nods as she follows me to the front counter where a woman with short, dark purple hair and square-framed glasses sits. She's the receptionist here, but I can't recall her name. Well, either that or she never gave it to me.

She eyeballs us as we approach. "Can I help you?"

I rest my arm on the counter. "Yeah, I was wondering if I could talk to Legend."

Her gaze flits to my hood, and then she reaches for the phone. "Hold on." She dials a couple numbers then puts the receiver to her ear. "Hey, there's a girl here who wants to talk to you." She bobs her head up and down, then her gaze zeroes in on me. "I don't know. Hold on." She covers the receiver with her hand. "He wants to know who's asking and the reason behind your visit."

"It's Mak. You've met me a couple times," I say as Embry moves up beside me. "And I'd just like to chat with him for a bit, like he used to do with my dad."

Her expression flashes with annoyance as she removes her hand from the receiver and repeats what I said. Then she nods, her irritation growing. By the time she hangs up, she's glaring at me.

"You can go on back to his office. Just make it quick. Legend is a busy man."

"Are those your words or his?" I can't help asking.

Her eyes flash with fury. "Just make it quick."

Smiling sweetly, I start toward the narrow, fluorescently lit hallway that leads to the backroom where Legend's office is located. Embry strolls beside me, peering around at the filing cabinets cramming up the space and the strange, skeleton-like wall art.

Embry leans in and whispers, "What's up with the bitchy secretary?"

I give a half-shrug. "I've only met her a couple times before, and she's always been like that. I think she might have a thing for Legend, but Legend's never been into her. I think she thought I was here to, like, *see* him, see him, and was being territorial."

"How old is Legend?" Embry asks. "Young, I'm guessing, or hoping since you're seventeen and she thought he'd date you."

"I think he's twenty-two."

"Holy shit, I thought he'd be, like, seventy and bald with a beer gut and a creepy mustache."

I chuckle. "Why?"

"Stereotyping from movies, I guess. And doesn't take like a long time to become a coroner?"

I stop in front of the office door and knock. "I think he was super smart and went to college really young. And FYI, I don't think he's going to fall into your stereotype at all."

"Why? What does he look like—" She cuts herself off as the door swings open.

Legend is standing on the other side, decked out in a pair of black pants and a matching button-down shirt with the sleeves rolled up. The outfit is topped off with a vest, the pockets decorated with chains, a series of steel and leather bracelets, and thick black boots. His black hair is a bit longer than the last time I saw him, reaching chin level, and like always, his dark, long eyelashes give the impression he's wearing eyeliner.

"Mak," he greets me with a small smile, motioning for us to come in. "Long time, no see." He eyeballs my hood drawn up over my head. "Nice get-up. Playing hooky, huh?"

"Nah. School's actually canceled today because of some security maintenance thing." I step inside his small, cluttered office. "Sorry I haven't stopped by. I've been meaning to, but just got caught up with other stuff."

"No worries." His gaze lands on Embry and question marks flood his eyes. "Who's this?"

"Oh, this is Embry," I introduce. "She's a friend of mine."

"Hey." Embry gives him the barest of smiles.

"It's nice to meet you, Embry." He smiles at her before redirecting his attention to me. "Mak, I just want to say that I'm so sorry to hear about your dad, but I have faith that he'll show up again."

"Really?" I scratch my neck. "Because no one else seems to think so."

"Well, screw what everyone else thinks." He heads toward his desk that's covered with stacks of papers, files, and folders. "I knew your dad pretty well, probably better than most of the people in town, and I know he's not the sort of man who would just up and take off like that with no plans on coming back." He drops down in a chair.

"He didn't say anything to you about leaving, did he?" I plop down in a chair on the other side of the desk.

Embry takes a seat beside me, her gaze skimming the room.

He shakes his head, strands of hair falling across his forehead. "No, but I'm not surprised he took off."

My brow pops up. "Why? Because I sure as hell was."

He presses his lips together then slants forward and lowers his voice. "How much do you know about the story your dad was working on before he disappeared?"

"You mean, his theory that this town was covering up murders and stuff?" I lean forward, too. "Because that wasn't a story. That was an obsession he had with trying to solve Sawyer's death."

"That's not what it was." He shakes his head, his gaze flickering in Embry's direction.

"She's cool," I assure him. "I promise."

He nibbles on his bottom lip, considering something. "Your dad was on to something big, Mak. Not just about Sawyer's death, but about a lot of the deaths here in Shadow Cove. Deaths not everyone knows about. Deaths I don't even get called in to investigate. Deaths that no one is supposed to know about."

"Then how do you know these deaths even exist?"

He nervously looks from Embry to me. "Because of the destroyed files your dad found."

"What destroyed files?" I ask. "And how did he find them if they were destroyed?"

"Because they weren't really destroyed." He sweeps his hair out of his eyes as he slants closer. "Someone—he never said who—was supposed to destroy the files, but they gave them to your dad instead so he could hide them. I'm not positive on all the details in those files—he never showed them to me—but he said a lot of the papers contained undocumented deaths in Shadow Cove. And not just that, but the cause of the deaths was strange."

I glance at Embry, who raises a brow. I'm fairly certain I know what she's thinking. That strange is becoming a common theme the further we dig into this.

"Strange how?" we both ask.

He looks back and forth between the two of us. "He never told me; said it was too dangerous."

"Are you just saying that to protect me?"

He shakes his head, but I still wonder if he's lying.

"I really don't know. And I only mentioned the files to warn you that you need to be careful." He slumps back in his seat. "Your father was chasing a dangerous trail, and he may have pissed some pretty powerful people off. You and your mom need to be careful."

I rest my arms on the desk. "Do you know who the people are?"

He shakes his head, but again, I have the feeling he is lying.

"But, considering we live in Shadow Cove, it could practically be anyone."

I search his eyes, questioning if he knows more than he's letting on. If he does, he doesn't want to cave. "What about Bria Brookenrose?"

His frown deepens. "What about her?"

"Is she one of the strange deaths?"

His lips part. "Mak, I really don't think you should go down this road. It could be dangerous."

"I'm not going down any road," I lie. "Look, there's a rumor going around school that Sawyer and Bria died the same way, and I want—no, need—to know if it's true, because people are saying awful things."

He massages the back of his neck tensely as he studies me, then lowers his hand and leans forward again. "Sawyer and Bria's deaths were very similar, but I don't believe they did it to themselves—never did. They may have had morphine in their systems, but they also had these scratches all over their bodies."

I swallow down the vomit burning at the back of my throat, feeling sick to my stomach.

"What caused the scratches?" Embry wonders, slanting forward. "Were they, like, animal scratches?"

Legend shakes his head. "See, that's the thing; it looked like an animal, but I couldn't identify the scratches myself, so I was going to get an expert's opinion." He shifts in his seat. "Then the mayor and Don Jennings showed up and took the files from me. They told me I was no longer to look into Bria's or Sawyer's deaths. They took my files on a couple of other similar cases, as well."

Nerves bubble through my stomach. "You think they were all killed by ... by the same animal?"

"If it was an animal, it's rare as hell," he says, "since I couldn't match up the scratches to a species."

"What else could've done it besides an animal?" Embry asks with a bit of fear in her tone.

"That's what I'd really like to find out," Legend replies, his gaze landing on me. "Mak, I don't want you to go looking further into this. I just want you to be aware that something odd is going on in this town and possibly something dangerous. You need to keep your guard up, okay?"

I nod, promising him I will. Well, at least keep my guard up. As for not looking into it, Ev said it best. Now that I know this sort of stuff exists in our town, I can't just pretend it doesn't, especially when the people I care about could be in danger.

After we leave the office, I call Kennedy to come pick us up. When she pulls up to the curb, Embry and I hurry into the car.

The moment Kennedy speeds off down the street, she says, "Well, the pills aren't vitamin B."

I take the bottle as she hands it to me. "What are they, then?"

Kennedy trades a worried look with Ev, and then Ev says, "They're laced with jade."

"Those sorts of pills actually exist?" I ask in horror.

"Illegally, yes," Ev replies quietly. "And the pills were manufactured here. Look at the bottom of the bottle."

I glance under the bottle, and my eyes widen at the *Made in Shadow Cove* stamp.

"Why the hell would Scarlett try to get you to take jade pills?" Embry questions, slipping off the hood from her head.

I shrug, lowering my hood, as well. "But I need to find out before she realizes I haven't taken them and tries more drastic measures."

I have to wonder if I already took some since Embry said they can be linked to necromancy and I can sometimes talk to the dead. But, since I've never taken them knowingly, that means someone had to have given them to me without my knowing.

THIRTY-FIVE

LOCATION: SHADOW COVE LAKE
TIME: 10:36 AM
DATE: WEDNESDAY, MARCH 24th

"I don't know ... It doesn't look very green to me," Kennedy says as she, Embry, and I stare out at the rippling lake.

Ev is sitting in the car just behind us, working nonstop to access Dixon's computer and Liam's phone while Kennedy, Embry, and I have spent the last ten minutes attempting to spot any sort of greenish tint to the lake, but we haven't had any success yet.

Clouds cover the sky, a thin fog laces through the forest enclosing the lake, and the air smells similar to the slime we found last night. Not to mention we're the only ones here.

The entire scene is beyond eerie and brings back memories of yesterday, when I woke up here all alone. I half expect Lispy Larry to pop out from the trees and attack me again. After all, I'm still digging around into other people's business. Although, I haven't done much that involved Lispy Larry ... *yet*. As soon as I find a way to do it safely, I'm going to find out what he's hiding in that damn ghost house of his that seems to be the town's hotspot to where people vanish.

"Maybe it's because it's cloudy." Embry tips her head up toward the sky. "If the sun was out, the water might not look so dark and we could get a better view."

"Or maybe we're going about this all wrong," I mutter, wrapping my arms around myself. "Maybe the only way to see what the lake truly looks like is to go up there." I lift my gaze to the mountains across from us.

Kennedy hastily shakes her head. "There's no way in hell I'm climbing up that mountain. Sorry, Mak, I love you, but I despise hiking."

"I'm not a fan, either, but I think I might eventually have to." My gaze scans the lofty trees around us. "The forest poses a bit of a problem, though."

Her brows scrunch. "Why?"

I lift my shoulders. "Because, if what Legend told me is true, then Bria and Sawyer were killed by some strange, unknown animal. And since their bodies turned up in the lake, the animal could very well be in these trees."

Tension ripples through her body. "Dammit, why did you have to say that while we are standing out here?" She whirls around and hurries back to the car, her heels getting stuck in the dirt.

After she's safely inside, Embry says, "You really think that's a possibility? That some strange animal is in these woods attacking people?"

"It's part of my theory. But, since Bria and Sawyer also had morphine in their systems, I don't think an animal was the only cause of their deaths."

"So, you think what? That someone doped them up, and then left them here by the lake and this animal got ahold of them?"

I swallow a shaky breath. "Maybe. Or maybe someone doped them up then hauled them in the forest *for* the animal to attack."

She drags her fingers through her fiery red hair. "Then, that would mean someone knows about this unknown animal. And that this unknown animal is dangerous."

"I know."

A moment of understanding fear passes between us that gets shattered by Kennedy squealing, "Guys! Get your asses in the car. Ev just busted into Dixon's computer and Liam's phone."

And just like that, my fear goes *poof* as eagerness rushes through me.

"You ready to do some snooping on the rich kids lives?" I ask Embry.

"You know it." We bump fists then hurry to the car and climb into the back seat.

"What do you have?" I ask Ev as I shut the door.

"Well, I've only had time to glance through Liam's

phone, but I did find a couple of texts that were interesting." She hands me his phone. "Read through the message thread I left open."

Swiping my finger along the screen, I begin to read.

Liam: I'm not sure which one of them has the video. It could be more than one.

AE: Well, you better figure it out, or you're going into the woods soon. Do you want that, Liam? You want to see what really lies in the dark?

Liam: All right, I'll find a way to figure it out. I'll steal all my friends' computers if I have to. Just please don't make me go out there, man.

AE: Maybe I should anyway. It's about time you and your friends learned the extent of what the society is willing to do to protect their own dark secrets.

Liam: Look, I get that we messed up, but you have to take into consideration the families we come from. Eventually, one day, we could be joining the society and that could cause a lot of problems for you.

AE: Careful, Liam, it's starting to sound like you're threatening me.

Liam: I swear I'm not. I'm just stating a fact.

AE: Well, fact or not, you should know by now that I don't give a shit about the society. In

the grand scheme of things, they're a blip in this arrangement. A very small blip that can easily be taken care of.

Liam: I understand. And like I said, I'll get the computers to you ASAP.

AE: Good. And I don't need to remind you of what will happen if you or any of your friends in that stupid club of yours repeat what they saw on that video. You all may think you're above their rules, but you're not.

The message ends there.

"Are there any more of these?" I glance up at Ev.

She shakes her head. "No, but from what I can tell, Liam is the sort of guy who doesn't leave messages on his phone for very long."

Crap.

I scroll through the message threads just to double-check, but nothing of interest jumps out at me. Then I go back and reread the message thread with AE again.

"Who do you think this AE is?" Embry asks as she leans over and skim-reads the messages.

"Well, I'm not positive, but I'm wondering if it might be Alexander Garyinford."

"The owner of the blue car that was following us?"

I nod. "Yep. But that's just a guess. I'm sure there are a ton of people in this town with the initials AE. I can look it up and create a list." I tap open the internet app.

"Um, guys," Ev says, worry cramming her voice. "I think I found something."

I set the phone down on my lap and lean forward. Embry does the same.

Ev positions Dixon's laptop so we can all see the screen. "It's a video file labeled: *What Lies in the Dark*. It caught my attention because it's the only file that has password access on it."

What lies in the dark.

What lies in the dark.

What lies in the darkness.

Liam had said that to me right before he doped me up; that I needed to let what lies in the darkness stay in the darkness.

Chills break out across my skin. "Did you figure out the password yet?"

She slowly nods. "Should we watch it?"

I rub my lips together, somehow knowing whatever is on that video is going to be terrible, yet I find myself nodding.

With a shaky finger, Ev clicks *play*.

The screen starts out dark, but then a flicker of light illuminates the screen. It takes me a moment to figure out what it is—moonlight.

As the light cascades across the surroundings, I realize the video was recorded in the very forest nearby.

Holy shit.

"*Do you hear that?*" the person recording whispers—no, Dixon whispers. I'd recognize his voice from anywhere.

"*What the hell is that?*" someone else says, his voice unrecognizable.

They grow quiet at the sound of branches snapping.

"*It sounds like it's getting closer.*"

"*Shh, you idiot. It's going to hear us.*" The camera lowers, as if Dixon ducks down.

More branches snap, then the most awful, inhuman growl rips through the air. It's followed by a scream. A scream that sounds like it belongs to a woman.

"*Shit, man, I think it saw us …*" The guy trails off as a pair of green, glowing eyes appears through the branches in front of them.

It snaps its teeth, growling, then charges at Dixon and his friend.

"*Run!*" one of them shouts.

Footsteps. Growling. Another Scream. Branches snapping left and right.

The noises continue until Dixon and his friend make it to a car. They set the camera down on the console, the sounds of their heavy breathing filling up the silence.

"*What the hell was that thing?*" Dixon's friend asks breathlessly.

"*I don't know, but whatever it was, I think it just killed someone.*"

A beat of silence ticks by, and then his friend whispers, "*You think this has anything to do with* them."

Dixon laughs hollowly. "*Oh, I think it has everything to do with them.*"

"So, what are we going to do with the footage, then?" his friend asks. *"If they find out we know about ... that, they'll probably fucking feed us to that creature."*

"We hide it while we find out more," Dixon says. *"Until we gather enough proof and figure out what the hell is going on in this cursed town."*

The video cuts off, the computer screen turning black.

"Holy shit," Kennedy breathes out. "What the hell did we just see?"

"A murder? A monster? The fact that Dixon and his unknown friend are digging around into stuff like we are?" I shake my head in shock. "I honestly have no fucking clue how to process any of this."

Ev looks like she's on the verge of crying. "Guys, can we please go somewhere else? I really don't want to be near these trees right now."

"Yeah, I think going somewhere else is a good idea," Kennedy agrees, starting up her engine.

As she drives forward, I twist around in my seat and stare at the trees behind us. I've never thought about it much, but now that I am, I realize I have never seen anyone going into those trees. There are also no trails. Same with the mountains around us. No one hikes in Shadow Cove, yet the scenery is prime for hiking. Why is that? What keeps people away? Especially when the mountains are supposedly filled with jade?

"Shit," Kennedy curses, slamming on her brakes.

When I turn around to see the reason behind her

sudden stop, I half expect a glowing, green-eyed creature to be standing in front of the car. Nope. Instead, I see Dixon's luxury car blocking the road. The only way around them is through the trees by foot which, yeah, is so not happening.

"Hide the computer," I hiss to Ev as I toss Liam's phone under the seat. "And lock the doors."

Ev fumbles to shut the laptop then shoves it under her seat right as four figures hope out of Dixon's car and head toward us.

My fingers curl into fists. "Dixon, Liam, Trysten, and Rylen. Why am I not surprised?" Though, I have to admit, the latter hurts like a bitch.

"What do you think they want?" Ev whispers, clutching the edge of her seat.

"I don't know, but I'll beat their asses if they try anything." Embry pops her neck and knuckles then glances at me. "You got your pepper spray and Taser on you?"

"Yep." I pick up my backpack, grab both, and hand Ev the pepper spray. "If you have to use it, aim for the eyes, okay?"

"What about me?" Kennedy asks as she eyeballs the guys as they start down the road toward us. "What should I use?"

Embry digs a pair of brass knuckles out of her pocket and hands them to Kennedy.

"Those won't do any good," Kennedy scoffs. "I don't even know how to punch."

"Like this." Embry demonstrates by tapping her fist against the palm of her hand.

When Kennedy frowns down at the brass knuckles, I snatch them from her and hand her my Taser. She gives me a grateful look as I slip the brass knuckles on.

"One zap should send them to the ground," I tell her, then glance at Embry. "Do I even want to know why you have this?" I lift my hand with the brass knuckles.

Embry shrugs. "I thought maybe they'd come in handy sometime. Guess I was right." She gives a pressing look at the four guys walking side by side toward us, all mafia style.

"Dude, I think they've seen too many mobster movies." I snicker, and so do Embry and Kennedy. Ev can barely breathe.

"Ev, relax. We got this." I pat her shoulder. "For all we know, they're only here to hang out by the lake." I don't believe my own words. Not even a little bit. Nor do I find it simply coincidental that they showed up here right after we watched that video.

Before I can come up with any theories as to why, they reach the car.

Dixon and Trysten eyeball us, while Liam glares and Rylen stands there, looking uncomfortable.

"What're you guys doing up here all by yourselves?" Dixon asks with a smirk.

Kennedy cracks her window. "That's really none of your damn business. And you better move your damn car out of my way before I decide to just slam into it."

Dixon's smirk only grows. "Will you get your sexy panties out of a bunch? I'll move my car in a minute." He pauses, chewing on his bottom lip before his gaze cuts to me. "Just as soon as you give me back my computer."

I crack my window with my fist balled. "I don't have your computer, rich boy, so move your stupid ass out of the way."

"Mak," he tsks me as he approaches my window. "Maybe you better think about what you just saw on that video before you start trying to lie to me." He crouches down, putting his face up to the window. "Or I might decide to take you for a little stroll in those trees."

The wheels in my head turn, like gears clicking into place. I was right. Them being here right after we watched the video isn't coincidental. They know we have his computer, just like they know we watched the video and looked through Liam's phone. Because, somehow, they bugged me. The question is: how? Since they just recently learned about it, it has to be something they did recently. Maybe they somehow did it to Kennedy's car? Or ...

My gaze travels to my skateboard resting beside my feet and zeroes in on the brand-new bearings I just put on last night. For the most part, I kept the bearings and board in my trunk, out of earshot, except for the last few hours. The last few hours my friends and I have spent talking about Dixon's computer and Liam's phone and all sorts of other crazy stuff. We also talked about going up to the lake where people rarely hang out. Where Dixon and his friends could easily get the computer back without being seen.

A wave of anger storms through me as I reach up and snatch the Taser from Kennedy's hand.

"What're you doing?" she protests as I grab my skateboard from off the floor and stuff the Taser into my jacket pocket.

"Lock the doors again after I get out." Before anyone can say anything, I manually unlock my door and hop out of the car.

"So, this is what the bearings were about?" I direct my question at Rylen.

He massages the back of his neck, guilt rising in his eyes. "Mak, I didn't just—"

I hold up my hand. "Spare me the details." I march over to the lake.

"Mak, don't," Rylen shouts, rushing over to me.

"Why? You afraid I'm going to ruin the bugs or something?"

"No, I don't give a shit about that." He strides alongside me, desperation gleaming in his eyes. "You can't touch the water right now."

"I'm not going to." I stop on the shoreline. "The board is." Even though it nearly kills me, I lift my arm, preparing to chuck my skateboard into the water.

Rylen moves in front of me, pleading, "Please don't do this, okay? I know you don't think you can trust me right now, but you can. I swear." He swallows hard. "And I can prove it to you." He bends down to pick up a small pebble.

"Careful, Rylen," Trysten warns. "Too much force will put their system back up. And we only have minutes as it is."

"Is he talking about the security cameras all over town?" I wonder, hugging my board against my chest.

Rylen crooks a brow at me. "You know about those?"

"Don't you already know I know about those?" I challenge. "After all, you've been listening in on my conversations."

"Not all of them," he assures me. "And I regret doing it, but I sort of had to."

"Why?" I demand.

"To see what you already know," he whispers. "To see if we should bring you in on this or not."

My heart thunders in my chest. "In on what?"

He puts his finger to his lips then chucks the pebble into the lake. It barely makes a ripple, but that motion makes the entire lake alter, the water briefly turning green.

I swallow hard, my fingernails digging into the skateboard. "What the hell is going on?"

Rylen turns toward me. "Nothing in this town is what it seems."

"Yeah, I'm starting to realize that." I blink away from the lake and focus on him. "What else do you know?"

He starts to reach for me then pulls away, only to reach forward again and tuck a strand of my hair behind my ear. "I know this entire town is controlled by something. I know there are things that only haunt people's nightmares living in these woods. I know hardly anyone can be trusted." He dips his lips toward my ear. "I also know that Trysten has been trying to get you to go to a post office box and try to unlock it because he thinks you have the key. Don't do it, okay? Trysten isn't a bad guy, but he'll do just about anything to get what's inside that box, even if it means *they* figure out you're on to them."

I think about the key I found that is currently in my pocket; how something had been filed off the front of it. Could it be to this post office box? If so, why did Sawyer have it and what on earth is inside the box?

"Who the hell is *they*?" My heart hammers in my chest. "And what the hell is in that box?"

"Some files he had your dad hide for him," he whispers, nearly knocking the breath out of me.

Files.

Files.

Like the destroyed files Legend told me about?

"As for the *they*," Rylen continues, "that's going to take a lot more time than we have right now to explain."

"Does it have to do with the society?"

"Yes and no."

"That literally makes no sense."

"I know. And I wish I had time to explain more." He moves away to look me in the eyes. "You know about the cameras all over town, right?"

"Yeah."

"Well, right now, they're temporarily shut down by a virus Trysten installed in the system. But it'll only last a few minutes before they figure out what's going on and reboot it. Once the cameras are back up, they'll be able to see us out here." Worry flashes in his eyes. "And if they know what we're talking about" —he gulps—"well, you saw what was in those trees, right?"

My chest constricts as I nod.

He lets out an uneven breath as he checks the time on his watch. "We don't have a lot of time left. We need to be long gone from here by the time those cameras come back on so they don't grow suspicious. If you'll meet us at the address on the note that was left in your pocket, we can explain more."

"So, you left the note in my pocket?" I ask, and he nods. "It looked like Trysten's handwriting."

"He wrote the note, but I'm the one who slipped it into your pocket." He acts like it's no big deal, yet it is.

A really big, annoying deal.

I grit my teeth, beyond annoyed that he snuck out to the lake while I was passed out, only to put a cryptic note in my pocket then leave me there alone.

"Why can you tell me more but not now?" My irritation seeps into my tone. "Are you going to shut down the systems again or something?"

"No, that address is the only dead zone in the entire town. You have to be careful going in and out of it. Take the back entryway. It's the safest, okay?" He starts to step away, but I capture his arm.

"Something's not adding up," I tell him. "When Lispy Larry attacked me, why did you drive all the way up to the lake just to leave a note in my pocket and put Dixon's computer into my back seat when you guys clearly don't want me to have the computer? And how did you even know I was at the lake?"

A pucker forms at his brow. "I didn't put the note in your pocket when you were at the lake. I put it in there when I was giving you the bearings ... And we never gave you the computer, Mak. We thought you stole it from Larry, which kind of helped us out since we were planning on stealing it ourselves after Liam was blackmailed into giving Larry all our computers."

I frown. "I didn't—"

Careful, Mak. You have to keep some secrets to yourself, or they might not tell you all of theirs. And trust me, you need to know what they know. You just have to be careful about it. Everyone in this town is playing a game. You need to start playing your own.

I can hear you again. Relief washes over me.

For now ...

Huh?

Rylen's watch begins to beep, tearing me from my thoughts.

"Shit, we have to go. The cameras are about to reboot."

He briefly hesitates then threads his fingers through mine and guides me back to the car.

Embry got out of the car at some point and is arguing with Liam, but she stops and eyeballs me and Rylen's interlocked fingers as we approach. Then her brow arches in confusion, which is pretty much how I feel right now.

When we reach the car, she asks, "Is everything okay?"

I shrug, completely unsure how to explain everything to her.

Dixon glances at me and Rylen, then smirks. "So, are you two a thing now?"

I open my mouth to tell him to eff off, but Rylen beats me to the punch.

"Be quiet," Rylen warns, then turns toward me. "Get in the car and have Kennedy take you straight to your house, okay? Stay there as much as you can until Friday."

I nod, but it's a total lie. Rylen clearly has a lot to learn about me if he thinks I'm the sort of girl who'll just believe everything he says. While I'm not saying he's not being truthful, it doesn't mean I'm just going to believe everything he said. No, I'm going to do what I do best and find out the answers for myself.

Find out what the bleep is going on in this town.

I motion for Embry to get in the car as I start to open the back door, when Dixon sidesteps in front of me and crosses his arms.

"I want my computer back," he demands. "And Liam's phone."

I place one hand on my hip, the other still holding my board, and stare him down. "Then give me the thousand-dollar reward."

He laughs in my face. "You think I can't just take it."

Rylen starts to step toward us to intervene, and so does Embry, but I hold up my hand, indicating for them to stop. I want to take care of this myself.

Then I stick my hand into my pocket, grab the Taser, and lift it toward his face. "Back the fuck off before I zap your ass and knock you to the ground."

Trysten laughs, apparently finding the situation amusing, while Liam looks a bit apprehensive.

Dixon offers me his stupid, infamous cocky smirk as he surrenders his hands in front of him. Then he lets out a dark laugh and sticks a hand into his back pocket. "Fine, you want your money?" He pulls out his wallet that's filled with hundred-dollar bills and hands me a thousand dollars in cash. "There you go. But a little warning. At the rate you're going, it's not going to matter soon if you have that cash or not."

I clutch the money in my hand. "What's that supposed to mean?"

With a wicked glint in his eyes, he sticks out his hand. "I paid you the money, now give me back my computer."

"Fine." I stuff the money into my pocket, open the door, and have Ev give me his computer and grab Liam's phone. "There you go." I practically toss the items at him, and he almost drops both. "Pleasure doing business with you."

"Anytime." Like an asshole, he winks. "And if you ever get into your mom's business, look me up. I might know some people who are interested."

I glare at him as he turns and hikes back toward his car. Trysten offers me a wink before he walks away, too, while Liam doesn't even so much as look in my direction, smiling instead at Embry who flips him off and calls him a fucker.

"Please don't let Dixon affect your decision to meet us on Friday," Rylen says, lingering behind. "I know he's an asshole sometimes, but it's mostly because he's stressed out."

"Yeah, I'm sure it is," I reply, recalling how I overheard Dixon telling Rylen at the skate park how he likes to get under my skin.

He takes a tentative step toward me and leans in. At first, I think he's going to try to kiss me and I just about Taser his ass, but then I realize he's just leaning in to whisper something in my ear.

"And be careful of the jade in the caves, Mak," he whispers. "Once you touch it, nothing will ever be the same again. And of the cameras. If you're within their view, don't do anything that will bring suspicion to yourself."

"How do I know where they are, though?" I wonder. "From what we found out, there are thousands of them."

He moves back, his cheek brushing against mine. Then he places a hand on my shoulder and steers me around. "See that tree over there with the markings on it?"

I squint at the cluster of trees, then frown when I spot

the marking of Greek-like letters surrounding a circle. "Yeah, I see it."

He moves his lips close to my ear again. "Wherever those are, a camera is nearby."

"I thought that symbol belonged to a secret society," I say, highly aware that his hand is resting on my hip. "That's what Liam told me. Was he full of shit?"

"No, it is. They control the society," he utters softly, his face brushing against the back of my hair.

WTF. Did he just smell my hair?

Before I can figure that out, he steps away, whispering, "I have to go. I'll see you Friday night."

I wonder if he's referring to the date or meeting at this secret place. Then I laugh at myself.

Why on earth am I wondering about our date? I'm sure it was all part of their setup to bug me.

Irritation pulsates through me as I watch him walk away, so many questions burning at the tip of my tongue. Like, if what he said is true, then why did Trysten see the doctor for jade poisoning? And where are these caves full of jade? What does any of that have to do with this town, the societies, the monster living in the woods, and the cameras all over town? And why the hell was Scarlett trying to get me take jade pills?

What about what Embry found out about jade? That it can give a person supernatural, ghost-speaking abilities? I thought jade is what is causing mine and Ev's little gift of talking to the dead, but now Rylen's suggesting jade is bad. It doesn't make any sense.

Instead of chasing him down and demanding questions, I climb into the car.

I may not know much about what's going on, but the best way to get answers is to find them myself. Plus, I don't want to be near here when the cameras come back on. That much of Rylen's story I believe.

"What the hell was that about?" Kennedy asks after Embry and I scoot into the back seat.

I motion for her to drive as I close the door. "I'll tell you when we get to my house. Right now, we need to get far, far away from this lake."

With worry written all over her face, she shoves the shifter into drive and presses on the gas, kicking up a cloud of dirt.

As we pull away, I give one final glance over my shoulder at the trees. My heart nearly stops in my chest.

Peering through some branches is a set of glowing, green eyes.

Now you see why you have to be careful? Sawyer whispers. *If you don't, you're going to end up there. You're going to end up like me. Promise me, Mak. Promise me you'll be careful.*

I wrap my arms around myself as Kennedy steers onto the road and drives toward my house. *I will.*

That doesn't mean I won't stop searching for the truth.

Like I said before, now that I know what's out there, I can't just walk away.

I'm going to find out the truth no matter what it takes.

As we make the drive home silently, I come up with a few ideas as to what is going on.

1. Shadow Cove is under an experiment ran by some government agency about the causes and effects of jade on humans. And those monsters in the trees are what happens when someone gets high dosages.
2. The society—who this Alexander is a part of—is luring people into the ghost house and injecting them with jade for various reasons.
3. The whole town is being watched by some agency, and whenever someone goes looking into the truth, they get doped up or killed or fed to the monsters.

Yeah, that's pretty much all I've come up with, and the theories are way out there. Until I can get more answers, though, I can't come up with anything else.

And I will get more answers.

Of course my determination deflates a bit as we pull up to my house to find my mom waiting on the front porch with a huge-ass smile on her face. A smile that looks an awful lot like the creepy one Scarlett had on her face the other night.

Mak, get your guard up!

What's wrong with her? I ask, eyeballing my mom as Kennedy parks in the driveway.

The necklace starts to burn against my neck, scorching my skin.

Sawyer remains silent for so long that I figure he isn't going to answer, but then I hear it. The softest reply.

She took the jade, just like they made Dad. Now she's one of them.

Just like that, my heart nearly stops.

You know what happened to Dad?

He doesn't answer, leaving my head crammed with questions. Like, what on earth is wrong with my mom? What did the jade do to her? And if the same thing happened to my dad and my mom, then why is my mom here and my dad isn't?

Most of all, I wonder: who *they* are? This *they* that everyone keeps referring to. Who is this group or person who seems to be controlling the entire town? Is it the society? Someone else?

Who's in control?

That's the number one question I need to find the answer to before I end up either dead like Sawyer, gone like my dad, or like the person standing on my porch, looking completely possessed like half the damn people in this town —my mom.

"Dude, what's up with your mom?" Kennedy asks as she turns off the engine. "She looks like she's trying out at a clown audition or something."

"I have no idea." I open the door to get out. "Honestly, she looks like Scarlett did last night—"

The words are ripped from my tongue as at least a dozen uniformed officers barrel from the trees and from inside my house.

"What the hell?" My heart hammers in my chest as I climb back in and shut the car door.

A tall, broad officer stops at my door while more cops surround the car.

Ev starts freaking out, nearing toward hyperventilation. Embry tries to calm her down, while Kennedy is the epitome of cool.

"Kennedy Lee Everprice," an officer says as he yanks open the driver's side door, "get out of the car."

"Kennedy, what's going on?" I hiss as I lean forward.

"I don't know," she mutters, then lowers her head and ducks out of the car.

I shove on the door to get out, but the officer standing there stops me.

Embry tries the same thing, but an officer stops her, as well, leaving us trapped.

"Let her go!" I shout as an officer handcuffs her.

"Kennedy Lee Everprice," he says, steering her toward the end of the driveway, "you're under arrest for the murder of Mila Everprice."

My heart nearly stops beating. "No, there's no way Kennedy killed her stepmom!" I shout, trying to shove the door open again. This time the officer lets me out, but

Kennedy is already getting shoved into the back of a car that's parked at the corner of the street.

She stares at me through the window, her face pale, tears dripping down her cheeks. "*Help me, Mak, please,*" she mouths.

I nod and mouth back, "*I swear I'll get you out of this.*"

Moments later, the cop vehicles zoom away, and all I can do is helplessly watch as my best friend is taken away by a group of people who could very well be part of the evil taking over Shadow Cove.

ABOUT THE AUTHOR

Jessica Sorensen is a *New York Times* and *USA Today* bestselling author who lives in the snowy mountains of Wyoming. When she's not writing, she spends her time reading and hanging out with her family.

For more info:

Facebook: Jessica.Sorensen.Author

Facebook group: Sorensen's Stars

Instagram: jessica_sorensenauthor

jessicasorensen.com

Also by Jessica Sorensen

Shadow Cove Mysteries:

What Lies in the Darkness

Untitled (coming soon)

Enchanted Chaos Series:

Enchanted Chaos

Untitled (coming soon)

Chasing the Harlyton Sisters Series:

Chasing Hadley

Falling for Hadley

Holding onto Hadley

Untitled (coming soon)

Tangled Realms:

Forever Violet

Curse of the Vampire Queen:

Tempting Raven

Untitled (coming soon)

Unraveling You Series:

Unraveling You

Raveling You

Awakening You

Inspiring You

Mystic Willow Bay Series:

The Secret Life of a Witch

Broken Magic

Untitled (coming soon)

Standalones:

The Forgotten Girl

The Illusion of Annabella

Rules of Willow & Beck

Confessions of Luna & Grey

Breathig Lies

Guardian Academy Series:

Entranced

Entangled

Enchanted

Untitled (coming soon)

Sunnyvale Series:

The Year I Became Isabella Anders

The Year of Falling in Love

The Year of Second Chances

The Coincidence Series:

The Coincidence of Callie and Kayden

The Redemption of Callie and Kayden

The Destiny of Violet and Luke

The Probability of Violet and Luke

The Certainty of Violet and Luke

The Resolution of Callie and Kayden

Seth & Greyson

The Secret Series:

The Prelude of Ella and Micha

The Secret of Ella and Micha

The Forever of Ella and Micha

The Temptation of Lila and Ethan

The Ever After of Ella and Micha

Lila and Ethan: Forever and Always

Ella and Micha: Infinitely and Always

The Shattered Promises Series:

Shattered Promises

Fractured Souls

Unbroken

Broken Visions

Scattered Ashes

Breaking Nova Series:

Breaking Nova

Saving Quinton

Delilah: The Making of Red

Nova and Quinton: No Regrets

Tristan: Finding Hope

Wreck Me

Ruin Me

The Fallen Star Series:

The Fallen Star

The Underworld

The Vision

The Promise

The Lost Soul

The Evanescence

The Darkness Falls Series:

Darkness Falls

Darkness Breaks

Darkness Fades

The Death Collectors Series (NA and YA):

Ember X and Ember

Cinder X and Cinder

Spark X and Spark

Unbeautiful Series:

Unbeautiful

Untamed